SAVAGE
ALLIANCE

The Nickie Savage Series

Book Five

R.T. Wolfe

Book and cover design by eBook Prep
www.ebookprep.com
Cover photography by S.J. Jones Photography
February, 2017
ISBN: 978-1-61417-892-7

ePublishing Works!
www.epublishingworks.com

CHAPTER 1

Dozens of patrons crowded the corridors. The museum accommodated the number with ease, but that did little to placate Duncan Reed. While greeting his admirers, he scanned faces and evaluated tuxedo jackets for possible hidden weapons.

His landscapes and still lifes replaced the customary artwork and would be on display beyond tonight's event and throughout the following week. However, since the event doubled as a fundraiser, Duncan reminded himself to be cordial.

He and one of the attendees locked eyes. The mayor of Las Vegas. Duncan nodded toward him as he stepped around one of his smaller portraits. It sat on an easel next to one of the massive marble beams that broke up the area. The mayor was safe. The subject of the portrait was not.

Oscar award-winning actress Coral Francesca didn't pose the kind of threat Duncan feared that evening. Nonetheless, a threat she was, and since she slithered her way toward him at that moment, he stopped and raised his guard.

He had been on her arm the evening she won Best Supporting Actress. It was one of many events that netted him the label Taste of L.A. Crooking her wrist, she closed the space between them and placed her forefinger on his shoulder. After a telling pause, she slid it down the arm of his jacket. "I'm terribly sorry to hear about the fire, dear." She shook her head and tsk'd. "Such a shame. I hope you didn't lose everything."

His everything appeared around a corner. He lifted the side of his mouth. The difference between the two women caused him to accept a more sensible view of the results of the fire. He may be temporarily living in a hotel, but his wife and family were unharmed. The crime ring responsible was depleted and on the run.

Coral glanced over her shoulder at the subject of his attention. His Nickie glided across the floor in an ivory sequined, tea-length gown. He'd purchased it for her during an undercover operation. The back was high enough to cover her lines of scars and old cigarette burns. In contrast, Coral's dress was fire engine red, a halter gown that exposed her smooth back from the clasp at her neck to just above her buttocks.

Nickie smiled and greeted each patron with a raised ivory-gloved hand. The gliding and the gloved hand—they were necessary. He understood this. However, he preferred her as the unrefined Detective Nickie Savage, the brassy, complicated and selfless woman who wore black boots, tight pants and often spoke like a sailor. Although he appreciated each hat she wore, tonight's hat was the most disconcerting.

"Hello, Coral," Nickie said as she approached. "Thank you for coming to the fundraiser this evening. I do hope you're hungry."

"Oh, goodie," Coral said and checked her manicure. "Small town food."

Nickie dropped her chin and nodded. "If you're worried about the menu, no need. I believe the chef has prepared braised duck in a red wine sauce with capers and lemon." She smiled and tilted her head. "On the other hand, if you're just being a bitch, don't eat."

Coral rolled her eyes. "I see Johnny and Bebe Lyons. I think I'll make my way to more suitable conversation." She rotated on the balls of her five-inch heeled, ice pick sandals and slithered away as slowly as she'd approached.

"There you are," he said and lifted a corner of his mouth.

Nickie's smile faded. "I shouldn't have done that."

"It was the highlight of my evening," he said and brought her gloved fingers to his lips.

She lifted her chin and pulled her shoulders back. "Tonight is important. The ticket price has a friggin' comma in it. I can't believe how many people showed up."

Her poised posture may have been unnerving, but at least she spoke like his Nickie.

"Child Rescue needs this money." She placed her hand over his heart. "Thank you. This will fund their next rescue jump to Central America. It could help save dozens of children."

"You're welcome."

"Jess called."

"Ah. Jess Larsen, co-founder of said nonprofit working to protect, rescue and rehabilitate victims of human trafficking."

"He's on his way to a trafficking rehab hub and won't make it tonight."

Duncan knew this. "Completely understandable." Nickie knew he knew this, but he understood her need to say so regardless. He leaned in and placed his lips to her ear. "Let us get through the evening. We leave first thing in the morning to start our search for Fu Haizi. You are right to continue your pursuit of the organization in its weakened state."

"Or I just thought it was a good time to go since we're homeless and all."

He noted a group that gathered around a portrait of the target of Coral's conversation. A-list power couple Johnny and Bebe Lyons had requisitioned Duncan to create a portrait of them in celebration of their tenth wedding anniversary, a milestone to be doubly celebrated for those working in their toxic profession. If Coral was aware that he and the Lyonses were the closest of friends, she might not have been quite as anxious to refer to them as more suitable conversation.

The group created a horseshoe around the painting of the couple Duncan affectionately called *Colliding Stars*. At four by eight, the portrait didn't fit on an easel and filled one of the largest wainscoted framed areas on the white painted walls of the museum. Some of the men gestured to it as they spoke.

"Shall we?" Duncan asked and offered his arm.

He judged the men to be an odd mixture of politicians, actors and fine art connoisseurs. Some he knew; others he did not.

"The details are like a photograph," said the new assistant to the governor of New York.

Duncan didn't recognize the man who responded. He also didn't notice any telltale bulges under any jackets that may have suggested weapons. "The sharp lines and true colors aid to the picture-like resemblance of the Lyonses, yes."

Deciding the group was harmless, he steered his wife from them into the next area. The art show had inadvertently saved almost all of his artwork from the fire that took their home.

Nickie nodded and thanked donors for coming as they strolled past a life-size painting of her in the same dress that hung from her shoulders. He preferred the painting he had created of her minus clothing. He laced her gloved fingers in his as they mingled. She'd posed for the nude on the settee in their master bedroom. The painting was now ashes, as was the settee, the master bedroom and the rest of their home.

"Duncan," she said as they strolled.

Burned at the hands of the same man responsible for the scars beneath the dress she wore. The backs of his eyelids stung. His lungs expanded and released.

"Duncan," she said louder. "Um, ouch."

He moved his gaze from scanning the patrons for signs of Jun Zheng's men to Nickie.

"You're squeezing my fingers," she said.

He let go and pulled away. "I am sorry."

"I know," she said. "Let's find out what they're talking about." She pointed toward a different cluster of visitors. Their closest friends and family stood in a circle that could be mistaken for a football huddle.

Brie and Nathan Reed, the aunt and uncle who raised Duncan and his brother as their own, anchored the group. Duncan's brother, Andy, and his wife, Rose, stood near her stepfather, who in a small town such as Northridge, New York, served also as the captain of the NPD. Nickie's childhood foster mother and brother, Gloria and Gil, completed the circle and dominated the conversation with emotionally driven volume.

Duncan's aunt interrupted Gloria and said in the warm yet firm voice only a schoolteacher could carry, "I raised Duncan from the time he was a child. We still have his room ready for him."

He knew for a fact this wasn't true as it was filled with his aunt's first grade teaching materials. He appreciated the sentiment nonetheless.

"I am the one who took care of Nickie during the hardest years of her recovery." Her former foster mother, Gloria, was referring to the years after Nickie's captivity in Fu Haizi's trafficking. Nickie balked at the way she responded so freely, with little to no warmth, about her highly personal past. "They will live with me." Splotches of red flushed through Gloria's caramel skin.

Glancing at Nickie, Duncan analyzed her reaction. She released his arm and set one hand on Brie's shoulder, the other on Gloria's. Separating the two, she stepped into the circle. "Although we appreciate the offers, they're too dangerous. Our home was not the target. We were."

"Which is why you stay with Rose and me at the ranch," Duncan's brother added. "It's away from town. There's room for surveillance. Nothin's getting by me and Rose."

"That would be less than ideal," Duncan said and joined the circle as well. "You have a child." He ground his teeth together before continuing. "Jun Zheng may currently be in custody, but an inside operation set him free once before. It could happen again."

"May I share our plan?" All heads turned to the voice behind them. Johnny and Bebe Lyons rarely carried themselves as the superstars they were. "Duncan and Nickie will be staying at one of our vacation homes."

Duncan wasn't sure if the group was stunned silent by the address from the power couple or the suggestion Johnny made.

"Bebe and I have films in production. We won't even know which home they choose. They'll be safe to do their police work and will be able to supervise their—"

"Rottweiler," Duncan interrupted before Johnny said too much. Positively no one could know that former Officer Dale Parker would stay with them under witness protection until the trial against Jun Zheng. "We appreciate each of you and your thoughtful offers nonetheless."

A cell phone rang.

"Nickie, my daughter," Gloria said, pointing at Nickie's cleavage. "Your dress. It rings."

Nickie blushed as she reached between her breasts and retrieved her cell. "Savage," she said into it as she turned away. "How many children? The Belmont Stakes? That's tomorrow."

Duncan looked around. Dozens of people were here to view his work and donate to Child Rescue. He was the host of honor.

"I'll be right there," she said and spun to face him, an apologetic expression written on her face.

They glanced at each other in silent conversation before he gestured toward the back door. She nodded and slid her hand in his.

CHAPTER 2

The damned dress was too bulky, and the sequins made it heavy. Nickie gathered the thing up so she could take the stairs two at a time. As she reached the top floor, she pushed open the door and barely made it into the commons area before the catcalls started.

Yeah, yeah, yeah. She didn't expect anything less from the guys at the Northridge Police Department. From the dudes working desk duty to the beat officers who filled out shift reports, each snorted with laughter as she stepped foot onto the Berber carpet.

Letting the dress fall, she gave a theatrical bow and said, "Thank you, thank you. I'm going to kick each of your asses as soon I'm out of this thing." Which only made the catcalls louder and more obnoxious. She was never going to live this down. Lifting her chin, she marched through the middle of the cluster of metal desks that faced each other in sets of two. Heads disappeared behind computer monitors as she passed. Damn straight.

Duncan followed. Guilt scratched the back of her consciousness. He left the art show. He left his art show. He'd joined her without a second thought. She could hear him and her captain whispering as they walked behind her in their formal dress. Why didn't they earn any catcalls?

Nickie's attention and interest moved to her office in front of her. A man waited. Singular. This was both a surprising and a good thing.

FBI Special Agent Hurst. She would know the back of his head anywhere. Buzzed, curly black hair. Dark brown skin beneath the white collared shirt under his suit jacket. Even though he was a fed, he'd earned her trust. He shot his former partner dead. Since said former partner had been holding a gun to Nickie's head, it was a thing—the kind of thing that places a guy in the trust category without question. Although she trusted him, it didn't mean she had to like sharing with a fed.

Federal agents weren't the sharing type either. With her experience both inside and out of human trafficking, she earned a spot as an asset. Yet, feds were feds and Hurst was a fed. Nickie's case was in his hands, and she could only push him so far.

Pausing before she reached him, she reminded herself that he sat in her damned office. Not her captain's office. Not in an interrogation room. Not even at her desk, but in one of her two guest chairs.

As the sound of her heels neared the room, he raised his head. He didn't turn around. "You got here faster than I expected," he said as she rounded the desk and sat in her chair. Her captain took the remaining seat. Duncan closed the office door, then leaned against it and crossed his arms.

"No worries," she said. "Tell me about this tip."

"Yes." His elbows rested on the arms of the chair, and he steepled his fingertips together. "The Belmont Stakes."

Louisville, Kentucky. It was one of the locations on the map of potential Fu Haizi sites Duncan's brother had created.

Hurst said, "Your informant is there."

Her what? She could feel the heat as it lifted from her neck and covered her face.

"Says he was propositioned with child pornography and an offer to have sex with a minor after the race tomorrow night."

Slippery Jimbo. That slimeball. She stood so fast, her chair toppled over. "Slippery Jimbo Spalding told you he was my informant? How the hell did he get your phone number?" He was going to die a slow, painful death. She wanted to crawl in a hole. She'd already been sweaty from the haul up the stairs in the three-thousand-pound dress. This was not helping.

"He said you would ask me that." Was Hurst smiling? Traitor. "Said to tell you the last time you, and I quote, locked him all up in your office, he found my card on your desk."

"I'll kill him. I'll break his face, and then I'll kill him."

"He said you'd say that too." He definitely smiled now. "Well, something like that."

She'd left out Hurst's card? She doubted it. Jimbo went through her drawers, was more like it. "I'm speechless, really. I apologize that he has your—"

"Nope. And I don't have time to talk about it. James was able to discern there will be girls." He paused and took a deep breath. His black eyes stared at her with little emotion, but the muscles in his jaw gave him away. They flexed and released three times before he continued. "Children," he corrected. "Children will be brought in." He swallowed hard. "Both girls and boys. I have six teams being assembled as we speak. We leave at o four hundred. You in?"

She nodded, then considered. Hurst had saved her life. He came all the way out here to include her in a bust. Should she? She turned her eyes to her office door. Duncan nodded.

"I have the map," she admitted.

"Here?" Hurst asked and looked around like they might be watched.

Leaning to the side of her desk in the impossible dress, she slid the crime map from its place along the wall, and smoothed it flat on the splintered wood. The thing was big enough to hang off both sides. A complex maze of hundreds of lines zigzagged from corner to corner.

Hurst leaned over the map that extended to the southern part of Canada all the way to the top portion of South America. He glanced to her and asked, "Each line represents one of the false internet trails used to conceal the emails from the NPD mole?"

She nodded. "Officer—" She stopped, and then happily corrected herself. "Former Officer Dale Parker reported my every move to his source at IEM."

The sound of her parents' business rolled from her tongue like boiling green tea. "Parker will be relocated to the Maine location as soon as we're done in Louisville."

"Louisville, Kentucky, is one of several locations clearly void of any lines." She pointed to it. Surrounded by dozens of the marker lines Duncan's brother had drawn on the poster board, Louisville was encircled with a clean, white bubble. "We believe the IEM employee deliberately avoided sending the dummy Internet trails through the cities that contained hubs of captive children."

"Too bad that employee is no longer available to question about this," said Hurst.

"A bullet between the eyes has that effect, yes," she said.

She slid her finger to Northridge, New York. "See? Another void. We think it's because of the downtown barbershop location that housed one of Fu Haizi's groups of captive children."

"Fu Haizi, as you like to call it."

She nodded. "Yes. You call it whatever. My Fu Haizi is run by Ivanna Monticello."

"Your mother."

She sat now and closed her eyes. She'd spent seventeen years never needing to explain this to anyone. Now, she'd had to do so more times than she could count. "As a young teen, I discovered my parents' involvement. So, they arranged for Jun Zheng to silence me."

Hurst nodded. "Abducted as a means to both silence you and make money off you. That shit ain't right."

"But, I escaped. Neither my parents nor Jun Zheng saw that one coming. They aren't willing to have me killed. I brought enough unwanted attention to them when I showed up after going missing for eighteen months. So, they had me watched. Orchestrated my moves within the foster system as a minor, within police departments as an adult."

She turned her attention to the map. Peru, South America. Ontario. Daytona. Vegas and L.A. She and Duncan had planned to leave first thing in the morning to start their investigation of each location. Now this. She realized the silence had gone on for too long and glanced up to find him staring at her.

Hurst pulled his phone from the pocket of his suit jacket. "That's cold, Nick." He looked pale, if that was possible.

She nodded. "So is kidnapping children and forcing them into prostitution."

He held his phone out over the map.

Nickie's brows dropped.

Click. Click.

She didn't say he could photograph it. Her eyes darted to her captain, then to Duncan as if they could do something to stop him. He didn't even have the courtesy of turning off the sound.

"You think children are housed, then, in Cleveland, Vegas, Daytona…"

Yes. The few cities where no false trails touched, and now he had pictures of it all on his phone.

She stated what she felt was the obvious. "I think the children who are held captive in Cleveland, Vegas and Daytona are on their way to Louisville, Kentucky."

His eyes moved to hers. He took a deep breath and fell back into the chair.

He was going into shock from putting pieces together. It was time to strike. "In addition to my captain and Duncan, I want my partner on my team in Louisville. He has experience with Fu Haizi and understands the MO."

"I can agree to Detective Lynx but not the civilian."

Duncan? "The civilian?" she yelled and didn't care that she did. "That civilian has clocked more hours breaking down Fu Haizi than all of you put together." Her eyes moved to Duncan, her face tight with fear. He shook his head at her.

"Nick. I can't, okay?" Hurst held up both hands, palms out. "They're coming up with another partner for me as we speak. I really should've been placed on leave on account of my shooting Goodrich in the back."

That was a low frigging blow, and it worked. It was like her lips were glued shut.

"Nickie," Dave interrupted. She'd all but forgotten he was there. "Duncan's not exactly clean. He killed men at your house fire. If it wasn't for the fact that they were on your property and active shooters, he would be posting bond."

So much for the glue. "I give him the map. He takes pictures of it, and now this?" Partner. Shot in the back. To save Nickie from a bullet in her forehead. She dipped her head from side to side in a figure eight, then let her shoulders fall.

"I can approve Captain Nolan and Detective Lynx," Hurst said. "And that's only if some new partner assigned to me doesn't show up before tomorrow morning and disagree. But a civilian? No way."

Legs crossed, Nickie sat in the middle of the white couch. Her wrists rested on her knees. She squinted as her eyes followed Duncan walking from the penthouse bathroom to the closet and then to his suitcase, which lay open on the raised king-sized bed.

She was in her fleece pants and cami. He wore an olive green button-down shirt with black pants and casual dress shoes. The dog nudged her hand for the dozenth time, making her arm fall beside her. "Not now, Xena. Sit." The girl obeyed but not without whimpering.

"I should be going with you," Nickie said as he tucked the few belongings he'd purchased since the fire in organized sections of the suitcase.

"You are needed here," he said and reached behind the nightstand to unplug his charger.

"How long will you be gone?" This time, she set her bare feet flat on the floor, held the sides of their Rottweiler's face and rubbed heads with her. The dog smelled better than the scent of the floral air freshener and hotel room cleaner that surrounded the place.

He didn't answer her question. e didn't answer but instead said, He"Andy is coming with me."

He hadn't answered her question, but she was too distracted with what he did say to call him on it. "Andy?" She stood and let her hands drop to her sides. "Since when?"

He zipped one of the two pieces of luggage they owned. It still had the tags on it. "He called as you and Special Agent Hurst concluded your meeting."

"I didn't want this."

He stopped mid-zip. "I know that." Standing tall, he faced her. He stepped to her and took her face in his hands.

She leaned into him and pressed her forehead against his. "This is different from one of your business trips. You're going out of the country."

"You might find yourself somewhat appeased to know there were no first-class seats available on my commercial flight."

She didn't want him to make her smile at a time like this. "Coach seat. How will you survive?"

He lifted her chin with a finger and set his lips on hers. They were warm and safe.

"Okay," she said between kisses. "But what if I get to Louisville and the whole things is a wash? Hurst is relying on a gig set up through Slippery Jimbo."

"There is that." He turned back to his suitcase, finished zipping it and set it on the floor. "Then, you'll join us."

She sat down on the edge of the bed. "Why Peru? I thought we decided to case the closer spots first. Peru is not close. Ontario is close, and you know L.A. like the back of your hand."

"Mariposa joven," he said and sat next to her.

"My Spanish isn't that good, Duncan."

"Mariposa joven is a term I came across when sifting through the files I stole from your father's workplace. It means young butterfly."

"A butterfly. The symbol pedophiles use to show they prefer children of either gender." His lanky fingers wrapped around hers. "Butterfly references are used in the marketing world all the time. That's a stretch. You must have more."

"The reference mentioned some kind of drop box containing files pertaining to importing and exporting materials used to create earth-moving equipment."

"You're thinking more like importing and exporting humans?"

"I'm going to find out." He rotated to face her.

She placed her cheek on his shoulder. "I don't like this."

"I don't like the idea of you and Eddy Lynx setting up former Officer Parker in the witness protection location."

She sighed. "Let's get this done once and for all, Duncan. Then, we can think about that starting a family thing."

He took her face in both hands this time. "Or we could work on that starting a family thing before I leave." His mouth met hers, and his fingers traced a line to the back of her neck. She climbed on his lap and straddled him, meshing tongues and lips. He pressed her back to the piles of pillows and they started.

CHAPTER 3

Going in blind was an understatement. Special Agent Hurst told her six teams, but Nickie had no idea how many men that meant, if they had notified the Louisville Police captain or what her role was in all of this.

A crackle over the intercom was followed by an announcement. "Ladies and gentlemen, welcome onboard Flight 487 with service from Rochester to Louisville. We are currently next in line for takeoff and are expected to be in the air in approximately three minutes."

She'd given Duncan shit about riding commercial coach, but when was the last time she'd had to? The air smelled like it had been recycled from the last sixteen flights, and the temperature felt like eighty humid degrees.

Only four feds were on board. That didn't make up six teams. They sat up about ten rows. Her seat was in the middle of the plane next to a mother and her toddler. Her partner sat in the far back next to two teenagers with their noses in their tablets.

She messed with the twisty air thing over her head as her phone signaled a text message. Pulling it from her pocket, she saw the text was from Duncan.

The stewardess announced, "Please turn off all personal electronic devices, including laptops and cell phones." Swiping her phone, she read.

Landed in Atlanta. Four-hour layover.

She started to respond when another stewardess stopped at her seat, cleared her throat and said, "Ma'am. Please."

Ma'am? Nickie wasn't old enough to be a ma'am, but she smiled and stuffed her phone back in the pocket of her slacks anyway.

The mom next to her shook up some concoction in a bottle. It smelled horrible. Powder, cardboard, fake milk something. Nickie must have been staring because the mom said, "So her ears won't pop on takeoff." Oh, the sucking. Or was it a special ear-popping-protection formula? How would Nickie ever learn this stuff?

Duncan was in Atlanta when he should be in on Operation Belmont Stakes with her. Or she should be on her way to Peru with him. Her partner should be setting up the witness protection location for the bastard Officer Parker, not sitting behind her with strange teenagers.

Everything was backasswards. She placed her head on the headrest as the plane took off. The kid happily drank from the baby bottle while she stared at Nickie like she was an alien. Nickie closed her eyes until they leveled out.

"Excuse me, Detective."

The voice was close and made her jump.

"I'm with the gentlemen up front." Polished shoes, white shirt, tie. As if she couldn't tell. "Mr. Hurst would like to speak with you."

Ah, she'd been summoned. "Coming," she said and unbuckled her seat belt.

The spot next to him was empty. She assumed it was vacated by the dude who delivered her summons. Maybe he would become best friends with the mom and her kid.

Hurst wore the same thing she always saw him in, which was the same as every special agent she ever met. "Good morning, Detective."

"Mornin'."

He tilted his head to her and spoke low. "Base is set up at the racetrack."

"They won't be at the racetrack."

"Yet. We will be reviewing the plan of action at base."

"Since I wasn't privy to the preview or the main view, I guess I should ask what the view is and what you want me to do."

He rotated his large shoulders in the seat and faced her. "Do we have a problem, Nick?"

"Nope." Yep. "Just want to be helpful and all that." She lifted a boot and set her ankle on top of her knee.

He leaned in and whispered, "We have sixty-five men on the ground, plus the six of us en route."

That's seventy-one. Did she hear him right? She wanted to hate the feds. It was practically in her job description, but seventy-one? She tried not to get her hopes up.

"Your informant will be—"

Her left eyelid twitched. "Slippery Jimbo will be taking part in the operation?"

"Yes. He's been instrumental actually. Says he's visiting family. He was hanging out at an OTB when a man in a mock turtleneck and black pants offered access to child porn."

The muscles in her face dropped. Mock turtleneck and black pants. That was the MO of Fu Haizi. She stuffed her hands beneath her thighs to keep them from shaking.

"You gotta admit, Nick. James fits the physical profile of a slimy pedophile."

And the personality of slimy all around. She shifted in her seat. "I'm trying not to like you. You are a fed, ya know. Then, you have to go and say something funny like that about Slippery Jimbo."

He laughed. It was surprisingly girly. "Yeah. Back at you, Nick. We're not sure of locations or how many hubs, but we have enough men for up to six teams. I'd like it if you'd guide that part of the base meeting, then take charge as leader of one of them."

"Have you involved the local LPD?"

"Yes."

She nodded. "Will they be included?"

"No, but they will be allowed on-site."

That earned him an eye roll. "It's not a lot to go on," she said.

"We'll go into more detail in the secure location on the ground. Honestly, you're the most qualified and ready for this, Nick. I need you. The children need you."

So much for not liking him.

Duncan wasn't sure about Internet access or power where he was going, so he used the airport power and Wi-Fi. His office manager had a few questions that needed to be answered before he boarded the flight to Peru.

He checked his phone again. No response from Nickie.

He sighed and scanned his surroundings. Hundreds of people bustled around him, most of them waiting in line at the hot dog stand across from the terminal. The scent of the grill was almost as distracting as the absentee text message from his wife.

He sent the final email to his office manager, then decided to take full advantage of the hot dog stand with a loaded foot long. His stomach growled as he opened a search engine on his tablet. Lima, Peru, was clearly one of the voids on the map Andy had created. The same map Hurst made a copy of via the camera in his cell phone, making his Nickie not at all pleased.

He checked his phone for the fourth time. Nothing. Searching for a map of the casinos in Lima, he noted there were dozens. Since casinos bred Fu Haizi types, he and his brother were looking at a potentially extensive search.

His brother sat next to him and nudged his arm as they waited. "What's the matter?" Andy asked.

He craned his chin a fraction of an inch. "What makes you think something might be the matter?"

"You're grinding your teeth."

Ah. "My wife and I have an agreement to communicate when flying without one another. Her flight should have landed over an hour ago."

"I get that," Andy said. "But she's kinda doing something big right now."

"Which apparently makes me grind my teeth."

"Point taken, man."

Duncan had an eidetic memory. Generally, it was annoying. Sometimes, it was terrifying. Today, it was perplexing. He knew the voice that spoke behind him. The voice wasn't only in the same airport, but in the same terminal, which meant the man was headed to Peru as well.

Closing his tabs, Duncan straightened in his seat and turned. Jess Larsen did a double take as well. He continued his conversation with the young woman next to him, then stopped altogether. He turned back to Duncan and pulled his chin toward his neck. "Duncan Reed?" he said.

Standing, Duncan walked the few aisles to him and held out his hand. "Yes. It's good to see you, Mr. Larsen."

"Please call me Jess. You're on this flight?"

"I am." He took Jess's hand and shook as he turned a shoulder to expose Andy. "My brother and I are investigating a possible lead in Lima."

"I'd love to hear about it. Please, sit," he said and gestured to the seats next to the young woman. "This is Bella, my fundraising and development intern."

Duncan took the hand of the woman who couldn't have been more than twenty-five. Her blonde hair and blue eyes made her look younger yet. Bella nodded and shook his hand.

"How is Nickie?"

"She is well, thank you. She's involved in an operation today."

"A bust in the States," Jess said. "Excellent. You can tell she loves what she does."

"Yes and no," he said. "The FBI confiscated the case. She is now a subordinate."

"Ouch."

"Yes. That seems to happen often. They are allowing her assistance for today's operation, but she has little knowledge of the plan. It doesn't sit well with her." It felt good to talk about it.

"Allowing or using her assistance?" Jess said.

"Exactly."

"So, Peru," Jess said.

"It seems to be a location used by the international wing of Nickie's Fu Haizi."

"She is determined."

"She is. And thus, more frustrated that the case has been taken from her."

"And yet, here you are."

Duncan smiled at that.

"It's one of the reasons we work internationally," Jess explained. "We have more freedom and less bureaucracy. Where are you staying?"

"I actually have no idea."

"You're traveling to Peru blind?" Jess pulled his chin back again. "Really? We have room. I can show you around."

A wave of relief covered Duncan. He nodded. "We would be most grateful."

CHAPTER 4

The sun promised to cook anyone who dared to step foot from the shade. They entered Belmont Park in groups of three and four beneath a wall of arched windows that were surrounded with vines. It was eight hours before the racetrack opened, and already people hustled around like ants. Special Agent Hurst walked next to her, but Nickie's partner was stuck a few groups behind.

She'd picked her brown leather boots with the thicker heels. The pastel orange button-down blouse was sleeveless, and she chose her belt holster rather than the shoulder one that hugged her shirt. Sweat dripped down her back anyway.

"We have a room in the clubhouse," Hurst told her as they walked past the entrance to a long line of stables. The scent of manure mixed with fresh hay brought her back to her childhood, and that confused her. Why not to Duncan's brother's farm? It was where Duncan's horse was kept. Abigail loved Nickie, and the feeling was mutual. Same smell, yet her mind went to her childhood?

She guessed her parents had stables too. Maybe it was the pristine cleanliness all around her that took her mind there instead of Andy's barn. She'd never been to Belmont Park before, and even after years of English riding lessons, she'd never attended any horse race or riding show. Her parents never took her any place where she might embarrass them. Nickie was never proper enough, never clean enough.

Glancing down the entrance to the line of stables, a few dozen men and some women worked in front of an endless row of doors, each with what she thought of as a flower planter that overflowed with hay. The help hustled through the corridor with ropes and horse brushes.

As she followed Hurst into the clubhouse, she looked over her shoulder at the track. Machines manicured the mass of dirt. Her questions were endless. Would Slippery Jimbo be part of the planning meeting? How many groups of children were involved? Fu Haizi. She tried not to get her hopes up, and with all of the breaches in security thus far, she kept her mouth shut about it for now.

A woman in beige slacks, an ivory vest and impossibly tall matching pumps nodded. "Good day, Special Agent." The frown on her face spoke volumes. "Do you really have to do this today?" As did her words.

Hurst nodded. "If you would lead us to our meeting room, we have work to do."

"The others are waiting. Some have been there for over an hour."

As he checked his watch, Hurst followed the direction of the outstretched arm that gestured to a door in the back of the building. The building was decked out in wide, light-colored floor trim and ceiling crown molding. Large floor plants rested in corners on the hardwood floors with framed, matted posters of Triple Crown winners lining the walls.

Nickie followed Hurst into the room. She was relieved it wasn't nearly as decorated. She first noted that Slippery Jimbo was there. He sat at a table near a line of windows with five special agents. Not that it wasn't disconcerting having him there, but she was more distracted by the unconventional balance between female and male federal agents. By her quick count, she noted it was about fifty-fifty.

Looking to Hurst, he must have read the expression on her face. "I went heavy on the female special agents. Since a majority of the captive children are girls, I thought it might help them feel more comfortable."

Nickie nodded. Another reason to like a fed. This was not going at all as she expected.

Jimbo didn't yell out to her, greet her as Detective Dude or cause a scene. She was back to disconcerted.

Six tables that sat twelve each were arranged in two lines. Miss Ivory Vest provided a dry erase board on wheels at the end of the two lines of tables. It had a pad of chart paper draped over it. The rest of the seventy-one federal agents filed in and filled the remaining seats.

Her partner took the seat next to her.

"For those of you who haven't been introduced," Hurst started as he walked toward the front of the room, "this is James Spalding."

Jimbo didn't look so great. Ghostly white, really. She couldn't blame him. The room was filled with people not to be trusted. Including himself.

"He is the Northridge, New York, police informant who—"

Nickie wanted to crawl in a hole. She dared not look but could feel Eddy staring daggers into the side of her head. After all the times she and Eddy put Jimbo away only to have his slimy lawyer get him off…

"—was approached at an OTB this week as a potential john. He's been able to infiltrate the organization with promises of bringing in friends who want…different things."

Nickie ran her hands over her face, then interrupted. "Can you be more specific? Girls? Boys? Either? Young? Not so young?"

For a federal agent, he sure did have issues with keeping it together for this. He winced like he'd just eaten a lemon. "James?"

"Me?" Jimbo darted his eyes from Hurst to her to Eddy and back again. "Oh. Okay. Um. I'm visiting my homies, ya know." His hands shook, and his voice cracked. "Like the man here said, I had a dude ask me if I wanted a piece of his stable."

"A piece of his what?" interrupted one of the agents who sat at the table with Jimbo.

Jimbo's eyes grew, and he looked to Nickie.

"A stable," she said, forcing her eyes not to roll. "It's slang for a group of prostitutes."

"You've got to be kidding me," the agent said and laughed out loud. It took him about twice as long as it should have to notice he was the only one laughing. "That's funny, right? The irony? Stables? We're at a horse race?" His voice dripped with sarcasm.

Eddy spoke up from the spot next to her. "Shut the fuck up, Asswipe. These are kids we're talking about," he said as he sat with his forearms on his thighs.

The agent jumped to his feet. He was all ballsy from across the room. "You shut the fuck up." His thighs hit the metal table, and it scraped against the tile floor.

Oh great. They'd turned into junior high girls.

"The only reason you and your girlfriend are here is because she knows all about stables."

Eddy leaped across his table. She wasn't about to stop him. In fact, she considered joining him. It looked as if the dude wasn't liked by his peers either. A few agents got to their feet, not to help out the agent but get out of the way.

"Motherfucker. I'll kick your ass," Eddy said as he jumped, clearing the last table all together. Asswipe darted his eyes around like he was planning an escape route.

The dude started swinging before Eddy even reached him. Eddy ducked, then fisted the jerk's button-down shirt with one hand and landed a solid punch to the side of his face. He held back; she could tell. No shoulder, no tork. And he didn't go for the nose or temple but the cheek. Regardless, he made his point. Asswipe stammered and fell back into his chair.

"Gentlemen," Hurst boomed. She thought it took him a little too long to speak up, and that it probably was on purpose. She'd also never heard anything so loud but didn't dare cover her ears. It was as if a mega magnet pulled her butt to her chair. Eddy and Asswipe too. "Detectives Savage and Lynx are respectable members of the Northridge Police Department with extensive clock hours and success with taking down and apprehending human trafficking crime rings. You will give them the same respect you offer me, or you can find yourself another operation."

Eddy made his way back to his seat, but not without kicking a chair on the way.

"Detective Savage will lead the meeting from here."

She will?

"I'd like to start with hearing James's testimony, if that's all right with you, Detective," he finished and sat down.

She looked around. The agents' faces said they wanted to listen to her about as much as she wanted to lead the meeting. Asswipe mumbled something she figured contained enough colorful language to make a rainbow.

Giving Jimbo a go-ahead nod, his chest expanded and released. "Right. Yeah. Um. The dude in the black came up to me and asked me about the stable. I was like, hell yes. No." He drew out the word and shook his head before correcting his statement. "I mean. I was like faking interested and stuff. Then, he showed me a picture. It was a kid. Can you believe that shit? So, I thought of Detective Savage, ya know? She rescues kids from that shi—from that stuff. I didn't call you, Detective Savage, on account of you having the case taken from you by the feds and all." He wrung his hands together. "So, I had this card, ya know. That you left…that I found on your desk. It had Mr. Hurst's here phone number."

"As we deepened into his testimony," Hurst interrupted. "James agreed to wear a wire. He promised the perpetrators he would bring friends."

Nickie stood. "You put a wire on Slippery Jimbo?"

"It worked."

"Promises of bringing in men? I want to hear the wiretap audio."

Hurst nodded. "Of course."

She made her way to Jimbo. "Did they tell you what they had to offer? Boys? Girls? Ages? Where and when are you meeting them?"

Hurst sat down. She'd moved far enough from her chair that she was the only one standing. It was awkward as hell.

"Jeez, Detective Dude."

Oh no. Jimbo was using *Detective Dude*. He was getting comfortable.

"Do you gotta be all calloused?"

"I'm sorry, Jimbo. How would you like me to sugarcoat this for you?" She placed a palm on the table between him and the agent next to him. "We have one shot at this. Tonight. That's it."

Turning to face the crowd, she said to Jimbo but loud enough for all to hear. "You won't be lucky enough tonight to wear a wire. No weapons or electronics. They will confiscate cell phones and run a metal detector over each of you."

She walked to the chart paper and lifted the bottom of it, looking for a marker. "How many friends did you tell them you were bringing with you tonight, Jimbo?"

He shrugged. "I didn't."

She let her chest expand before releasing the air completely. "Okay. We're going to plan on five since with you that'll be six undercover johns. One for each team." She turned to Hurst. Since Jimbo's table was the only male-only, she said, "I assume the five sitting with Jimbo are the other undercover johns?"

He nodded.

"None of you are repeat customers. That means you'll have to prove you're legit."

Using her teeth, she uncapped the marker and drew a horizontal line near the top of the chart paper. In the space she'd created, she drew three shapes. The first was a spiral triangle. "This is the symbol used by johns who want boys."

Several agents turned their gazes away from the symbol and not just the ones designated as undercover johns.

Next, she drew a spiral heart. "This is the symbol used by johns who prefer little girls. And this—" she said, drawing two large and two small hearts depicting butterfly wings. She paused. Mariposa joven. In the back of her mind, she banked the connection, then shook her head back to the present. "—means the john will go either way."

She turned to a room full of flushed and pale faces. "A tattoo of one of these on your person should be convincing enough."

The eyes from one of the men from Jimbo's table widened and he asked, "Henna?"

"No. These need to be color, but they will clean off your pretty little arm." She turned to face Hurst. "Too bad we don't have an artist on hand." She hoped her voice dripped with sarcasm. "You know the men best. I assume you have a plan as to who teams up with who?"

Hurst answered, "I have you and Detective Lynx heading up one of the six."

She knew he said this out loud for the sake of the others. Using the rest of the space beneath the symbols, she drew six boxes. She wrote Jimbo's name at the top of one of them, with hers and Eddy's names directly beneath.

After some quick dividing in her head, she said, "Each group will have an undercover john, a team leader and three to nine additional men. Hurst, you decide on groups, then we'll go over strategy. I've got an errand to run."

CHAPTER 5

The flight was nearly empty yet the air stale after six hours enroute. Duncan loosened his tie.

As the plane descended over the Lima, Peru air space, Andy offered commentary only he could provide. "This is crazy, man. You've got to see this."

The brilliant white clouds that stood in front of the blue sky were, indeed, spectacular. However, Duncan wouldn't think of taking Andy's place at the window.

"The mountains and villages are insane, brother. You could seal this shit in that memory of yours and paint for decades."

Spoken like a poet. Duncan's stomach left him as the plane began the final descent. "Do you have your TAM card ready?"

"Yes, big brother. And my baggage paper thing." The tires skipped along the runway. "Get a load of the cops. They know how to carry."

Duncan lifted his chin and checked through the window. He spotted a row of police officers each carrying a Heckler and Koch 416 assault rifle. Interesting.

"Ladies and gentlemen, welcome to the Jorge Chavez International Airport. Local time is 4:35 p.m., and the temperature is sixty degrees Fahrenheit."

Duncan leaned back and inhaled deeply, his mind racing with the goals he planned to fulfill in the next few days. He needed to be certain about their theories regarding the holes in the map Andy had created. The voids surrounding the nearly dozen cities were obvious, but were they truly hubs containing Fu Haizi trafficked children?

The Nevada and Maryland locations certainly were hubs at one time but were abandoned. The void around Northridge was both accurate and current. If he were able to find a hub of children in Lima, it would solidify the theory, at least in Duncan's mind.

He and Andy would start with his short list of casinos with questionable reviews and locations. Tonight. Although he didn't speak the language, he had been able to pick up some Spanish phrases from his time spent with Nickie's Hispanic foster family. He could only hope to discover some connection and get some answers. Was Lima the mariposa joven?

"For your safety and comfort, please remain seated with your seat belt fastened until the captain turns off the Fasten Seat Belt sign."

"We meet Jess and his friend as soon as we exit."

"Are we arming ourselves?" Andy asked.

Duncan lifted a single brow as he glanced in front and behind. "Not if we don't have to," he answered in a low voice. "Only citizens are allowed to carry with a license."

"I repeat," Andy said, as if Duncan hadn't just explained. At least he knew to lower his voice this time. "Are we packing?"

"Possibly. First, I want to case the larger casinos. I have to go with what we know, and what we know is that Fu Haizi has a history of soliciting potential johns at large sporting events and in casinos. Since we don't know of sporting events in the next few days, I have both a short and long list of casinos."

Andy nodded as his expression morphed into the one that scared Duncan enough to second-guess his decision to allow his brother to join him on the trip. He could be reckless. South America was not a place for recklessness.

"One thing at a time, little brother. Jess Larsen's connections will save us precious time."

"And will save us finding a place to stay where we won't be mugged, beat up or pickpocketed. I almost lament missing the challenge."

"You're not funny."

"I am completely and consistently funny."

Duncan closed his eyes and rested his head against the seat. It would be more helpful to ignore Andy until departure.

Nickie stood facing the auto java machine in the stable-hand-only section. It stood along a corner with little air movement. Her blouse was damp and sweat formed around her hairline. Who drank coffee in this heat? The world carried on around her. More people showed up to pre-race shenanigans. More stable boys. Yet, her dilemma for this moment stood in front of her.

She'd always considered herself a healthy person. She exercised regularly—had to—and ate well. Fruit, raw vegetables, Greek yogurt, protein. Her only vice was Diet Coke. That's it. One.

Now, she was all about this…this thing she and Duncan were doing. No birth control meant no sweeteners, no caffeine, no fake fat, and no artificial anything. She didn't want to nuke some potential human. The kid would have enough strikes against it just being her kid. Except all of it meant no Diet Coke.

She sighed, placed the palm of her hand on the decaf button, closed her eyes, and pressed. She heard the cup drop. The machine screeched and let out a stream of something that might smell okay but would taste awful. When she opened her eyes, she found a paper cup with steam coming from dark liquid. Rolling her eyes, she took it and sealed a lid over the top.

With her free hand, she bent down and retrieved the bag she'd gotten from the nearby drugstore, then headed back to the meeting room. Eddy had a single hip sitting on the table inside the door. Most of the other agents had returned, too, and were huddled around the area in groups like in a high school cafeteria. She'd never been privy to any cafeteria huddle in high school or now.

He tilted his head when he spotted her, looked at her cup of coffee, albeit decaf, then up to her face again. Nickie shrugged and stepped around him. She placed the plastic drugstore bag behind his butt on the table and turned to investigate the chart paper.

First names had been added to the six boxes Nickie had created. "The undercover john is the name on top," Eddy affirmed.

She nodded and assessed the rest of the room. A map of the park had been added next to the chart paper. A circle was drawn in black magic marker around an exit. "And the name under that is the team leader?" she asked about the list of names. Her name was under Slippery Jimbo's.

"Yep." He must have spotted where her gaze landed. "And mine is under yours. We are listed under slimy Slippery Jimbo. What the fuck is that?"

It was true; that was messed up. She shouldn't smile at a time like this, but she couldn't help it. Until she considered Jimbo in danger.

Mock turtlenecks and black pants. The description kept coming back in her head. He'd taken a beating by Fu Haizi once before because of her. He could have squealed. He didn't. Goose bumps formed over her arms and electricity ran through them.

She didn't believe in coincidences. Since there wasn't a dress code for human traffickers, she was quite likely going to face the crime ring responsible for her abduction as a young teen.

She pressed her hand to the side of her jaw until her neck cracked, then did the same for the other side. Eddy set his hands on her shoulders and rubbed them up and down over her arms.

"You cold?"

She shook her head. "No."

"Freaked out?"

It was a better assessment, but no. "Just anxious. This is big. A lot of children are counting on us."

"You put too much pressure on yourself."

She wished she had more to give.

Hurst came in and walked to the wall of windows. The crowd thickened. Nickie thought of it as high-class tailgating. Using an electronic pad on the wall, he closed one set of blinds after another, shutting out the women in lace dresses and wide-brimmed hats and men roasting in three piece suits.

The last few special agents filed in, and everyone sat. Nickie noted each had moved seats. Since people rarely did that, she assumed they were grouped in their assigned teams. Two chairs sat empty at Jimbo's table. As the NPD outcasts, she and Eddy took them and waited.

"Nickie?"

What? Already? Okay. She stood and walked to the front of the room. "Tonight is likely going to look like this…The agents posing as johns—"

Jimbo cleared his throat.

She amended. "Each agent and police friggin' informant posing as a john will hang together at the exit. Those of you chosen to case the interior of the park need to be dressed to fit in. Hopefully, the trafficking scum assigned to escort johns to remote locations will show. Remember, no electronics on the undercovers. That part is crucial."

Hurst held up a finger. "I put a lot of thought into that."

She didn't like the sound of that.

He stuck a hand in his pocket. She opened her mouth to argue, but he held up his other hand with his palm out, facing her. "Everyone except the johns wears one of these audio devices." Holding up his arm, he pinched a lapel pin between his thumb and forefinger. "For the johns, I decided on GPS trackers."

"Absolutely not. I told you, Hurst. They'll be made before they ever leave the parking lot."

"They're ingestible."

Had he just said ingestible?

"I'm not willing to risk losing a man. We have a civilian," Hurst said.

Ingestible. Wow. This fed thing looked more promising by the minute. "No audio or visual. When the johns arrive at the locations, we won't have a signal as to when we can move in."

"Give them fifteen minutes," she said.

"Fifteen minutes?" Asswipe snorted. "That won't be enough time to get to the perps."

Her left eyelid twitched. "Turnover is quick. You can't imagine how fast. But the ass—the agent isn't far off base. There will be little time to get to the perps. Since we don't know where the undercovers will be taken, we won't be able to case the locations or surround the establishments ahead of time. As soon as each team is certain their john has arrived at the crime scene, they will have fifteen minutes to surround, assess and infiltrate the traffickers." Most of them were looking at the closed window, the ceiling or the floor. So, she upturned the contents of her plastic grocery bag, spilling out colored eye pencils and a few travel bottles of maximum-hold hair spray.

"One of you gets the spiral triangle." She drew the symbol in one of the six squares on the chart paper. "I think on the inside of your wrist. You are posing as a john who prefers boys.

"One gets the heart spiral. Inside forearm. It means you prefer little girls. Don't forget this. The remaining four johns get the butterfly-heart symbol saying you can go either way. How about two forearms and two biceps. We don't know what they're bringing and want as much flexibility as possible." She sighed and looked out over the crowd. "Anyone out there know how to draw?"

One of the females raised her hand, fingers together and only as high as her shoulder.

"My search engine told me eye pencil covered in hair spray lasts twenty-four hours."

Nickie walked to the front of the room, away from the door. She stood with her legs locked and barked, "The rest of you listen up. These people are seasoned and know how to take precautions. Anyone not wearing a big hat or a bow tie will be marked by their scouts. So, use your audio devices to communicate and anyone not undercover, keep the hell out of sight. I'm going to estimate three to six guards per location, which means we should be well staffed. Many of the children will be heavily drugged. Some cuffed."

Taking a deep breath, she waited until each looked up to her. Their eyes said it. They found this shit as sad and as sick as anyone. They weren't bad people.

"Any questions?"

CHAPTER 6

◆

"Never flag down a taxi," Jess said as Duncan followed him and his intern through the single terminal into customs.

The area was wall-to-wall musty plaster and concrete. Not at all the plastic, tile and carpet that seemed to cover American airports.

"Anyone can put a taxi sign on the top of their car," Jess continued. "Always call for one to pick you up. I will text you the names of the three trusted companies."

The flight had been somewhat barren, yet customs was filled shoulder-to-shoulder with people.

"We're going to make a copy of your passport. Carry the copy with you and leave your passport in the safe at the dorm."

Dorm. It was the place Jess was headed. Not a headquarters but a rehabilitation and work study assistance location. The man had several irons in the fire. His preventative Backyard Broadcast program, rescue missions, police training, and rehabilitation assistance.

"We already have copies," Duncan said, "but will graciously accept your offer to keep our originals in your safe."

"Good to hear, but you're dressed like high-class white folk. It puts a bull's eye on your back. If you're looking to come off as slimy gringos looking to rent children, you'll need to dress the part."

"We are looking for a specific MO, so to speak. I am not at all sure of our plan, but I feel the need to stick with what I know of this specific organization."

"Okay."

Andy walked next to him and behind Jess and his friend. He approached baggage claim and waited behind the row of people who had pushed to the front.

"We'll use the airport services to exchange your money. For now, it is the safest way to get the best exchange rate."

Duncan had been to a plethora of countries, yet this was humbling.

"Never go out at night. Always stay together." Jess reached between people and took hold of his suitcase. Setting it on the floor next to him, he didn't let go of the handle but continued. "Be wary of children who approach you. They often run in packs and are excellent pickpockets. I mean excellent, excellent."

"Point taken. We have money belts laced with wire that cannot be cut. We are most grateful for your help."

Andy grabbed both of their suitcases as if they weighed a fraction of what they did. He passed off Duncan's suitcase as he helped Jess's intern, Bella, with hers.

"Jess?" A male voice came from behind them.

"Samuel, my friend." Jess held out a hand to a tall, lanky man with a dark head of hair.

Samuel looked to be in his mid-thirties. He wore holey jeans and a T-shirt that read: There are two kinds of people in this world, and Peruvians are better than both of them.

They were still shaking hands as Jess turned his head. "Samuel, these are my friends, Duncan and Andy, and you remember Bella."

Samuel took Bella's hand in a much less vigorous shake, and nodded to Duncan and Andy.

Andy spoke to him. "You've got a beautiful country here, man."

Samuel dipped his chin once. "Welcome."

Samuel and Jess turned toward a set of double doors, and Duncan followed with Bella, Andy following close behind. As the doors opened, he inhaled the thick air common in heavily populated areas. It was damp and cool. Peruvian winter.

There was no taxi waiting but a 1990, severely beaten, red Toyota Corolla. Duncan eyed each member of their random group, then back to the Toyota. At least it had a luggage rack. Another man that could be Samuel's younger brother sat in the passenger seat. He exited the car and, without introduction, piled the luggage in the hatch and atop the vehicle.

Bella squeezed in the front and Duncan, his brother and Jess in the back. The car lowered several inches from the weight, but off they went into the bumper-to-bumper traffic regardless.

It was time. Nickie ground her teeth as she marched through Belmont Park to the clubhouse. To her left, cheers erupted from the crowd. Perspiring women who refused to take off their wide-brimmed hats waved white handkerchiefs at the track. Alcohol and sweaty perfumed bodies added to the scent of the manure and hay. Nickie paid little attention to which after-ceremony was going on. Her attention tunneled to the next few hours.

Lives were at stake. Children's lives. What if they didn't have enough men? What if the location of a brothel was missed? She stopped before she turned the last corner to the meeting room and squeezed her eyes shut. Not helping, Nick.

After cracking her neck, she shook out her shoulders and continued. As she made the corner, she realized the clothes she'd chosen weren't much smarter in the heat. Kevlar vest, sky blue blouse, black pants, and boots would make her stick out.

Eddy was there, waiting for her in the hall. He leaned against the wall next to the entrance. Other than a darker blue shirt and lower heel on his boots, they were a matching pair. He squinted as she approached.

"What?" she asked.

"Your hair is up."

"I'm sweating like a pig."

"Do pigs sweat?" He glanced at the ceiling and shrugged. "Never seen you with your hair up."

Never? She considered, then listened to the voices that came from inside the meeting room. "How many do you think are in there?"

"All of them. I'm waiting for you. They smell bad."

"Like pigs," she said and pushed open the door.

The five special agents posing as johns stood out. They looked surprisingly a lot like Slippery Jimbo. Plaid shirts with the top button fastened. Greased hair. A few in trench coats. Others wearing gold bracelets and chains, Chuck Taylors and baggy khakis. She was impressed…relieved really, but would never say so.

Each table also contained a single fed who wore either a bow tie or a large pastel hat with matching bellbottom slacks. The rest were in standard navy blue pants and long-sleeved shirts. She caught Asswipe's glare but didn't dwell on it. There was always a jerk in every group. The FBI had one like everyone else.

"Detectives, it's so nice of you to decide to show up." It wasn't Asswipe but one of the women. It looked like the FBI had more than one in this group.

Tipping up her chin, Nickie scanned the groupings. Jimbo's table had only nine. Her plus Eddy made eleven. This was good.

Hurst didn't acknowledge them. She preferred it that way. "All but the six unmarked vehicles are off-site," he said as she and Eddy slipped into the empty seats at Jimbo's table.

"You left me," Jimbo whispered. "You left me alone with feds." Spit sprayed from his mouth and his eyes were like saucers.

Nickie leaned away as she nodded her head up and down. He wasn't wrong.

"They made me eat this...this thing, Detective Dude. What if it stays in me forever? They can track my every move forever."

"Karma, Jimbo."

"That's not funny, man. Or what if I shit it out before this is all over?"

"There, there. You're not going to shit in the next few hours."

Eddy leaned in. "Stop talking, Jimbo."

"Hey, dude. I'm on your side." Jimbo's face relaxed. "We're like partners."

Eddy closed his eyes and shook his head. "I really hate you."

That made Jimbo smile.

"Post-race ceremonies will conclude in approximately forty-five." Hurst stepped next to the map of the park. "The undercover johns meet...here," he said, tapping the spot on the map circled in black. "The plainclothes agents will be stationed—"

Asswipe cleared his throat.

Hurst spun on his heels. "Do you have something to add, Special Agent?" Hurst barked at him.

"No, sir. I just wasn't sure if plainclothes was an accurate description of a man in a bow tie."

Too bad Eddy hadn't hit him in the mouth.

"Vehicles from group number one and two are staged here." He moved his finger to a spot a few hundred yards east of one of the parking lots. "That's you, Savage. Three and Four are here, and Five and Six, here. Load up for our first audio check at the conclusion of this meeting."

"Detective Savage?" Hurst lifted his hand to her.

She hated when he did that and swallowed. "Let me see the tats," she said and scanned the room as the undercovers rolled up their sleeves and rotated palms. Damn. She was both impressed and relieved. Nodding her approval, she continued. "Do each of you remember what your tat represents?" She mentally checked off each one as she made eye contact from table to table.

Her left eyelid twitched. "Follow Jimbo's lead," she forced herself to say. "The traffickers might have you drive your own car, but will likely take you to an off-site location in their vehicles. You may be in pairs or groups with other johns, maybe each other. Be ready for anything." She glanced at Jimbo. His face turned a shade of green. "You've each been given five hundred cash. The price will be negotiated and agreed upon before you leave."

Her upper lip started to sweat. Not from talking to a room full of special agents but from the subject of her discussion. Slipping her hand behind her, she grabbed hold of the top of her chair. Eddy's gaze went to her hand, then to her face. She looked away from him and continued.

"Those of you following the johns," she addressed the group as a whole, "even though the tracers are ingested, I am told you can get the signal up to a mile away. Keep it at a quarter mile minimum. Those black SUVs scream FBI."

She would not stick her head between her legs. She would not stick her head between her legs.

She was going way out on a limb here. Fu Haizi didn't use hotels. Other pimps did. "The children have likely been brought to large homes or warehouses. When the trace says the john stops moving, give them fifteen minutes as you surround the place with the remaining vehicles. There should be between three and six guards. They will be armed. Incapacitate them first. Keep watch for any you missed while the rest of you get the children out."

She was done. Whether or not she was done, she was done. She sat and gripped her knees until her fingers cramped. The contents of her stomach tasted like it was at her throat.

Hurst stood. "We rendezvous at the LPD." She didn't look at where he pointed and stared at the only spot on the floor that wasn't spinning. "Your team leader will give you your walkie channel assignment. Any questions?"

CHAPTER 7

Nightlife in Lima appeared much like nightlife in any large city. Lights that made it seem like perpetual dusk. People as thick as bees in a hive. Duncan watched out the closed passenger window as Jess Larsen's local contact drove them to the first casino on the list. He wanted to roll down his window, but assumed Lima was like any large city. Open windows in sketchy areas encouraged stoplight robberies.

"Gringos are targets for a smash and grab," Samuel said as he gunned the engine past a group of locals. "This is when men smash a window and rob us at gunpoint."

Yes, much like nightlife in any large city. Nothing good happens after midnight, especially if alcohol was involved. This was precisely why they were here.

"The two of you are dressed like you have a lot of money." His English was excellent, possibly a little too much so as he enunciated each syllable. "When you leave the car, you will also be a target for an express kidnapping."

"A what?" Andy asked from the backseat.

Samuel explained. "You are taken by force to an ATM and made to empty your bank account. Then, you are left there with no money or cell phone."

Express kidnapping. Duncan retracted any thoughts of matching nightlife with large cities anywhere.

Tiny lights scattered over the sides of the mountains that loomed behind the city. In the daylight, they provided a most picturesque backdrop to a colorful and breathtaking country. Now, they seemed like freckled giants who kept them prisoner.

"The casino is a block away. You may call me when you are ready for me to pick you up, or you may use one of the taxi companies Jess listed for you. Are you sure about this? You are ducks that are sitting."

He was sure. The cowboy hats and boots may be considered overkill. That was a good thing. They needed to stick out.

Samuel pulled to the side and double-parked, causing a number of cars to zip around them, holding their horns down as they passed. The more negative attention, the better.

"Good luck, Duncan and Andy."

"Thanks, man," Andy said.

Duncan handed him the tip he'd placed in his money belt. Samuel's eyes grew as he took it from him. "Thank you," Duncan said as he exited the vehicle.

As Samuel drove away, Duncan stood with his brother and scanned the rows of multicolored, flashing neon lights all around them. It was the first time doubt blew through him. Where could he possibly start? An image of a needle in a haystack appeared clearly in his mind.

Andy jabbed an elbow into his rib cage. Duncan glanced his way.

A boy about the age of nine stood in front of them and smiled as he stared. In the chilly winter Peru air, he wore a holey T-shirt and dirty pants. His expression was that of innocence and interest. It would be quite convincing if not for the hour of night and location the child chose to browse.

"Gotcha," Andy said as he grabbed the wrist of another that had come up from behind.

They were like ants. Four of them came out of nowhere. Andy craned the arm he'd grabbed and rotated it behind the boy's back. "Nice try, man. I gotta say I'm impressed."

Duncan doubted they understood Andy's English words, but his brother's expression and tone spoke volumes.

"Now, shoo," Andy barked and gave the boy a push.

The children ran east down the street, then scattered. Duncan imagined they would regroup and try another man or men within minutes.

"Come on," Andy said. "It probably won't be any better inside. At least they can't get these suckers off us," he said and wrapped his hand around his metal wire-money belt.

"Yes, but there is the express kidnapping thing. Please stay vigilant."

"I live for this shit."

Duncan wasn't sure what he was hoping for exactly. A poker game? Men in black pants and mock turtlenecks? "Let's try blackjack. It will give us a chance to first survey our surroundings."

"Okay, but can't you just say, 'case the joint?'"

"Never."

The looks from the other patrons were telling. He and Andy were not welcome. He ignored the glares and, without speaking, tossed a few Peruvian bills on the table. Andy did the same.

The dealer hesitated, then set chips in front of each of them. The man was twice Duncan's age with a full head of hair dyed black. He twisted the long ends of his mustache before picking up the cards. He, too, scanned the reactions of the men to the presence of the two gringos as he executed a complicated shuffling and fanning of the cards.

As the cards were dealt, a head appeared between Duncan and his brother. "You're not welcome here," the voice said in steeply accented English.

Duncan lifted the corner of his cards. Six of clubs and five of hearts. He motioned for the dealer to hit him with another. "We're not here for the gambling."

Another voice came from the other side of Andy. "Hit me. You gringos can find that at any corner. Out. Side." This man's English was flawless.

Two of clubs. He motioned a hold. "My tastes are more specific than what is found at corners."

Silence ensued before the cards were overturned. He and Andy lost and surrendered their chips. It went on like this for another half hour. The men around them spoke in a Spanish that differed from what was spoken at Nickie's childhood foster home. The men made a point to make it obvious that they spoke of him and Andy. Jeers, stares, pointing. Little did they know, this only helped Duncan with his cause.

A seven of hearts and a four of hearts. He estimated about eighty-five percent of the cards left in the remaining deck of six decks would be tens or face cards. He folded. A large win at the blackjack table would draw the wrong kind of attention.

Roulette, poker. He and Andy shifted through the entire establishment.

As well as the one across the street, down the street and around the corner.

It looked like a presidential motorcade. Lines of black SUVs staged at staggered off-site intervals. They made Nickie and Eddy take the one farthest from the park. Special Agent Hurst had given her the audio channels for each of the team leaders but not the GPS signals for the corresponding undercover johns. Jimbo only.

Relinquishing control was a bitch, but there was no denying the euphoria that raced through her body. Her knee bounced furiously. Girls would be saved. Girls that right at that moment either shook with fear or lay perfectly still in hopelessness. Some would be tying knots in their hair. Others, rocking back and forth or hugging their knees close to their chests.

By this time tomorrow, they would be free of it all.

Eddy dangled his wrist over the top of the SUV steering wheel. The windows were down as they waited in the first of their assigned four-car motorcade. The breeze helped to both cool her off and keep her mind from spinning in too many directions. Hurst had programmed the built-in screen to Slippery Jimbo's GPS tracer. It blinked at the pre-planned location within the park but didn't move.

He tapped his thumb against the wheel.

"What are you thinking?" Nickie asked.

Sniffing, he said, "I'm thinking this rig cost the feds forty grand stripped. There are twenty-four of them. That's almost a million dollars in cars for this one operation."

"Damn," she said in two syllables. She hadn't thought about it.

He craned his head to look at her. "I could do a lot with a million dollars."

She thought of his apartment, then of the home she and Duncan lived in. Or, lived in before Fu Haizi blew it up. Was the explosion her mother's idea, she wondered, but only for a moment.

Static from the audio attachment interrupted her train of thought. "Bogey at nine o'clock," the plainclothes agent assigned to their detail spoke into the bug.

Eddy grunted. "Did the dude just say, bogey?"

"Oy."

"Did you just say, oy?"

"Oy." She blinked and squinted at the screen. Did Jimbo's trace just move?

Speaking into her assigned channel, she alerted the rest of her team. "This is Savage. Be ready to go."

"Vehicle Three, affirmative."

"Vehicle Two, affirmative."

"Vehicle Four, affirmative."

"That's going to get old real fast," Eddy said, but she wasn't really listening to him.

She sat up straighter and scooted her butt so she could be closer to the screen.

Static. "Three men. Black pants. Black shirts. Black suit jackets. The five undercovers are standing behind the civilian." The civilian as in Jimbo. "One of the men in black is stepping to the civilian. It's like a posturing of the clan leaders in the Lord of the Rings."

Nickie ground her teeth together. Children's lives were at stake. She was in no mood for this. Her breath picked up. She checked the volume on the audio for the tenth time. All the way up.

Static. "And we have a launch."

She bent her nose closer to the screen. "Jimbo is on the move."

Eddy turned over the ignition.

"This keeping us in the dark to the rest of the plainclothes audios and undercover GPS trackers is bullshit."

"Hell, yes," Eddy said and shifted into drive.

She didn't realize she'd said that last part out loud.

The damn blink moved in slow motion. Her jaw ached from the pressure of her grinding teeth by the time Jimbo's trace moved fast enough to be in a car. Was he alone in the unmarked they gave him? With the other johns? In a car alone with the transports? Had he been made?

Static. "James is alone and headed north away from the park." She wanted to know about the others.

Eddy pulled out on the highway.

"Not too close."

"I know."

"Not too far."

"I know."

"This sucks."

"I'm—"

"Don't say you know."

"I was going to say I'm sorry. I know this sucks."

Buckling her seat belt, she inhaled, lifted her chin and rolled up her window.

It didn't take long before the oncoming traffic became scarce. "Two, Three and Four. Increase distance with us and each other."

"Vehicle Three, affirmative."

"Vehicle Four, affirmative."

"Vehicle Two, affirmative."

Eddy moaned. "Shoot me now."

Since she couldn't see a taillight, not even in the few straightaways, she kept her eyes glued to the screen. Her head shook. It's been too long. "Hurst, do you copy?" she said into her audio. No answer.

The blinking slowed and turned. Eddy backed off. The blinking stopped.

"Over near those bushes," she said and pointed off the shoulder. It was one of the few miles of road that wasn't lined with a white picket fence. Trees, bushes and shrubs almost completely concealed the entrance road that was more of a gravel driveway.

He did as she said, then turned off the engine. The search engine map said there was no back way for the perps to escape, but she found it hard to believe that they would be that stupid.

She spoke into the channel. "Two, Three and Four. Fifteen minutes. Check your watches. Numbers three and four, stage north a hundred yards from the next turn. I will text you the coordinates of our immediate rendezvous. Get your asses down here now."

"Vehicle Four, affirmative."

"Vehicle Three, affirmative."

Nickie's left eyelid twitched. She spoke into the police channel. "Hurst, do you copy?"

Nothing.

She rechecked the channel. "Hurst, we're going in fifteen."

Sighing, she blinked and shook her head. "Suit up," she said and pulled a dark cap around her head and face. "Let's do this, Lynx."

Before she could open her car door, he grabbed her hand. She looked at his fingers, and noticed he was fooling with the controls to his left.

"Don't open the door. I can't find the switch to turn off the inside lights in this damned vehicle."

She didn't have time for this and, focusing on her breathing, closed her eyes. He released her arm, and she opened her door to the humid night. The scent of fresh-cut grass filled her nose. The sound of the door clicking as she pressed it shut was quickly followed by Eddy's. With soft knees, they shuffled through noisy crickets and the brilliant starlight.

It was hot as hell. The long sleeves and pants weren't so bad, but the face mask was a bitch.

Three minutes in. While they waited for the rest of the team, she tried texting Hurst this time. "You there? Are the others safe? Are they in?" Were captive children saved?

She checked that her phone was on silent, turned the brightness down and stuffed it back in her pocket. The sound of soft feet came from in front of her.

"Vehicle Two approaching on foot, sir."

Because they might have driven through the bushes and trees?

Four minutes. More feet.

"Vehicle Three approaching on foot."

"Vehicle Four approaching on foot."

"Do you have the bullhorn?" she asked the vehicle three driver. The agent nodded as headlights came from the highway. The nine of them hit the grass and lay still. It slowed down and turned onto the road leading back to Jimbo. As it passed, she spoke into the microphone device attached to her vest. "Audio check. Number off if you can hear me in your earpiece.

"Group one takes the north, two the east, three south and four west. Stick to the plan, but be flexible. We have ten minutes. Let's go." She checked her phone one more time for a response from Hurst, and this time hoped he wasn't hurt.

CHAPTER 8

Nickie's group scattered low and quiet. The trees were thick, but she spotted the cars around the brown trunks. Bimmers Jags and Vettes were parked in a circle. It was a lot of cars. Sweat ran down her back, and she motioned for Eddy that they were going to go wide. A warehouse. Considering the clientele, the place was ghetto. Dirty white. The packed gravel surrounding the place could hold a few dozen cars easily. This place was used regularly.

"No more," she muttered under her breath.

No windows. This was a good thing. Johns and perps would have few escape routes. It was a huge structure. This was bad. There were less than a dozen on their rescue team.

She paused at the site of the white box truck. "Really?" she said mostly to herself. "They use those things all over the country?"

Eddy didn't question her rambling but elbowed her rib cage as they got close enough to hear. The metal walls seemed to amplify the cries. Screams echoed.

Nickie couldn't get her feet to move. Her knees gave out, and Eddy caught her left armpit before she fell to the ground completely. Ducking her chin to her neck, she tried to shake away the memory of the inside. The metallic odor of blood mixed with stale cigar breath, alcohol and the body odor of old men.

Eddy tugged on her arm. "You can do this," he whispered.

As if she had a choice. She could. She would. She willed her legs to stand and pointed to the back door. It was wide enough to fit a small vehicle. A single guard stood leaning against the side of the open frame. He wore black pants and a mock turtleneck. A white cigarette dangled from his coffee brown lips, and he grasped his rifle with two hands.

Fu Haizi scum.

Her breath quickened. She thrust four fingers in front of Eddy, signaling the number of minutes they had before they rushed the place. He nodded. Her eyes had adjusted to the dark and could see the structure from the dim light coming from the stars.

She whispered to the others in her audio device. "Other than the white box truck, I don't see any other vehicles to the east or west that seem like they could belong to the perps."

Static sounded in her ear. "This is Vehicle Three. We don't see the unmarked that transported your friend. There are two burgundy SUVs that could belong to the perps."

"When the perps use the same cars as the feds," Eddy whispered to only her, "it should be a considered a red flag for Langley."

Light talk was not going to help, but Eddy didn't know that. Instead of responding, she held up two fingers.

Taking her gun off safety, she reached down and made sure her spare was secure under her pant leg. "I have visual on a guard standing in the door in the back," she said into the audio. "Group two, you are clear to approach."

It was nearing midnight in a foreign country. Duncan had taken his little brother through a total of seven smoke-filled, questionable establishments in this third world country, threatening their safety at every moment. Andy should be home with his wife and baby, and Duncan should be curled up behind Nickie in a hotel in Kentucky, not twelve hours away, sweating in casino after casino.

They headed down the center of a dirty floral carpet toward the exit of one of the more high-class establishments in the line of bars, strip clubs and casinos.

"They're all beginning to look the same, brother," Andy said.

Not to someone with an eidetic memory, but Duncan nodded anyway. Roulette and craps to the left. Slot machines to the right. He had to persevere. Children were being used. His Nickie would never rest until she dismantled Fu Haizi. Duncan's need was nearing his wife's.

A man dressed in designer jeans and a cotton shirt with rhinestone-covered buttons stepped in front of them. "Guys, hey," he said and held out his hand. "Let me pay for cab fare back to your hotel. You do have a hotel, don't you?"

He was definitely a local. His accent was steep, but his English fluent. A thief? Scam? Child trafficker feeling them out as potential johns?

"No thanks, man," Duncan said. "We haven't found what we're looking for yet."

"You may think you can come to our country and exploit it for your bad habits. That no one will do anything about it. But you're wrong." He pulled his shoulders back and stepped within inches of Duncan's face. "We don't need your kind."

Yes, you do, he thought but dipped his head and maneuvered around him. He and Andy made it nearly out the door before another local stepped in front of them.

"You don't fit in here, Gringo."

This time, Duncan absorbed the extent of this statement. Hope died with each step. They hadn't gotten a single lead. He shrugged and looked at the man. He had salt and pepper hair that curled over his ears and a beard that matched in color. His clothes were similar to what Duncan wore. Pressed pants, casual dress shoes and a button-down shirt.

No black or mock turtleneck, but Duncan responded to him regardless. "What we're looking for does not include fitting in."

The man stuck his hand in his front pocket and, legal or not, Duncan regretted his decision to go unarmed. The local didn't pull out a gun but his phone. It was opened to an app with a picture of a young girl. She was without clothing. Duncan clenched his jaws until his teeth nearly chipped.

He blinked slowly, then glanced up at the man. The silence should have given him away yet he found himself speechless regardless.

"Close, but no cigar," Andy said as he held the door for the man.

It was hard to argue with anyone as muscle clad as Andy, yet the man nodded and swiped the pic away only to retrieve a new one. This was of a boy. Andy had a son waiting for him at home, and Duncan noticed as he clenched his fists.

Duncan found his voice. "How much?"

The man nodded and lifted a corner of his mouth. Five hundred American.

Duncan halted and craned his head away from both of them. He grabbed his jaw and massaged his five o'clock shadow. "That's steep, and your English is good. How do we know you're not a cop?"

"I look like a fucking pig?"

"Suit yourself," Duncan said and tugged Andy's sleeve before walking away.

"No. Gringo, I—"

Duncan lifted a hand over his head and waved once as he and Andy walked down the sidewalk. He bumped his brother into the doorway of the next casino, then put his arms on Andy's shoulders and turned him so they faced each other. Andy would be able to see where the man went.

"He watched where we went. Now, he's stuffing his hands in his pockets and rocking back and forth on his heels and balls of his feet." Andy knew what Duncan was after.

"How will we follow him?" Duncan asked. "We have no car. A taxi won't work."

"Got it, brother," Andy said.

His eyes fixated on something behind Duncan.

"Don't turn around," Andy said. "He's talking to a local."

People passed them in the doorway. Mostly men, but some had women with them. A larger man who smelled ripe with liquor shoulder checked Duncan on the way in. "Gringo. House."

Duncan didn't need the English to get the message. With the way he and Andy behaved and were dressed, it was the theme of the evening.

Andy grabbed his upper arm. "He's getting in a car. Follow my lead."

It killed Duncan not to turn and look. What the hell were they doing? Andy was completely reckless. It had always been his worst fault.

"Come on."

"Where are we going?" Duncan whispered. "How are we going?"

He soon found out as Andy gestured to a moped.

"A moped?" Duncan asked. "A moped with a lock." It was an ancient model and may be able to go twenty-five mph downhill.

"And you're a lock and explosives expert. Hurry up. This is a good spot. No one can see us. The dude is pulling away."

Duncan dug in his pocket and pulled out his key chain. Attached were miniature picks and files. He had the lock off in seconds, but the car was already out of sight. Andy jumped on and kick-started the bike anyway. "Get on."

The weight of the two of them kept the machine even under twenty-five miles per hour. They crawled down the road as they scanned in front and the side roads for the vehicle. Duncan had it memorized. It was a blue Durango with red duct tape covering the right brake light. He estimated it was about a 2001 model. Fu Haizi didn't drive shit cars, but this wasn't the U.S.

Andy slowed at a red light and hadn't even stopped before a man jogged over. The streetlight reflected against the knife in his hand.

"Wallet. Phone," the man ordered. The English was broken, but Duncan understood.

It came out of nowhere. Andy twisted on the seat and landed a left-handed hook to the side of the man's head. It wasn't enough to flatten him but worked well enough to deter his plans of the smash-and-grab Samuel had described.

He accelerated as much as the pitiful bike could stand with the two of them in tow. "I believe we've lost him, Andy. It was a valiant effort, and you were able to punch someone. So, it wasn't a complete loss. There." Duncan spotted the red duct tape through the traffic. "I see him. Three blocks ahead in the right lane."

"Ha. I knew it." There was no gunning any gas pedal, but they continued their path. Andy swerved between a few cars, earning volumes of Spanish protests through open car windows.

"Stay back," Andy said to himself. "Don't draw attention."

He followed the Durango for miles. He didn't stop for anyone or anywhere. Traffic thinned, and they wound around on increasingly disheveled and thinning roads. They reached the base of one of the mountains. Regardless of the mountain on their right, the absence of the tall city buildings allowed the wind to pick up and whip dust in small circles around them.

Andy turned off the single headlight. Above them, single-room homes with rusted metal roofs butted against each other. Looking up, Duncan noted the top of the mountain was barren. This was a slum hill. Duncan had heard of these. Peruvians who came in from the bush looking for work. The steep mountainside served as a back for the homes. It provided a wall and safety. And was extremely dangerous. There was no water and no stability in the case of a mudslide or fallen rocks and dirt.

"Stay farther back," Duncan said as he spotted a dense cluster of lights beyond the mountainside. It was in the middle of an open plain beyond the mountain in the distance. The line of packed dusty dirt showing a road was barely visible, but the Durango drove along it.

The backdrop of light showed a passenger in the blue car. "He must have picked up a passenger when we weren't looking."

"A customer, you think?" Andy asked.

"I don't know."

The terrain lacked bushes or trees for any kind of cover. The towering hills behind the cluster of lights were much too far away and much too big to use as shelter from view. "Pull behind the boulder."

"What boulder?"

"The one at two o'clock."

Andy rotated his head slightly to his right. "Ah. That's a ways away. Hold on."

They rode without use of the headlight. Andy had to slow to a snail's pace to keep from crashing as they hit each rock and dip in the hard earth. Duncan kept his attention to the cluster of lights.

It was like a miniature town. A few dozen vehicles were parked randomly. From this distance, it seemed some were rusted out and possibly hadn't moved for years. The polished paint from others shone in the scattering of overhead lights. A large warehouse-like structure stood to the left of a handful of smaller sheds.

Andy had slowed the moped down enough that the dust did not scatter as they rode toward the boulder. Duncan took mental note of each rock, vehicle and structure, painting a map in his head. A scattering of men walked from the warehouse to the cars and sheds. He didn't spot any children, but the area screamed danger.

As they reached their pathetic shelter, he took note of the entire three-hundred-sixty degrees around him. He didn't spot any lookouts or traffic approaching from the highway. What he did spot was a small green, metal structure. It was about four foot in height, rusted and with a myriad of wires tangled into it.

As they approached the boulder, Andy slowed the bike to a crawl. "Did you see that?" he asked.

"I did." Duncan slid off the back before Andy came to a complete stop. "I can't see where the wires lead."

"Only one way to find out," his brother said. He propped the bike against the rock and duck-walked toward the metal structure.

"Damn him," Duncan said. Andy had gotten far too brazen as of late. He squatted through the wind as it stirred around him. Duncan motioned toward him, pointing to the bike, waving back to the rock, but Andy didn't even turn to notice. As he reached the structure, Duncan could barely recognize the outline of his body in the swirling dust.

Now that Andy stood next to it, Duncan noted it was more like five foot tall. Through the blowing dust, he could barely see as Andy lifted wires. There seemed to be a bundle of them that led toward the miniature town and a group that led in the opposite direction.

Leaning his back against the boulder, he checked the time on his watch, then reached in his pocket and retrieved the Peruvian cell phone to see if Nickie had returned his message sent through social networking. What could she possibly be doing that would cause her not to touch base with him all this time? Closing his eyes, he attempted to keep his imagination at bay.

He sensed a presence a fraction of a second before the blow hit the side of his head. His eyes opened to the butt of a rifle. The pain was moot. His vision and his mind raced into much more pertinent details. His brother. His wife. He saw the men just before everything went black. There were two of them, and they were dressed in black pants and mock turtlenecks.

CHAPTER 9

It was time. It killed Nickie to sit back. Trusting others wasn't her specialty, but it wasn't her time yet. She watched as a single agent from team two rushed in low toward the guard. The agent must have trusted her description because, without looking, he reached around the door opening and grabbed the guard who leaned against the doorjamb with one ankle crossed over the other. The rifle in his arms shot out in front of him, but it was too late. The rest of Vehicle Two charged on the balls of their feet. She and Eddy joined them.

The agent thrust the guard from the doorway and around to the back of the structure as wails of both screams and laughter carried on inside. With several H&K MP5s pointed at the man, he raised his arms high as the cigarette dropped from his lips. Eddy lifted the M14 that hung around the man's neck, released the magazine and tossed it toward the woods.

The black clothing. The mock turtleneck. Smells that blew from the open doorway. Sex. Body odor. Alcohol. Drugs.

An agent grasped one of the guard's lifted wrists and wrenched it behind his back, then repeated with the other. Couldn't they hear the sounds? How could they function with the sounds? The screams. The laughter. It pounded in Nickie's mind, her memory, her ears. She clasped her eyes shut and shook her head in attempts to clear her thoughts, her focus.

The sound of a zip tie made her open her eyes. Eddy stood next to her with an arm dug under her pit. She watched as the agent secured the guard's wrists, then looked down at Eddy's hand. He was holding her up. When had her legs given out again? Several sets of soft-moving feet rushed into the building.

They were going in without her. No! Grinding her teeth together, she shoved Eddy's arm from her and took off into the structure.

Inside was an equally wide hallway that traveled the entire distance through the building and out the south side. A smaller hallway split perpendicularly through the center. She estimated close to a dozen agents entering from the opening at the south.

Two groups of special agents gathered and squatted, one to the north of the perpendicular hallway and one to the south.

She stood and held up a bent elbow and closed fist. The signal to halt. Pressing her back to the wall, she inched closer to the cross hall. Cries echoed throughout the area. A staggering john seemed oblivious to the cries or the cluster of men and women in Kevlar.

Making eye contact with the agent leading the group on the other side, she pointed to her chest and toward the west. Then, she pointed to him and the east. He nodded.

"Back to back," Eddy whispered to in her ear. She nodded. They couldn't rely on feds to have their backs.

Feedback announced the presence of the bullhorn. "This is the FBI. We have you completely surrounded." Organized chaos ensued even before the brief warning was done. Eddy pressed into Nickie, and they turned to the hallway as the announcement finished. "Come out with your hands up."

The command was answered with gunfire. Like a crab with four legs, she and Eddy made their way down the west wall as they shot at anything that wasn't a fed or a kid. Agents grabbed Fu Haizi and dragged them out the north entrance to join their friend there.

It wasn't that Nickie didn't care about the guards. They could be considered key. She needed them alive to interrogate and find out how to take down Fu Haizi as a whole.

But her mind and her memories did not allow room for that now. Now was about the girls.

A john came running from the first doorway. He was partially dressed, skinny and pale. The man was tangled in both the shower curtain that had covered the opening to the room and the pants that gathered around his ankles. As he freed himself from the curtain, he exposed his gray hair, gold chains and a tat of a butterfly on his hairy pectoral. A special agent snatched him up and dragged him down the hall.

The girl inside sat on the bed in her underwear. Short, black curls rocked back and forth. She was too drugged to notice the war that went on around her.

"I've got her," Eddy said and ripped the shower curtain from the doorway. He threw it around her exposed body and lifted her beneath her knees and shoulders.

Sirens sounded in the distance. Hurst had gotten her message after all. A short wave of relief was replaced at the sight in the next doorway.

Agents gathered johns and guards as Nickie burst around the shower curtain. This girl had blonde hair. She estimated her to be about thirteen. The girl held up her fists as tears ran down her cheeks like a running faucet.

Nickie holstered her gun. "You're free, honey. I'm going to take care of you." Holding up her hands, Nickie felt a tear of her own fall down her cheek as she inched toward the child on the balls of her feet.

Strands of straight, blonde hair fell over the child's shoulders before she fell forward completely. Nickie ran and caught her before she hit the ground. Tucking an arm around her shoulder, Nickie stuck out her hip and used it to carry the collapsed girl's weight and hefted her toward the door.

"We're here." Nickie smiled and crooned. In the midst of gunfire and shouts, peace ran in waves through her body. "Everything's going to be okay."

Eddy stood outside the door. Screams of girls, howls of johns and gunfire continued. Yet, Eddy stood with the girl wrapped in a shower curtain still in his arms. Nickie peered around the opening of the crude doorway. Special agents led girls from rooms toward the south hallway.

Instinct made Nickie's right foot step back into the room. The focus of her sight zeroed in on the hands of the girl in front. Handcuffs. They circled her wrists. Her arms wrapped tighter around the blonde child as her eyes bulged and darted her gaze to the next and the next. Shiny silver wrapped around each.

Panic. Air ceased to enter her lungs. She froze and checked east, west. In front of her and behind.

She tossed the girl toward Eddy, only remotely noticing the way he stumbled as he attempted to juggle both of the girls. "What the hell are you doing?" Nickie screamed and, in the midst of deflating gunfire, bolted toward the line of special agents. "Take those cuffs off. That's a direct order." Three steps from the first in line, she jumped and took air. Her fingers were spread. She was going to dig her thumbs into his eye sockets. Take his head off. Snap his traitorous neck.

But she was clotheslined from the side.

Flat on her back, she saw stars but thrust to her feet anyway. "You son of a bitch, I'll kill you." Ready position, she ducked beneath the arm that came from her left, then propelled her weight with a direct elbow blow to the agent's ribs. She rounded on the next man in Kevlar with a hook that sent every bit of her strength square to the side of his head.

She could hear the sound of Eddy's grunts and the fighting muffled under the cries that came from terrified and confused children, but she didn't dare take her focus from the group that closed in on her.

"Easy now, Detective," she heard someone say as if she was a rabid animal, but it was muffled behind the blood that pumped through her head.

Roundhouse boot to the face of one, back handed punch to another. Blood spurted from noses and dripped from ears. Skin peeled from her knuckles as she aimed for areas without protection. Jaws and noses, necks and arms.

Reaching the agent in front, she curled her fist and landed a solid punch to the center of his nose. Nickie bent and caught the girl he'd taken as she threw her boot out and dug her heel into the diaphragm of the one that closed in on her.

"These are children," she screamed like a crazed woman to the agents who stood behind, each with their handcuffed teenager. "Get those handcuffs off them before I have each of you suspended indefinitely."

Three of them closed in on her at once. She clung to the girl like a child with her blanket. "Don't you touch her," she screamed until her throat was raw.

One of them kept his distance and held his arms out. "Detective, it's okay. This is pro-to-col," she said like Nickie was hard of hearing. "The girls will be safe and warm in a certified juvenile detention facility. This is protocol. See? Safe."

Nickie's arms were wrenched, one to the left and one to the right, as heavy weight thrust her back to the concrete floor. Her wrists were pulled far from her sides and her face pressed into the cold floor. She opened her eyes, looking for the girl.

That was when she spotted it. The paddy wagon. Red lights circled the top of it. The children were being herded into a paddy wagon like cattle. Like criminals.

From around the front of the vehicle came polished black boots. Special Agent Hurst. Between the fingers that held her face to the ground, she searched his face but found nothing.

"Hurst," she begged. The backs of her eyes burned with betrayal. "Please."

"Bring her to the north side," he said. "And bring my car around."

She thrashed her shoulders and hips as four of them lifted her. The children were led to the van. "You liar!" she screamed. "Traitor! Bastard!" Skillfully, they secured her arms and legs so all she could move was her gaze. She spotted Eddy in a similar hold as he was dragged out the same side of the building as the children.

Her toes scraped the floor as they hauled her outside. As they tightened a zip tie around her wrists, she spit on the closest agent. "Zip ties for me? Did you use all of the cuffs on the victims? On the children?"

They shoved her head into the back of a vehicle, then the rest of her. She kicked the window as they shut it behind her. As the door closed so did the will of her arms and legs. Of her heart. Her lungs beat in and out, but the rest of her drooped forward. Her head, her shoulders.

It seemed like hours, maybe days, but was likely minutes before the front passenger door opened. Hurst slid into the seat, then rotated to face her. Her chin remained against her neck, but she followed his movements with her eyes.

He, too, sat with shoulders forward and head down. He wiped something from his eyes before he finally had the guts to look at her. It was an expression she didn't understand. On his face was a mixture of shock and helplessness. She watched as the whites in his eyes turned to a bright pink and water spilled over his cheek. "Nick," he croaked, "I don't…I can't…It was protocol."

Her breathing slowed, but the disgust that filled her soul seethed and percolated. Something she couldn't identify was in his hands. She stared at it through the steel mesh that separated the front and backseats. Something black. It was cloth with sparkles and a long string.

He opened his grasp and showed her. It was a small black purse with fake rhinestones lining the open zipper. Inside, she spotted it.

"Nick." His voice cracked. "Condoms and Pokémon cards. The child was carrying condoms and Pokémon cards."

CHAPTER 10

Duncan woke to blinding rays of sunshine that beat down on the other side of his closed eyelids. Everything hurt; everything except his arms. They were numb. He blinked, then squinted in the blinding light. It shone through an opening that seemed to have been a garage door at one time. Blinking from one side to the other, he realized he was not alone. And he was hanging.

A man sat on an overturned five-gallon bucket surfing through his smartphone. Duncan feigned sleep and closed his eyes again to assess his situation. Although his mouth cracked with thirst, his shoulders were the most concerning. They ached with pain and may both have been dislocated. He couldn't feel the rest of his arms or his hands and only knew they were still attached to his body because they were what kept him from falling to the dirt floor.

The throbbing from his shoulders was little compared to the pounding of the side of his head. Turning away from the light, he opened his eyes and scrunched his face. Dried blood from the side of his head cracked and pulled his hair.

He tilted his head upward. It took several seconds before his dizzying focus cleared enough to see his wrists. They were secured with zip ties and hung by rope from a low-hanging wooden ceiling joist. A barn swallow shrieked and narrowly missed his head before landing in its nest along the joist.

The balls of his feet barely reached the concrete floor, keeping a small portion of his body weight from pulling at his wrists and shoulders.

The man glanced up from his phone and spotted Duncan awake. He blinked a long blink. Pressing the side of his cell, he stuffed it in his pants' pocket and stood. He was long and lanky with skin the color of caramel. Sweaty brown hair stuck to the man's forehead. A small, decrepit wooden table stood next to him. A handful of bloody blades, knives, a mallet, a handful of zip ties, a machete, and Duncan's cell phone lay in a line on the splintered and dirty wooden top.

Without so much as another glance toward Duncan, he walked out through the large garage door opening. Duncan heard a conversation spoken in Spanish. It might as well have been the barn swallows talking, because Duncan made out only a single word from the entire conversation. Gringo.

He didn't know what time it was and hoped he hadn't remained unconscious more than overnight. He may have been dehydrated, but he decided not enough for more than a night of captivity.

His brother. Andy. Oh no. His mind cleared and everything came rushing back. With the way his head was wedged between his arms, he could hardly turn to look around the room. Had they captured Andy? Where was he?

Duncan jutted his chin forward the fraction of an inch his arms allowed and used the balls of his feet to rotate to the right. It was, indeed, a garage. The Durango sat empty next to a newer Jeep Cherokee. It wasn't the largest structure Duncan had spotted from his boulder vantage point, but it was large enough that it could have fit a half dozen cars if needed.

Wall-to-wall dirt floor. Corrugated metal walls with a single window centered in each. Two on the side with the garage door. Outside of the door opening, the place seemed deserted. The sun was barely over the horizon, but since the horizon was above a mountain, he estimated the time to be maybe 10 a.m.

He scuttled his feet in the opposite direction to the left. A wooden picnic table covered in empty cans and cigarette butts sat in front of three white box trucks. The man from the overturned bucket came back with three other men. Each dressed in black except the one in front. He wore tan linen pants, a white shirt and a tan blazer.

He walked to the spot in front of Duncan and stopped. He stared at him, tilting his head one way, then the other as he slid his cell phone from the outside pocket of the blazer. He spoke something to the men behind him, then lifted the phone and clicked some pictures of him.

Duncan was in a Fu Haizi lair in South America. The magnitude of this brushed the sides of his mind, but his brain was clouded with thoughts of Andy and his Nickie. Their safety and whereabouts.

His eyes must have wandered in his thoughts, because the man reached up and grabbed his face with a thumb on one side of Duncan's mouth and fingers on the other side. He turned his face to the right, then left before tossing it to the right, making his entire body swing in almost a complete circle.

"Who sent you?" the man said in a thick Peruvian accent.

Duncan stared at him through half-opened lids as he noticed a head peer around the opening to the door.

Andy. No, Andy, no.

The man closed his eyes in a long blink as he turned his gaze toward the bucket guy, then gestured a thumb at Duncan.

Bucket guy stepped forward, pulled his arm back and dug his fist into Duncan's gut.

He sucked air as if he'd just come up from three minutes under water, and coughed as he swung from his hands.

"I asked question."

It was hard for Duncan to concentrate. Not from the pain or the threat, but because Andy's head had disappeared. He sucked air and said between gasps, "I wanted...to watch."

"Who sent you?"

Duncan winced at the impending next blow. "I came to watch the kids. I like to watch." His brother was about to be captured and tortured. His Nickie was who knew where. It was all he could come up with.

The man squinted, his eyes black and lifeless. "Alexander say you have friend with. Tell me where is friend."

Bucket guy slipped on a pair of brass knuckles.

"The friend said I was a sick motherfucker," Duncan croaked, then raised his voice. "I told him to go back to his woman." As he spoke, he twisted his fingers, wrapping them around the ropes that held his wrists. "I think he found a whore instead."

The man gestured to Bucket guy and Duncan braced. This punch was metal and it was followed by two more. He heard a crack. Then, came the pain.

Spitting blood, he opened a single eye. The man poked the screen of his phone with his index finger. Andy appeared in the window opening next to the garage door.

No, brother, no.

Duncan's Spanish was sparse, but he understood enough pieces of the next conversation between the man in charge and Bucket guy.

Pit boss. Plane. Early. Then, a slew of expletives.

Pit boss. Duncan remembered this term. It was a Fu Haizi term used for someone higher up.

The man in charge spun on his heels and lifted his phone to his ear as he barked orders to everyone around him. The others scurried behind him like ants. They couldn't have been more than ten steps away when Andy emerged from behind the Durango, a large machete in his hand. Duncan's eyes opened wide, and he shook his head back and forth.

Andy smiled from ear to ear. If they got out of this alive, Duncan was going to kill him. With both hands, he lifted the machete over his head and ran straight for the ceiling joist. Duncan increased the space between the balls of his feet and braced. In one large swipe of his arm, Andy cut the rope that held Duncan's wrists.

With soft knees, Duncan landed and froze. He and Andy turned their gazes toward the backs of the men as they stepped out of the garage door opening. Duncan's shoulders screamed. His wrists were still confined with the zip ties, but there was no time. Andy slipped into the driver's seat of the Hummer painted camo in green and brown.

Duncan's eyes burned. His brothers. His platoon.

He yanked at the zip ties on his wrist as he braced. Bogies in the doorway. One of his platoon in the Hummer on the sand. He spotted the table of enemy weapons and ran to it. Keeping his eyes on the insurgents, he used his restrained hands and grabbed a bloody blade. He stuck it between his teeth, then bit hard and cut the zip ties with the steel of the blade.

He picked up the mallet and rushed the men. The sand beneath his feet muffled the sound of his approach. The soldier in the Hummer waved his arms and shook his head like a mad man, but Duncan only had this one chance. The insurgents sensed him as he jumped with one knee and kicked with the other, but it was too late for them. He handed a solid roundhouse to the side of Bucket's head. As the adversary dropped, Duncan swung the mallet at the bodies that came at him. The man in charge stepped back as Duncan connected the hard, rubber head of the weapon with the shoulder of the taller one, then the head of the shorter one.

The tires of the Hummer spun behind him. The man in charge stepped next to the building, and Duncan to the other side of the moving vehicle. "Holy shit, brother. Get in," the solider yelled as he skidded to a stop.

Duncan opened the passenger door and spotted an enemy plane approaching as he dove in and the vehicle sped away. A trail of glass followed them as bullets shot out the taillights and back window of the Hummer.

His chest pounded and his breathing came in long, deep gasps.

"It's okay, it's okay," the driver said in a panic. The voice didn't sound like anyone in his platoon. He looked down at his hand. Lines of deep red circled the outsides of Duncan's wrists. He remembered the zip ties. He remembered looking up at them when he hung from the ceiling joist. He remembered the man who sat on the bucket. The men in black pants and mock turtlenecks. Not from the Middle East.

Andy.

"Brother," Duncan croaked. A quick rush of agony stabbed Duncan's shoulders, his ribs, his head. Ignoring the pain, he forced his head to the side to look at his brother.

Andy's hands clasped the steering wheel of the Durango as he darted his eyes from the rearview mirror to the side mirror and back again.

"Brother," Duncan repeated.

"I know, I know. It's okay, man. They're coming."

Andy swerved around barrels and vehicles. Andy would never speak of Duncan's flashback. Not this one or the ones in the past. Duncan twisted and sat; his head nearly hit the roof of the car as they bumped over the primitive road. Craning his head around, he spotted the dust from about a half-dozen vehicles as well as a small plane that came in low toward the south side of the village.

"I need a gun," Duncan said under his breath.

Regardless of the noise of the ride, Andy shouted, "And add using an unregistered firearm to trespassing and grand theft?"

"Is that why you came at me with the machete?"

Andy didn't answer. It had been dark when they arrived the night before, but Duncan remembered well the turns and distance of the path they'd taken. "The highway is at the end of this road."

Duncan patted his pockets. His local phone was on the table in the garage. If he hadn't had a flashback, he would have been coherent enough to take it and slip out in the

Durango instead of attacking with the rubber mallet. Fu Haizi scum. If not for Andy, it would have been worth it.

He spotted the corner of Andy's local cell phone from his front jeans pocket and took it. Dialing Jess Larsen's cell from memory, he pushed send as Fu Haizi men rushed the plane.

"This is Jess."

"Jess, this is Duncan."

"Duncan! You never showed last night, man. It's good to hear from you. I was worried about you."

"Yes, well, we are, indeed, in a bit of trouble. Can you pick us up?"

"Samuel is here with me, yes. Where are you? Is everything okay?"

The Durango was old, dirty and sounded like it was choking on something. He glanced at the rearview mirror at the variety of vehicles that were gaining on them. "Everything is well. Let's plan on the same place he dropped us off. How about in fifteen?"

Duncan could hear Samuel's voice from the background. "Let me finish my coffee and I'll be on my way."

Duncan squinted in the side mirror at the people who climbed from the plane. The man in charge held the hand of a large woman dressed in a coral pantsuit, helping her from the plane. Ivanna Monticello.

CHAPTER 11

Nickie sat in the break room of the Louisville Police Department. Yesterday's donuts sat next to her in a white grease-stained box. The smell of burnt coffee came from somewhere on the counter behind her. She glanced at the pop machine, then tapped her fingers on the table.

An old tube television hung from the ceiling in the corner near the door. The sound was off, so she couldn't hear what the anchors said, but the breaking news scrolled along the bottom.

LOUISVILLE, KY...FBI RESCUES 63 CHILDREN FROM HUMAN TRAFFICKING...

She let her eyelids close. The voice of Special Agent Hurst came from somewhere outside of the break room. It had been like this for hours. She didn't have the energy to find him. What good would it have done? Everyone was going through debriefing. Everyone except her.

She stood and grabbed a hard donut on her way to the television in the corner. Even at 5'10" with two-inch heels, it was just out of her reach, so she sat back down in the chair on the other side of the table so her back was to the screen. She shut her eyes anyway.

She wanted to get home.

Home.

She didn't have a home. Not that brick and mortar was what made a home, but everyone needed some form of shelter. The sixty-three girls booked in juvie may never have a home again.

Her partner was due to escort former Officer Dale Parker to his next witness protection location. Now that Nickie wasn't in Peru with her husband, he would have to wait for both Eddy and her to get him there.

Eddy.

She had no idea where they kept him. They took her phone, her keys, her ID. She had nothing to keep her eyelids open except silent television and stale donuts. She took a bite.

The feet of the chair across from her scraped along the floor, so she opened her eyes.

Hurst slouched as he sank into the chair. He looked terrible. The top two buttons of his shirt were open, exposing the dirty inside of his collar. Five o'clock shadow. She was certain she didn't look any better. They had a complete conversation without speaking a word. It's funny how rescuing sixty-three captive children only to take them in and book them could do that to two people.

"Am I in custody?" she finally asked.

"None of the guys would press charges against a fellow…" His voice drained away.

Fellow what? Agent? She wasn't one.

"I'm sorry."

"Yeah, you said that. Am I free to go?"

"Yes, but I need you."

He'd never come right out and said it like that before, but she didn't care anymore. "Thanks for your help with the mole at the station and all that, but we're done here. I'm out." And thanks for taking away the captured men so she couldn't interrogate them. And for booking sixty-three trafficking victims.

"I don't know what to do." His eyes were doing that pink thing again.

Leaning back in her chair, she slung a boot over her knee and stuffed the rest of the donut in her mouth. She knew she was frowning, but didn't care about that either.

Running her hands over the top of her hair, she grabbed the back of her neck. "You're the one who dropped Jess Larsen's name to me. He's the only one I can think of who can help you with this."

"Jess Larsen of Child Rescue? He has retired FBI and Special Forces who help out with local emergencies. He takes them to third world countries to do rescues. Things are different in the U.S."

And there lies the problem.

"Right now, there are sixty-three children in a detention center instead of safe houses that could help them learn to be human again. You have no idea what's it like. They've been brainwashed." Her voice got louder and louder, and she didn't care about that either. "It's like a cult. These kids are made to believe they are bad. That no one will want them. Including their parents. Mostly their parents. What about the ones who don't have parents?" She pushed herself away from the table and stood.

"They're going to end up in foster care or a group home. They'll escape and end up right back in the arms of their captors." She paced, dragging her exhausted feet along the tile floor. "Or else they'll go home before they're ready. Their parents won't have the training to handle them, and they'll end up back in the system. That—" She leaned her head close to his, pointed to the television as it scrolled the news about the bust. "—is bullshit."

He dipped his chin and nodded.

She paced. "Jess has people who can come in and conduct trainings." She spun to face him. "You think feds are going to listen to a nonprofit trainer on how to do their jobs?"

"I'll call him, Nick. Condoms and Pokémon cards. I have to try."

* * *

Duncan took a deep breath. "The driver is going to finish his coffee before he leaves to pick us up."

"I heard," Andy said as he fishtailed onto the highway.

Duncan placed one hand on the dash and grabbed the passenger door with the other. They bumped and sped for several minutes, both checking their mirrors, before either spoke of the elephant in the room.

"I failed you, brother," Duncan said.

"Stop it," Andy answered as he took the first right into the city center. "Did you notice who came out of the plane?"

"I did." Duncan pointed to the left. "There is an alley in the middle of the next block on your left. Take it. To the public, Nickie's parents run an international import and export service. Lima is one of the locations on the map you created." Duncan checked the mirrors. No sign of the vehicles that chased them. "Take it. You're clear."

Andy slammed on his brakes and spun the steering wheel to the left. The car rocked back and forth twice before slowing down inside the alley. It was short and populated. People smacked the hood of the car as the two white tourists crawled through their territory. They were soon swallowed by passersby.

Duncan turned and watched over the heads of the locals. "I discovered mention of a mariposa joven in the files we stole from the IEM building. Young butterfly. It makes far too much sense that Ivanna arrived at the location."

He spotted the tops of two of the vehicles that had followed them. One was a conversion van and the other an old-model SUV. They passed the alley without slowing down. He hoped they'd shaken them. "Left out of the alley," he said to Andy. "The casino Samuel dropped us off at will be on the right side of the street. Let's get out of here."

Andy pulled the car to the curb a few blocks before reaching the casino where it had all started the night before. "We are a moving bull's eye in this car. Let's ditch it."

Duncan checked his mirror and spotted the conversion van as it turned onto their street. "We've got company, little brother. Move."

He and Andy ducked from the Durango and rushed down the sidewalk. At the sound of an accelerating engine, Duncan pulled Andy into the first store available. It was more of a small room and held shirts handmade by locals. Duncan and Andy stepped behind a rack. "I can't believe I let you come with," he said.

"Be glad, big brother. Wait 'til I show you what I got."

"What did you get?"

"Duck," Andy said.

Watching between shirts, Duncan spotted the man in charge of his interrogation. He spoke with locals on the street who pointed inside the store. Duncan grabbed Andy's arm and pushed his way to the back.

Peruvians sat at rows of manual sewing machines. Two supervisors carrying clipboards yelled and shook their fingers at them. One at the end of the rows reached beneath a desk.

"Here," Andy yelled and yanked Duncan out a screen door.

Duncan looked down the street to the left, then the right. He spotted Samuel's car and stepped into the middle of the street. At the sight of them, the driver jerked to a stop. Duncan and Andy jumped in and ducked low as Duncan said, "Go, go, go."

Samuel pulled out into traffic. "Good morning, men. I'd rather not know."

That was good since Duncan would rather not tell him.

"Look," Andy whispered from behind the front seats. Duncan watched as Andy scrolled through his cell phone. The notes feature of his phone contained lists of names, dates and locations. He forgot all about the fact that he was crouched down in the back of Jess Larsen's car in the middle of Lima, Peru, with a half-dozen Fu Haizi vehicles searching for him.

Several of the locations listed July 2nd next to them. Locations from Ontario to Vegas to L.A. to Daytona. "Are these what I think they are?"

"Yep," Andy said and peered over the back of the seat. Sitting up tall, he leaned close to Duncan and whispered, "I tapped into the electrical box while I waited for the village to go to sleep. Which it never did," he added as a second thought and shook his head. "When the scary dude showed up and made his way to the garage they had you in, I had to cut off my file copy program and save your ass."

Duncan continued his scrolling. There were numbers, estimates and names. Leaders of the sub groups?

"Wait," Duncan said and took the phone altogether. He scrolled back and found a name he recognized. Goodrich. His name was next to July 2nd, Daytona Beach Resort and Casino Poker Tournament. Duncan guessed Fu Haizi would need to find a replacement since the crooked FBI agent lay in a morgue with a bullet in the back.

Nickie.

He loaded up the social media app and sent her a message.

Special Agent Hurst set Nickie's belongings on the table and slid them toward her. She didn't care if she looked like a teenager who couldn't live without her phone. Her husband was in South America, and she hadn't heard from him in over twenty-four hours. Grabbing her stuff, she pocketed her badge and ID as she punched in her security code to the cell.

In the midst of several dozen messages from her foster mother and brother, sister and mother-in-law, and captain, was one from Duncan. Relief swept through her followed by a wave of peace that only her husband provided. Before she swiped it open, she spotted another. And another. The relief turned to curiosity laced with worry.

Nearly forgetting Hurst sat with her, she leaned back in her chair and opened one in the middle.

We found a schedule. July 2nd seems to be an international day. Lima, Ontario, Vegas. Names of FBI.

She read it repeatedly. Each time, her hopes grew with the possibilities. July 2nd. That was in three weeks. That was enough time. She was hungry and needed a shower. None of that mattered. Her entire body came alive with ideas. This could work. The more she thought of her plans, the more she needed to jump up and get started.

Movement from across the table brought her back to the present. Hurst sat with his forehead resting in his palms. Hurst. She could use this.

It was unethical of her, but she said it anyway. "You've not only screwed up this bust," she said, "but my chances with Fu Haizi." Yep. No guilt whatsoever.

"Yes." He moved his forehead back and forth against his hands.

"I have conditions," she said as she read the message again.

He froze, then looked up to her, cautious hope written over his face.

"If I might happen to have information about another bust…"

Her phone vibrated. Another message from Duncan. He was on the phone right then? For a fleeting minute, her mind wandered to where he was at that moment. In a car? Working undercover? Trailing the perp who gave him the intel? All of the above?

Then, her stomach growled. She grabbed another donut and swiped open the message.

Horse races, boxing matches and casinos. Poker tournaments?

"And if I happen to share this potential information," she continued. "I want equal access to any and all planning and details."

"Done." Done?

I found headquarters. They got a pic of me.

Headquarters? The hair at the back of her neck stood on end. She typed out a question.

Headquarters? As in FH headquarters.

Electricity ran through her body. Headquarters? She'd spent the past several years chasing her tail. Taking down one Fu Haizi hub only to have another pop up. This could be permanent. "And I want each and every agent involved trained under Jess Larsen's Child Rescue on humane and proper procedures for trafficked children after they are rescued."

"Agreed."

Her phone vibrated.

Yes. Your mother was there.

In Peru? At the Fu Haizi headquarters. Her headquarters.

Her euphoria went to despair to sadness to fuming in seconds.

"This is my house," she said, barely remembering that was her captain's coined phrase. "I know these people." She raised her voice and pushed away from the table. "I know the business, and I know what I'm doing." She stood tall and remembered the time Jun Zheng took her foster mother hostage. The shot Duncan took to his shoulder. The beating Slippery Jimbo endured on her behalf. The bullet to the gut that nearly killed her partner.

She finished. "I want my choice of civilians."

He dropped his chin. "I'll try, Nick. You have my word."

Headquarters. She had a location.

"There's a car waiting for you. The driver is also your pilot. Eddy is waiting. The plane will take both of you home."

She grinned, not from the thought of going back to New York but the hope that she might put her mother, Jun Zheng and all of Fu Haizi away for good. And place each and every victim in a safe place. She stood and spun on the balls of her feet. "Don't call me. I'll call you," she said as she made her way to the door.

Her legs stopped. Snapped a pic of Duncan?

CHAPTER 12

The plane ride from Upstate New York to the witness protection location was short. Shorter than the one from Kentucky to New York. The plane was smaller too. A four-seater. Eddy rode in the passenger seat. Nickie and Parker rode in the back. Short ride or not, the seat belt nearly left bruises from where it hugged her pelvis in the turbulence.

The pilot wore big enough headphones; she assumed he wouldn't be able to hear a thing other than whatever was going on in the receivers.

It didn't matter. There wasn't any top-secret talking going on between her, Parker and Eddy. She was busy answering the mountain of text messages from her friends and family.

Nathan and I have reserved a spot at the kennel for Red anytime. We are ready to help whenever you are.—Brie

You are my daughter. You have not called. You will call.—Gloria

Hey, sis-in-law. Itching for a fight over here. Ma says she'll take Andy Jr. anytime. Have you heard from the men? Andy hasn't messaged me since last night.—Rose

We deserve to be there for you, baby foster sister, and if you shut us out, Mom will kick your ass herself. Lol. Call me.—Gil

"We're here already?" Parker asked as they descended.

Johnny and Bebe Lyons' vacation home was more of an estate. Miles of white picket fence surrounded acres of green grass, making the land look like one big puzzle piece.

"Where are we?" he asked.

Maine. But she wasn't going to tell the backstabbing scum.

The pilot aimed his plane for a short runway to the south.

Parker craned his head in every direction. "There's nothing out here," he said as he rubbed his hands over the thighs of his FBI-issued jeans.

Nothing but trees, mountains, lakes, and winding deserted roads. She could stay here indefinitely.

Parker asked, "How will we get food?"

"Shut up," she and Eddy said in unison.

She grabbed the side of her seat just as they touched down on the hard dirt. The top of her head hit the roof as they bumped along the runway. The brakes squealed, and the plane skirted to a stop.

While she waited for Eddy to open the side door so she could slip out, she assessed the surroundings. Not a single person in sight. Just what the doctor ordered, or in this case, her.

Sliding out, she leaned over and opened the storage compartment. She and Parker had one thing in common. Both held every material object they owned inside a single piece of luggage. She watched as he came around the plane and took out his single...no two...make that three suitcases. So much for common.

In her still unshowered state, she made her way across the manicured lawn toward the home. It, too, was painted white and looked like it had a number of wings. One-story ranch. A white wooden porch covered nearly the entire front of the house with a handful of white, wicker rockers that swayed back and forth in the Northeast wind near the front door. Something short and evergreen-looking clumped at the corners of the place.

It was nothing short of anything she would expect from a superstar power couple like Johnny and Bebe Lyons. It was good of them to let it be used to house Parker until he could testify against Nickie's mother, Jun Zheng and all the other scum. He was the only witness they had, but he was a jackpot of a witness and was going to put them away for two hundred and fifty years each.

The Lyonses had sent the help away. Where, Nickie didn't know. She pulled up the Berber front door mat and found the designated key. Unlocking the front door, she pushed it open, hauled her suitcase over the threshold onto an ivory marble floor.

The inside may have been the most beautiful home she'd ever stepped foot into. She didn't know. The sight in front of her combined with the weight of the last forty-eight hours, the last few years, the last few decades…it all came crashing down.

Her fingers didn't leave the handle of the suitcase. Instead, she dropped to her knees and sat on the back of her heels. There in the center of the foyer stood a black, metal stand. And on the stand was a cello. A Stradivarius. A gift tag had been tied around the neck. She didn't need to read it. She knew who would do this for her. Who would know what she'd lost in the fire that burned down her home and everything in it. The one who knew the only thing in that fire that meant anything to her.

It might have been the horrors of last night's bust, or maybe the lack of sleep. Maybe the fact that her husband was in Peru without her. The loss of her home. The ultimate betrayal of her mother. She wasn't sure, but tears started falling down her cheeks, and not just a few. Buckets of them.

She heard footsteps. Her body wouldn't move, and she couldn't get the frigging tears to stop. Nickie wasn't a crier. She heard Parker start to say something behind her. A loud rustle happened, and then silence. Thank you for that, Eddy.

Pressing her weight on the luggage, she stood, then let it fall on its side on the marble. She stepped forward and squatted down in front of the cello, running her hand over the bow that was propped next to it.

He bought her a cello. The one she'd had was gone. The one her mother purchased for her as a child in an attempt to refine Nickie into the uptown bitch her parents always wished she would be.

Not the kind of daughter who slipped away in the night so she could take out the family English riding horses and ride them bareback. Not the kind of kid who sneaks around in secret basement rooms she'd been ordered to stay away from. Not the kind who would find the room her mother used to keep children captive until it was time for them go out and be rented to pedophiles for money.

Squatting like a catcher behind the plate, she put her face in her hands and sobbed. Her shoulders shook, and she cried like a little girl in captivity who responded like a normal kid should. Nickie hadn't. She had fought and spit and swore.

She was no longer Nicole Monticello, daughter of Edward and Ivanna Monticello. She changed her name to Nickie Savage. She did that in honor of all the girls she left behind. The ones she vowed to save. She was a cop now. A detective cop.

Wiping her face with her sleeve, she stood. She would find the strength to touch the damned, sweetest, most thoughtful and personal gift she'd ever been given after she'd gotten her shit together and quit crying like a hysterical girl in need of years of therapy.

She leaned over, grabbed the handle of the fallen luggage and marched down a hall, looking for a bedroom to shower and sleep. Or else sleep and shower.

The sun was nearly down. Nickie put the finishing touches on her hair. She could accomplish a lot more in life if she didn't take so long in the bathroom. And if she didn't skip entire nights of sleep. Onward.

She zipped her boots and looked around the room she'd picked. It was nice. Superstar power couple nice. King-sized bed with a down comforter and Egyptian cotton sheets. Everything smelled like a clothes dryer was being used somewhere. She should probably make the bed, but then no.

Standing, she secured her gun in the holster around her shoulder and headed for the door. Duncan was due anytime and would answer the thousand questions she had about the Fu Haizi information jackpot he hacked into while he was in Peru.

July 2nd. International sting. It both overwhelmed and excited her. She couldn't decide whether she should jump for joy or puke. So, she chose option number one.

Her boots clicked along the white-washed hardwood hallway, then changed pitch as she hit the ivory marble floor of the main living area. The place was nice and all, but the colors would make her nuts. White, ivory, cream, beige. She was almost too scared to wear shoes.

She found Eddy in the kitchen. His black work boots were propped on the Lyonses' glass kitchen table. His head was behind the newspaper he held, but his raw and swollen knuckles were front and center.

"Sup?" he asked without dropping the paper.

As if the fiasco in Louisville never happened. Eddy was a good guy. He was rude and inappropriate. His ethics in the female department were marginal, but he was a good guy and great partner. She had doubted him.

She fell for the false trail Fu Haizi had left for her. She accused Eddy of being the mole. Then, she was a sobbing mess in the foyer of a witness protection house over the new cello she still hadn't touched. Train wreck.

Eddy moved the paper away from his face and repeated, "Sup?"

Nickie smiled and took a deep breath. "Where is he?" she asked.

He tilted his head out the window next to him. It overlooked a pool in the shape of an hourglass. She might have missed him if Eddy hadn't pointed him out. He sat in front of a dozen fake potted plant tree things. Bent over, he leaned with his forearms on his thighs, fiddling with a quarter.

Eddy took a sip of his bottled water. "It's not like he can get away."

She didn't need an explanation, but she did find Parker's proximity to the water disconcerting.

"I have the keys to the only car, and my gun is on me."

The gun Eddy hadn't used on Parker, even though Parker had shot Eddy in the gut and left him for dead in a stairwell. She definitely didn't need the explanation.

Places to house witnesses weren't generally luxury vacation homes or even this big. Still, Parker was out of reach, so she let Eddy explain.

"Thank you for taking babysitting duty," she said. She meant it.

"Yep," he said and shook his paper straight. "You owe me big," he said with an emphasis on the word big.

She smiled again. "I'm gonna talk to him."

He nodded and kept reading.

The air was thick enough to cut. She dodged leftover rain puddles on her way to the pool deck. She stopped and looked around. There was no fence around this pool. Is that what you got to do when you lived a million miles away from anything? He didn't flinch when she approached. He sat in the heat in the jeans and T-shirt the FBI had issued him.

At one time, she thought of him as straight-laced Officer Dale Parker. Smooth, confident Parker. Now, he was unshaved, in great need of a haircut and wearing a plain white T-shirt. His feet were so close to the edge of the water, she wondered if he contemplated falling in.

"Parker?"

He didn't answer.

She scraped one of the white painted wrought iron chairs closer to him and sat.

"I don't want to die," he said.

He should have thought about that before he helped child traffickers, became a mole at the station and shot her partner.

"They're everywhere, you know."

"I know."

He stared at the water as he shook his head. "I don't think you do. She's got people in high places."

She, as in Nickie's mother. What a cluster.

"Police, feds, politicians," he said in monotone and squinted his eyes as he stared. "Some are in it because they want the kids. Most just want the money." Mindlessly, he flipped the quarter between his fingers. "I was supposed to kill Lynx."

She sat up and straightened her back.

"I moved the kill shot. I didn't know he would lie there bleeding for so long. I really liked Miranda." He'd used the ADA. It was a struggle to sympathize.

She'd seen the look in his eyes before. Mostly from little girls forced to do things little girls shouldn't know existed. He was about to snap. His arm reached around his back.

In the blink of an eye, Nickie stood, released her gun from her holster, took it off safety, and pointed it at him.

He nodded in acknowledgement of why she aimed her Smith and Wesson at him, then slowed his movements. An index card appeared in his fingers. A quick glance told her it was filled with numbers.

"These are coordinates. There are grave sites, Nick. It's all I've got to give you."

"Okay," she said slowly and took the card from him. There were four pairs of numbers that could definitely represent latitude and longitude coordinates. "We'll check it out," she said and pocketed it. "You're going to testify against the bad guys, then live the rest of your time in witness protection. You have a chance here, Parker."

"No, I don't. And neither do you." He lifted his other arm, palm up. In it was the quarter. Except it wasn't a quarter.

She jumped to her feet and stared at it like it was alive. In a way, it probably was.

"I found this in the pocket of these pants." Now he tells her?

She didn't know if it was an audio bug or a tracking device. It didn't matter.

Grabbing his wrist, she took the thing and tossed it onto the cement pool deck. As she smashed it with the heel of her boot, she waved in Eddy's direction. His nose was in the newspaper.

She put an arm around Parker's back, pulling him down as she ducked and headed for the house. She barely took the first step when a bullet buzzed over her head. A single shot from the north. Sniper. At the top of her lungs, she yelled to Eddy, "We've been made!" His face appeared from behind the newspaper. He took one look and bolted from his chair.

Another shot came from the north followed by one from the west. A chunk of the clay pot holding one of the fake trees exploded in front of them, making her run a little lower and a lot faster.

CHAPTER 13

Parker was a big man, and while he didn't fight her, he wasn't exactly in a hurry either. As Nickie ran for the house, she dragged him along low with one arm while keeping his head down with the other.

The door to the back of the house opened before she reached it. "You motherfucker," Eddy said, wrapped his arm around the back of Parker's neck and punched him in the face.

Blood dripped on the marble floor as Nickie rolled her eyes and yelled, "I don't believe he did this, Eddy. We're wasting time."

He let go of Parker with a push to his chest. "The car is out front," he said and turned toward the entrance. A window in the back shattered. He ducked and yelled, "Move!"

He and Parker ran toward the front door. She veered left.

"What the hell, Nick?" Another window shattered in the back. "We don't have time for you to get your shit."

She didn't care about her shit. Her yet-to-be-touched cello was in the foyer still in its stand. As the two men ducked out the front door, she opened the case and gently placed the beauty in it. She finished snapping the latches as another window shattered at the side of the house.

Protecting the case like it was a child, she ran to the open door.

They'd left the passenger door ajar for her. If anyone shot her cello, they were gonna die a slow and painful death. She dove in, slamming the door behind her as a single bullet sank in the metal.

Eddy spun the tires on the police-issued unmarked. "Pretty boy's cello? Are you fucking kidding me?"

"It's a Stradivarius."

Two more bullets, one right after the other, hit the headlight and the passenger window. Glass flew at the back of her head.

The car fishtailed, and Eddy yelled, "There's only one way out."

"I know."

"The drive is almost a mile long."

"I know."

"There are frigging trees everywhere." Chips of glass blew into the backseat. Parker slouched with one arm covering his head and the other holding his FBI-issued T-shirt to his bloody nose.

Then, there was nothing. Only the wind blowing through the gaping space left from the back window.

Eddy didn't let up off the gas. "This can't be good," he said.

As they flew down the drive, she scanned the trees and the road in front and back. The trees blocked out the last bits of setting sun and the beams of light made the shadows move and seem as if things ran all around them. Her phone vibrated, and then rang. It was Duncan's ringtone. Oh no. It was Duncan telling her he was here.

"Duncan, it's me," she said as she answered while hanging on to the bouncing dash. "Stay away, please."

"And a hello to you, my lovely wife."

"I mean it, Duncan. We've been made. We're on the run."

"Where are you? Ah, I see you."

He saw her? That was when she heard it. A helicopter. "Eddy, pull over."

He didn't stop.

"Stop here now!" she yelled.

Eddy slowed but didn't stop fast enough for her liking.

"That's Duncan. Pull over!"

"Oh, hell," Eddy said and stopped the car. He craned over the steering wheel and looked out the space where the windshield had been. "Frigging knight in shining armor."

Ignoring him, she checked the surroundings. Road, trees, bleeding witness in the backseat. Her heart beat out of her chest. It might have been from the thought of Duncan coming to get them out of this mess, but she would never admit it.

He landed in the road ahead of them. She glanced at the cello case, then back to Parker, then to Eddy.

He threw up his arms and said, "I'll get the scum in the back."

She ran in low, cradling the case, with Eddy and Parker on her heels. The wind from the helicopter blades blew the trees, making their whereabouts visible for miles.

She recognized the pilot. Andrew flew helicopters as well as small jet planes?

"Incoming at nine o'clock and six o'clock," Duncan said. "Off-road vehicles." He paused and stared at the only thing in any of their arms. He grinned as he guided her into the copter. "You brought the cello?" he asked with brows lifted high.

"It's a Stradivarius," she argued. "Thanks, by the way."

He held out a hand to Parker, then to Eddy.

Eddy held his arms up and said, "Touch me, and I kick your ass."

The first shot struck the tail and was followed by a sea of bullets. "Move it, move it, move it," Nickie ordered. They lifted off before Eddy's butt was in a seat.

Duncan lifted a weapon from between the seats and started shooting out a side door. It was a machine gun. AR-15. Andrew spun the copter as he lifted off, allowing Duncan to spray the perimeter of the area.

"Holy what the fuck," Eddy screamed like a girl as he covered Parker's body with his own.

"I have grenades in the box," Duncan yelled over the sound of the wind, the helicopter and gunfire.

She dug in and grabbed two. Pulling the pins, she hauled one and the other out the door on the opposite side of the copter. Vehicles appeared out of the trees and skidded on the road next to the deserted police-issued unmarked.

"Black SUVs," she said. "I'm really tired of black SUVs." Long, lanky fingers wrapped around hers. Oh no, Duncan. He was taking fire from inside a helicopter. Her glance darted to his face. She scanned every inch of it, judging his mental and emotional state of mind. This was how his platoon died in front of him. The reason for his PTSD.

She read calm and collected. She also spotted a large goose egg bump on the side of his head. He didn't smile with his mouth, but he did with his eyes. She had a thousand questions but decided to take the moment to be thankful. Thankful they escaped. Thankful Parker wasn't floating in a pool with a bullet in his head. Thankful they had a plan for taking down Fu Haizi and that the new cello her husband bought her rested safely next to the AR-15.

Duncan had much to share, to plan. The clock was ticking, and he found himself in unfamiliar territory, that of impatience. His Nickie was alive and unharmed. She sat next to him with the wind blowing the scent of her freshly washed hair over him. She was busy reviewing the events of the past twenty-four hours with the disgraced Officer Dale Parker. Although he heard every word, as she spoke, she mindlessly tugged at the inseam of his pants, making his mind travel to places it shouldn't in such a scenario.

He hadn't seen his Nickie naked in nearly forty-eight hours. The time frame may be brief in regards to the direction of his thoughts, but a lifetime of events had happened in that forty-eight hours. Some events sent them forward in their quest. Some pulled them backward, which only served to send his mind into thoughts of pulling forward and backward.

He opened his eyes wide and shook his head three times, which caused her to stop talking and turn to him. She must have read the inappropriate expression on his face because she said, "Oh." Thankfully, no one else seemed to interpret the situation.

Pulling her hand away and to her lap, she continued, "Parker found a transmitter device in the pocket of his FBI-issued pants."

"What kind of a transmitter?"

"I'm not sure," she said.

Duncan extended both arms, one behind Nickie and the other on his knee. He looked to Dale whose nose swelled as they spoke.

"It was in the watch pocket," Dale said around the crusted blood.

"The what?" Eddy asked as Nickie moved her legs so her thigh brushed against Duncan's.

"The watch pocket," Duncan answered. "The small pocket inside the right side pocket of jeans. Take off your shoes." They could hide a transmitter as well.

Eddy huffed. "I'm not taking off my shoes."

"Not you, Eddy. Dale. Take off your shoes, Dale."

"Me?"

Duncan ignored the question. "And the jeans." They had a button fly. "The T-shirt can stay."

Dale opened his mouth as if he might try to protest as well, but Nickie and Eddy both lifted from their seats, chests out and arms wide, so he quickly toed off the shoes and slid off the pants.

"Whitey tighties?" Nickie snorted as she sat back down close enough that her hip pressed into Duncan's. An electric current connected the fabrics.

Dale nodded. "FBI issued."

"I liked him better in the hospital gown," Eddy said and sneered.

Duncan lifted the shoes and jeans and tossed them out the open side door. "I have a pair of pajama pants you can wear in the storage compartment. I'll get them to you when we arrive."

"Where are we going?" Nickie asked.

"My brother's home."

"Oh great," she said. "He's never going to let us live this down."

Duncan lifted the corner of his mouth.

"There's gonna be a lot of I-told-you-so goin' on."

Glancing to the cello case that rested on the floor beneath his seat, Duncan said, "You are worried about jeers from my brother regarding the use of his home and not the fact that you risked your life to bring an instrument in an escape vehicle?"

Her beautiful chin dropped for several seconds before she smiled and shook her arms in the air. "It's a Stradivarius!"

"Does it play well?"

The smile faded. "I maybe haven't played it yet."

He touched her cheek with the backs of his fingers.

Her lids closed, and her chest expanded.

"You two are making me wanna puke," Eddy said.

The sound of heavy boots came from the mudroom between the garage and the kitchen. Nickie slid her hand from the top of the kitchen table and placed it on her gun.

"Shoes off," Rose said, holding Andy Jr. on her hip at the kitchen sink.

It was Andy. Nickie placed her hand back on the table. The kid squirmed at the sight of his dad and wiggled from his mother's arms. It was like his legs were the only thing that moved as he ran to Andy, who was back in the mudroom.

He came back wearing house slippers with A.J. bouncing on his shoulder. Xena padded through the kitchen and ran to Nickie as if she hadn't just seen her a half hour ago. Her tail wagged furiously as she did her half whine, half cry thing and wiggled in a figure eight.

Andy spoke as if a kid wasn't squealing at the top of his lungs on his shoulder. "Perimeter is secure. Abigail or Xena would have sensed if something was out there."

A horse and a dog. Both loyal and with senses that beat any electrical security system.

"Okay," Rose said and hefted a diaper bag over her shoulder. "Off to Grandma's we go."

The kid couldn't talk yet, but he seemed to know what that meant as the squealing increased, and he started doing figure eights with the dog. It was all a little overwhelming for Nickie, and she stayed put in her seat at the kitchen table.

"Mamaw, mamaw," A.J. said and jumped up and down with both feet. So, maybe he could talk some.

Andy kissed Rose longer than was comfortable for everyone else in the room. Was Nickie the only one who noticed how Rose held her stomach low like she carried a shirt full of berries?

"Is this what I'm wearing?" Parker said as Rose and A.J. left. He had on the sweats Duncan used as pajamas and the bloodstained white T-shirt the FBI had given him. Duncan hovered around six feet tall, but he was no comparison to Parker's height. The pants were too short, and no one had shoes that fit him.

Struggling to keep a straight face, Nickie said, "We'll get you something tomorrow. Be glad you're not full of bullet holes."

"Yet," he mumbled and sauntered away to the adjacent room.

"Don't go out of my sight," Nickie called. Parker waved a hand over his shoulder.

Eddy, Andy, Duncan and she sat around the kitchen table. In that order. The seats were the bench kind and wound around the table like a horseshoe. It was simple and rustic and sat in a bumped out nook that overlooked the back of the Reed Ranch, as they liked to call it. She slid her hand on Duncan's thigh. It was warm and flexed beneath her grasp.

The black out there was endless. Had they missed a tracer somewhere on Parker? Was something slipped onto Nickie or Eddy when they teamed with the FBI? Were there dozens of men in the trees, ready to breach the farm at any moment?

Andy glanced in Parker's direction, then leaned in and said, "What did Special Agent Hurst have to say for himself?"

Nickie sighed. "I haven't told him." She hadn't even told the Lyonses yet, since the news of the breach would go directly to Hurst.

Andy popped the top of his beer and threw back a gulp. "You gonna wait 'til the morning?"

Duncan elaborated. "She may not tell him."

Andy stopped mid-sip. "Nice," he said and nodded. "Stick it to the man."

"Or at least I'm going to wait until I'm on the road. I interrogate my father and Jun Zheng first thing in the morning. I'll call him when I'm well on my way. I'm not saying he leaked the Lyonses' location, but it might be better for everyone involved if he doesn't know where the witness is being held." She really liked her job, but her tendencies to break the rules and direct orders made her wonder how much longer she'd be able to keep it.

Duncan wrapped his hand around the inside of her thigh. Her eyes grew wide and she looked away, brushing a thumb to the side of her nose. "It's late. I'm beat." She'd just slept for hours at the Lyonses' now bullet-filled vacation house.

Eddy rolled his eyes. He was doing that a lot lately. "I'll take first watch."

"Thanks, man," Nickie said and left the three of them at the table. She wasn't used to covert flirting and hoped Duncan took the hint. As she headed for the room Rose had prepared for her, she recognized the contrast between this and Lyonses' place.

The floors were stained wood instead of marble or whitewashed hardwood. The walls were covered in family pictures framed in matching wooden frames of different sizes and shapes. Animals were in the frames as well as family. Ouch. There was one of Nickie at her first family Fourth of July party. She looked like a deer stuck in headlights.

Her room was the one right after a framed photo of Rose holding a bald eagle tethered to her gloved arm. On the edge of the bed, Rose had placed a shower kit and change of clothes and…she would kiss her sister-in-law the next time she saw her…a curling iron.

The sound of familiar steps walking down the hall sent chills from her head to her toes.

CHAPTER 14

Duncan knew his feet moved at a regular pace, but it felt as if they waded through molasses. His wife waited on the other side of the door in the middle of the hallway. If they'd been alone, he would have picked her up in his arms and took her there on the kitchen table…if they'd been alone and if his rib cage wasn't covered in bruises.

They hadn't been married long enough that he could yet judge her unspoken signals, and the times they'd needed to communicate covertly rarely included sex. His feet paused as he doubted his interpretation of her kitchen table gestures and expressions.

She'd survived the past forty-eight hours on little sleep, a horrific failed rescue operation and narrow escape with a prisoner in witness protection. Yet, the news of a Fu Haizi headquarters and the potential July 2nd international sting operation appeared to give her a sense of hope Duncan had not seen in her before. His feet continued. The door was open. He stepped in, and she was there.

When she brought her face to his, she pulled her shoulders in tight and rested a hand on each side of his jaw. Her hips pressed against him, challenging his patience as man and husband.

He dug the tips of his fingers into her back and set his forehead to hers. He would be here for her as she was for him. A single palm left his face and trailed a line down his chest. His mind crossed over to a place of no return before her hand reached its destination. He used their joined bodies to close the door behind them and dug in.

The air left his lungs, and his head dipped to her shoulder. He slid a hand around from her back and cupped her in his hands, grabbing and kneading.

Her mouth was warm and needy. Lips and tongues joined, fought, meshed, and taunted as he and Nickie worked buttons and zippers and released fabric. Flesh. The heated, needy flesh of his wife.

Her eyes grew large. "Duncan, your ribs."

"It's nothing," he said and, for now, it was the truth.

Her fingers traced the ruby red bruises, then the outline of the tattoo on his left pectoral. A single, silky leg lifted and twined around his backside, pulling heat to heat.

"My Nickie, my wife," he crooned and trailed his tongue down her neck and over her shoulder. His hands couldn't be in enough places at once. The door served as a brace, and he pressed against her, raising her arms above her head.

Drawing his hand down her stomach, he didn't stop until he heard a quick intake of air. He covered her mouth with his to muffle any cries or moans.

"There, there, there. Oh, Duncan." She clung to his shoulders as the muscles in her legs collapsed under her weight. Her body shook. She left his lips and pressed her teeth into his shoulder. Lifting her other leg, he dove in. His Nickie, his wife. Joined. They rocked and moved. He had to see her face, her eyes. He held her as he craned his neck away to look into the steel gray.

The sight of a tear that dripped from the corner of her eye made him pause, but she moved closer to him, around him. And she smiled. The smile sent him over. It was instant and powerful and more than he could have expected.

Her thighs squeezed around him as she linked the backs of her feet together. They remained joined, and he pressed their cheeks together, supporting her weight with both hands on her butt. As she came down, he felt a sigh that seemed to come from her entire body.

"Thank you," she said. "I feel much better."

He grinned. "I'm happy to be of assistance, but my ribs…"

"Oh," she gasped and slid her legs down, one at a time. "I'm so sorry. That must have hurt."

The smile was more than a grin this time. "I feel much better actually. Thank you."

"I'm in love with you," she said and made everything else in this life obsolete.

Leaning over, she gathered her clothing. "Can we lie together for a few minutes? I've only been up for six hours, but I could use some Duncan time." As she stood, she grinned and bit her bottom lip. "Some of the other kind of Duncan time."

As she shut the adjacent bathroom door, he pondered their sex life and how much it had increased since she quit taking birth control. He slipped on his boxer briefs and pulled down the sheets of his brother's guest bed.

Their moments of discussions regarding a family had become fewer ever since the fire. Or was it because Nickie had discovered her mother was the one who had pulled the strings of Nickie's life since her escape from trafficking captivity? Or was it the plethora of other obstacles that kept barricading forward movement in her life?

She stepped out of the bathroom wearing only the shirt from his back she had removed from him moments before. Lifting his arm, she crawled next to him and shifted her back into him. His arm snaked around and pulled her into him.

"Duncan," she mumbled. "What if they find him? What if Parker's right and they find him and kill him?"

"What if they don't and he testifies?"

She pulled his arm closer to her chest. "What if I can't get Hurst on board with July 2nd?"

Kissing the top of her head, he said, "What if you do?"

"What if we rescue the children only to have Fu Haizi take more?"

Whether she had slept for hours at the Lyons home or not, she sank into a sound sleep.

The drive south was long. This was a good thing. Nickie needed time to sort through the past few days and the possibilities that lay in front of her. As the sun tipped over the horizon, she slipped on her sunglasses and rotated the visor to block the glare.

Chopin Internet radio station played low as she activated her hands-free. An occasional car passed her on the northbound side of the highway. "Call Special Agent Hurst, personal cell," she said to the device.

"Calling Special Agent Hurst, personal cell."

The sunlit drops of dew glistened on every surface. She wasn't comfortable leaving Duncan, Eddy and Andy in charge of Parker. Duncan and Andy would be busy sorting through the goldmine of information they hacked from the Fu Haizi site in Peru, and although Eddy was qualified and able to guard a witness in protection, it wasn't fair to dump on him like she'd been doing.

It took Special Agent Hurst six rings before he answered. "Nick," he said in a low voice. "How is everything?"

If he only knew. "Are you alone?" she asked.

"Yes, since you're calling on my personal number, I moved to the hallway."

Trust, Nickie reminded herself. He earned it. "One of your guys planted a device on the witness. We were swarmed. I spotted a total of four vehicles. Black SUVs. And at least six men. Two were sharp shooters."

Silence. She got that. She waited for the long list of questions. Where was the witness now? How did she know it was an inside job? Was the witness given the opportunity to contact an outside source and give away his location?

He didn't ask any of that, but instead said, "Is everyone okay?"

"Parker has a broken nose."

"Where are you?"

Translation: Where was Parker?

"I think we need to speak in person."

More silence. "Where are you?" he repeated.

"I'm driving. I'm going to question my father and Zheng."

"When?" he asked. "I'll meet you there."

"I'm a few minutes away."

"Oh," he said and paused.

She'd waited until mid-morning to tell him about the breach and until now before she told him she was coming to question her father and Zheng. She was scum.

"I'll be there in an hour," he said and disconnected.

"Text Duncan," she said to her hands-free.

The device acknowledged, "Texting Duncan Reed."

Made it here safely. Don't beat up the witness, no matter how much he deserves it.

The place was much like any jail or prison. Increased security through each door, searches that borderlined molestation, empty pockets, sign and wait. She couldn't remember the last time she entered any room without her gun.

A young prison guard stepped into the room and looked over Nickie's head. "Detective Nickie Savage?"

Nickie was the only one in the area. Since the gal didn't call her ma'am, she would give her a break. She stood. "I'm Detective Savage. Shall we?"

The woman nodded, turned and walked back through the same door. Nickie followed and grabbed it before it shut in her face.

The hallway was short. The tile floor, the walls beige painted poured concrete. Tiles broke up the ceiling above her, and the guard stood in front of the door she'd opened and held for her. Nickie knew who was in there. She just couldn't get her feet to move.

Duncan's shrink would have a field day with this. She cracked both sides of her neck, then dug the heels of her boots onward.

The guard clasped her hands behind her back. "Call when you're done. I'll be outside the door."

Nodding, Nickie turned the corner. She might not have recognized him. Same frown. Same defiant posture. But his skin was as gray as the roots of his hair. He didn't look up. She swore he'd lost thirty pounds. She couldn't remember the last time she'd seen him out of suit pants and a dress shirt.

She forced her feet to move. Pulling out the chair, she said, "Hello, Father," and swung a leg over the top of it. She lifted her foot and set her ankle on her knee. Hopefully, it hid the way her chest expanded and released.

"This is all your fault," he mumbled. His voice was nearly unrecognizable. Hoarse and soft. His eyes darted from place to place around the table but not to her.

"As usual," she said.

"Where is your mother?"

"I have no idea." Or else in Peru coordinating an international trafficking mission.

He tapped his thumbs on the metal table that separated them.

"Tell me about the basement," Nickie said.

He rolled his eyes and threw his head back. It didn't produce quite the same effect dressed in an FBI-issued jumpsuit. "The one you destroyed?"

She sighed. "I don't have all day. We know the basement was used to hold children between sex trafficking operations and sub group crime rings. We have evidence that it was remodeled and painted as a way to cover up evidence thereof."

"That is something you concocted. That's all you've ever done since the day you were born. Dad is a criminal. Dad hurts people." His voice turned childlike. "Dad covered up what I did while I was gone."

"While I was gone?" Nickie sneered. "Is that what we call forced child prostitution now?" She pulled out her picture of him and Jun Zheng standing in front of one of her father's buildings and slapped it on the table.

His chest was still panting from his tirade as he looked down his nose at the picture. "Why are you showing me this?"

"You're in quite a mess, Pops. Earn yourself some leniency. Tell me about your relationship with Zheng."

"Dr. Li? He's a delivery boy. You make it sound as if we are romantically involved."

She filled her lungs, then exhaled. "Is Li an alias?"

"I am done with your questions. Guard!" He pushed the picture away. "You're not making any sense, just like always. I am going to get out of this place, find your mother and sort all of this out."

"How can you possibly expect me to believe you don't know about the room in the basement? About the children that were kept under your roof?" Nickie had never known.

"Guard!"

"You expect me to believe you don't know Zheng's role?"

He lifted from the table. His feet were shackled and his hands cuffed. "You're incorrigible," he barked. "We gave you everything. The finest upbringing." Spittle sprayed from his mouth as he spoke. "How do you thank us? You go and…and…and do those things for those men."

Her arms were like weights. They sat heavy on her thighs. Jun Zheng was next. She couldn't afford to be off her game.

The guard came in and glanced from Nickie to her father and back again. Nickie shrugged and the woman escorted the Edward Monticello as he shuffled his way out of *the* room.

Her arms still weren't moving. Or her legs, or her heart. The backs of her eyes burned. If one single frigging tear escaped over her lid, she was going to kick somebody's ass.

The sound of an alarm jolted her from her stupor. She checked her surrounds and said, "No. Way." Her head shook back and forth in disbelief, then shook some more at her disbelief that she even had disbelief.

She had her suspicions, but she got her butt off the chair anyway. In defiance of the alarm, she took one slow step after another on the way to the hallway. It was empty, of course. The door shut behind her as the sound of the alarm changed pitches. With this, the sound of doors automatically locked came down both sides of the hallway.

The young guard came jogging around the far end. Out of breath, she stopped in front of Nickie, who swore the gal was about to salute. Standing tall, the woman said, "Sir. Detective, sir. I'm afraid I need to ask you to come with me."

"Jun Zheng?" Nickie asked flatly.

The guard's brown eyes grew wide and her mouth opened in a small O. She didn't answer. Steps came from behind Nickie. She turned and spotted Hurst just as out of breath as the guard.

He dropped his chin to his chest and nodded. "Jun Zheng, yes. He's missing."

"Of course he is," Nickie said.

CHAPTER 15

It was Eddy's turn to ride the perimeter, and since Andy was sharing a meal off-site with his wife and son, Duncan was in charge of watching the witness. Abigail had turned out to be an exceptional watch horse. With Xena at her heels, Duncan was confident they would signal if outsiders were present.

The sound of the ancient piece of junk Nickie drove pulled up to the house. With earbuds in his ears, Dale didn't seem to hear it. He sat in the adjacent family room listening to a book on tape while Duncan analyzed the sparse text messages Nickie had sent him during the course of the day.

She knocked, then pushed the door open and walked in. Her stride was without the purpose and confidence he'd grown accustomed to from his detective. Dark circles lay beneath her eyes. Her honey wheat hair was straight rather than the large waves she spent considerable time creating each morning.

Without speaking, he rose from his seat at the kitchen table. She made a direct line to him and threw her arms around his neck. Her body was warm, too warm. As she clung to him, he trailed his hand over her shoulders and felt the back of her neck. No fever.

Her face turned into the crook of his neck, and her chest expanded. He waited. Patience. Acceptance. He inhaled and closed his eyes, reading her need. She had not shared the details of her time with her father or Jun Zheng through her phone call or text messages. He would not question and would wait until she was ready.

They stood like this for several minutes, arms clinging and fingers pressing into muscle. Outside the ranch was alive. Whinnies from the horses in the barn. Songs from the birds in the woods. Chatter from the squirrels. The song seemed to soothe her as her body relaxed in his arms.

"I want to hear about the data you compiled from Andy's hack job in Peru."

He lifted his brows.

"And I need to tell you what I learned today," she added.

The door opened without a knock this time. Four paws with nails that needed to be trimmed ran through the mudroom to the kitchen. As she whimpered sounds of joy, Xena walked in a figure eight as she lifted her chin up and down. Around Duncan's legs, then Nickie's, then repeat. Nickie squatted and sat on her heels. "I wasn't gone that long, girl," she said, grabbing the sides of Xena's cheeks and pressed their foreheads together.

Eddy appeared from the mudroom as Nickie turned her chin in the direction of the witness. "You," she yelled to Dale. "Out to the patio where we can see you."

"Xena." She turned to their dog and said, "Go with him."

Parker sighed, shook his head and dragged his feet out the back door. Xena followed but failed to appear as much of a watchdog with the dancing and the tail wagging.

Eddy opened the refrigerator as Xena and Dale appeared through the patio window. Nickie said, "My father was a wash." She slid into the horseshoe bench seat that wound around the table. Duncan positioned himself next to her.

"He's cracked up," she continued. "Not making much sense."

She slung a boot on her knee. There were two times she did this: when she needed to make a specific impression of calloused and brazen during a meeting or interrogation, and when she attempted to convince herself she was calloused or brazen. Duncan assumed this was the latter.

"And he looks like he's got one foot in the grave." She paused before she continued.

Eddy closed the door to the refrigerator with his foot as he popped open the tab of a can of beer.

Rubbing the side of her nose with her thumb, Nickie said, "Jun Zheng escaped again."

It gave Duncan a sudden desire to sling a boot on his knee. Eddy's arms froze away from his body as the carbonation escaped the can.

"I know. I know," she said, "but you have to admit. No surprise there."

Worry crossed her eyes. She checked where Dale sat in a patio chair with the earbuds in his ears. Xena lay at his feet. "Except, I think it happened while I was there. The guards were a mess. Alarms were blaring." She waved her arms in circles above her head. "Hurst showed up. He's feeling like shit about it all. We talked for a long time."

As Eddy slid around the table, he threw Duncan a look as if he worried about his partner. Her eyes grew big and moved to each of them, but she continued. "He led a team of seventy-one to rescue sixty-three children from trafficking only to have them booked through the juvenile detention process." She seemed to have forgotten about her unrefined, brazen façade. She placed both feet on the floor and folded her hands on the table. "The witness protection location was breached by one or more of his own, and now Zheng escaped while under their watch. His hands are tied regarding allowing civilians in on any operations. Hurst feels trapped and at a loss of options. I sense he truly wants to do the right thing, but recognizes the corrupt agents and realizes how much the red tape of the business ties our hands."

It was a lesson that his Nickie had endured almost weekly as of late. She shook her head and took a deep breath. "I wouldn't tell him where we're keeping Parker."

Eddy leaned forward. "We gonna have the feds on a massive manhunt for us, partner?"

"I don't think so," she said and stared at a spot on the table. "It was a hard day on both of us. We need some time to process."

"That doesn't make me feel much better, ya know."

"So, are you going to tell me about Peru, or what?" she said to Duncan at the still silent table.

The sound of the opening door in the mudroom was followed by Andy's voice. "You didn't start without me, did you?" Ah, the hacker himself.

"Yes," Duncan said to Nickie. "Let's get started." He turned his chin and spoke louder. "The coffee is decaf." He'd made it that way for his wife.

"What's the matter with you, brother?" Andy opened the door to the cabinet above the coffeemaker. "I'm going to need something stronger than that."

"I can make a cup of caffeinated for you," Duncan said.

"After a visit with my mother-in-law, I'm going to need something stronger than that too." He took out a bottle of whiskey from the top shelf.

Nickie wondered if all parents were supposed to put the liquor on the top shelf. She should give up and pour a few fingers of whiskey for herself. Duncan set a hand on her thigh and squeezed gently. Damned observant husband.

Andy brought his glass to the table. "I made the mistake of telling my mother-in-law about the botched up trafficking bust, Nick. Bad idea."

Rose's mother was not only married to the NPD captain, she ran dozens of homeless shelters all the way up and down the East Coast.

"She's seen her share of mistreated youth." With the glass of whiskey in hand, he paused. "And from the look on your faces, Duncan did not tell you what we found in Peru."

"What you found," Duncan amended.

"Yeah, you were busy being captured."

"You crawled off into the wind to explore the cable box. I stayed behind the rock we had agreed upon as our hideout."

"And got yourself caught."

"Is this what siblings do?" Eddy asked. "I wouldn't know."

She shrugged. "Me neither."

"Sorry," Andy said and pulled a few notecards from the inside of his jean jacket. "And I didn't get everything. I had to go rescue the captured brother. How are the ribs, by the way?"

Red. Purple. Bruised. She had to make sure and keep her hands on his shoulders in the bedroom while they were—

Duncan would never say. He just lifted a brow.

"I need to get back in there," Andy said and placed the notecards on the table. "I've categorized these into three subjects."

She craned her face closer. They were titled: Customers, Employees and Dates/Locations.

"I hacked into the server using the phone we bought in Peru, so I was only able to screen shot some lists. They are partial and cut up."

She was trying to listen and read at the same time, but she was distracted by what she was looking at. Names, dates, locations. July 2nd listed several locations and events. Car races in Daytona, boxing in Puerto Rico, horse races in Cleveland and Vancouver, and poker in Vegas and Lima, Peru.

Andy pulled out his phone and unlocked it with his thumbprint. The screen shot was a list of names. She took it from him. Craning her head close, she read several names out loud. "Strong, Lewis, Moody, McKinney, Tanner." All names of crooked cops and politicians.

"Yes," Duncan said. "There are others."

"Special Agents Strong and Lewis," Eddy said and pretended to spit. "The only thing worse than a dirty cop is a dirty fed." He looked over his shoulder and out toward former Officer Dale Parker. He was still on the patio, safe and sound with Xena facing him, alert and in a sit.

"We've got to get back into that server," she said.

"There is no we," Duncan retorted.

She craned her neck and glared at him.

"You are not privy to the location, and I'm not sharing."

It was like an alien had invaded his body. She jerked her gaze to Andy.

He held up his hands. "Oh no. Bros before…well, brothers first, Nick. You understand."

"Like hell I do. This is my—"

"I'm not implying that you will be left in the dark, only that you are needed here. You said it yourself. Special Agent Hurst cannot allow us in on his operations, but he can allow you."

She huffed out a breath and had to force her arms from crossing in front of her. "There isn't any operation. I haven't told him anything yet."

"But you will," Duncan said, "because it's the right thing to do. He works July 2nd from the States. We deal with Peru."

July 2nd. That was less than three weeks away. "We could take a trip down there before the 2nd, just you and me."

"Hey!" Andy interrupted.

Eddy's expression said he felt the same way.

"Okay, the four of us," she amended. Fu Haizi was her case, not her captain's. Not the FBI's. Her entire life's purpose. Her why.

CHAPTER 16

Thirteen donuts seemed like overkill, but the bakery had this thing called a baker's dozen special on Wednesdays, so Nickie went with it. They wouldn't compare to her mother-in-law's scones, but at least Nickie wasn't empty-handed. It was the first time they'd had Sunday morning scones on a Wednesday morning. She needed to get to work, but Duncan had insisted and he was damned persuasive. As they drove, she bounced a leg inside her dress slacks and boots.

Unfortunately, Xena also knew she wasn't empty-handed. The dog could sit and stay, heel and keep her head out of the toilet water. But donuts were more than she could resist. Whine, drool, stick head out window, rinse and repeat.

Duncan chose his Barracuda that morning. His chest stuck out further whenever he drove this car. It was the first time he'd allowed Xena in it, and now there was drool over everything. The windows were down, so while shaking her leg, Nickie gathered her hair around her shoulder over her holster and kept it from flying in her face.

The heat was stifling, but the scent of fresh air made the open windows worth it. They bumped onto the Black Creek Bridge and stopped. Nickie leaned in and checked her side mirror for any cars coming behind them, then asked, "Why are we stopping?"

"Listen," he said.

She didn't hear anything except Xena panting, so she glared at Duncan. He smiled. That didn't help her concentration on whatever she was supposed to be listening to. She turned her head and closed her eyes. "Why do people close their eyes so they can hear better?"

"It is difficult not to focus on what you see when it is in front of your eyes."

She grinned. Zen Master Duncan.

He said, "When we blacken our sight, our focus moves to the senses still available."

Water rushed over the rocks, echoing beneath the bridge as it hurried out the other side. Ah. This was a memory for Duncan. Not just a memory, but an eidetic memory. The sound from his childhood would be as crisp in his memory as if it happened yesterday.

As she expanded her lungs, she opened her eyes to view what she heard and spotted a Great Blue heron. Its stealthy walk was better than Nickie sneaking up on a perp. Xena barked, and the bird squawked like a flying dinosaur, bent down and opened her wings. As she flew to a location free of barking dogs, Nickie noticed the cattails and tall grasses along the bank that cast shade over the water, making it seem even darker than it was.

The car started moving again, and Duncan placed a hand on her knee. Both of her feet rested on the floor mat. The quiet breeze blew her hair around her shoulders, and the soft curls rubbed against her cheeks.

They turned up Duncan's aunt and uncle's drive. Brie and Nathan. He never called them by their first names. It was Mom and Dad.

Family didn't have to mean blood.

As they passed the scattering of towering native trees, the house came into view. And so did the cars that were there. Her eyes squinted at what she saw. Scones at the Reed house meant Andy and Rose. She got that. And when her in-laws' biological children were home from college, it meant James, Jonathon and Hannah. So, their vehicles made sense too.

It did not mean Nickie's foster mother or brother. Yet, their cars were parked along the garage as if they belonged there. She glanced at Duncan.

He returned the look and shrugged.

Now, she was scared.

Xena was inconsolable and uncontrollable. She danced circles in the backseat until they parked when she tried to escape out the window. "Xena, sit," Nickie said to deaf ears.

Nickie got out before the car came to a complete stop. She opened the back door. Xena lunged as the front door to the house opened. Brie and Nathan's Lab bounded out.

The barking. The whining. An outsider would think the two of them were doomed for a head-on collision. Nickie watched through her fingers, but both Red and Xena skidded safely to stop, sniffed butts, circled each other three times, then took off around back.

"It's like a ritual," she said.

"Indeed," Duncan responded and took her hand.

She took a deep breath. "Okay." She grasped his hand while balancing the flimsy white box on the other. "Let's find out what this is all about."

The smell of coffee blew over her as soon as she stepped through the front door. How could something so awful smell so good? Her steps slowed as she approached the kitchen. "It's too quiet in there," she whispered to Duncan.

"Agreed."

There was more than her foster mother and brother. Gil had brought his wife. Teresa was there too. Andy and Rose were here. None of them had their children with them, which was another red flag. She was glad she'd brought her gun.

It was more like an intervention, rather than Sunday-turned-Wednesday morning scones with the in-laws. They sat around the enormous cherry kitchen table Nathan had made with his own hands. The only two empty chairs were one at the head of the table and one on the other side. Each person had a small plate and drink in front of them. None had taken a single bite.

Step by careful step, Nickie approached and set the box of donuts in the middle of the table.

Andy reached for the box. "Daily Baker's Dozen from Northridge Bakery. Score."

Daily? Not just a Wednesday deal? It was like who was going to be the last one standing when the music turned off in Musical Chairs. Nickie was not going to be stuck with the head spot and quickly took the one at the other end of the table. She carefully avoided eye contact with Duncan since she'd just thrown him under the bus.

Gloria took a deep breath. Nickie winced like she'd just sucked a lime after a shot of tequila. "We have learned of this Peru. And of this July 2."

Nickie's mouth dropped open and her eyes darted to Rose who held up her hands and said, "Wasn't me."

Andy was next. "She was really scary," he confessed.

Nickie sighed. "Yes. We have an international bust we are scheduling in a few weeks." How many resources they would have was yet to be determined. "I have a meeting with an FBI agent in the morning to plan that very thing."

"I told you a week ago. I come with you."

Hurst wasn't around. Nickie would throw him under the bus. "The FBI agent has a strict no civilians policy. He won't even let Duncan around anymore."

"I want to speak to this agent person."

"Oh, wow. Right. Okay. No." Nickie shuffled in her seat. Where was the soothing creek water when she needed it?

"I am coming to Peru," Gloria said in her way that said she wasn't going to budge.

"You know," said Duncan's uncle, Nathan. "That's not such a bad idea."

Gil jerked his head from Gloria to Nathan. "Oh no. I'm not gonna be left home."

Nickie was speechless. Flattered, but speechless. "As much as I'd like you to come—" And all get your heads blown off, "—you can't get a Peru visa on such short notice." There. That was perfect. How did Nickie come up with that so fast? She sniffed and sat up taller.

"I have already made arrangements. These Fu Haizi. They have identified you, Duncan. Yes? They know my Nickie's face. They not let either of you near this place." She pointed to the spot above her sizable chest. "I can get in. I speak the language."

Nickie's eyes grew large. "Peruvian Spanish is a bit diff—" she started to explain.

"You cannot keep me from this, my daughter. I would die for any of my children," Gloria said. "And this man. This Jun Zheng. He kidnapped me. This. It is personal."

Nickie's brain hurt. She sat at the desk in her office. Today was the day for her and Special Agent Hurst to have it out, and her head was still spinning from the railroading she received from her family at Sunday scones on Wednesday with the in-laws.

The desk clerk's station just outside of Nickie's office still remained empty. They hadn't replaced Lucinda. Her family hadn't even come to get her personal items yet. It made everything too real. Much rode on Nickie's shoulders. Most of it on this meeting.

Officers, desk clerks and detectives began to arrive for the day. Lights flickered and computers powered up. All except her partner. He was stuck babysitting former Officer Dale Parker at the secret Reed Ranch current witness protection location. When had her life become such a mess? When had she become emotional about every damned thing?

She had a plan. This was the day both the captain's wife, Amanda, and Jess Larsen could join them. The clock on her phone said seven. An hour to go.

Hurst was going to have to figure out a way to allow the civilians, or she would simply keep the whereabouts of the

July 2nd operations to herself. She would withhold Parker's location. Let him arrest her.

There wasn't room in her small office for the six of them, so they would meet in Dave's. She glanced over at the pop machine on the other side of the commons area and sighed. The opening elevator caught her eye. Jess Larsen of Child Rescue stepped out and looked from his left to his right.

She stood and walked around her desk. Jess caught sight of her and tilted his chin up in greeting. He followed her back into her office.

"Thank you for coming," she said and cleared off a chair for him.

"Of course."

He opened his arms and stepped toward her. Oh, boy. Ignoring her obvious and inappropriate reaction to being hugged, he held on and patted her on the back three times before letting go and sitting in the only empty chair.

She could still smell his cologne. It wasn't so bad. Jess was a good guy. After taking a short moment to recover, she chose pacing. He sat with his feet flat on the floor and his hands on his thighs. He nodded as he looked around.

"Do you think it will work?" he asked.

She sat down and closed her eyes. "I don't know. I am without a Plan B."

They reviewed the proposal, then re-reviewed it. She'd already done so with her captain's wife, Amanda, the night before.

The elevator opened. Dave stepped out with his wife. He stood over a foot taller than her and placed his dinner plate-sized hand on the back of the blue scrubs she wore. Glancing in Nickie's office window, his eyes landed on Jess before he kept walking.

Nickie pulled out her phone and sent him a text.

Ready for company?

He answered almost immediately.

Yep.

"We can head on in," she said to Jess. "It looks like just about everyone is here."

"Hello, Nickie," Amanda said as Nickie walked in. "It's good to see you." She walked up and wrapped her arms around her. It wasn't a pat-on-the-back hug. It was tight and lasted for hours. Or possibly a few seconds but seemed like hours. Nickie tried not to be too stiff and hugged her back.

"Thank you for coming," Nickie said. "I know you're very busy."

"This is important. I am here for you."

"Jess, I'd like to introduce you to Amanda Nolan. She's the person I mentioned who is highly involved in shelters around this area. Amanda," she said and gestured to Jess. "This is Jess Larsen, co-founder of Child Rescue."

They exchanged pleasantries, then together helped Dave arrange his leather guest chairs in a line in front of his desk. "Let's turn the chairs so the backs face Dave's desk. I want them to face the wall of dry erase boards."

Low vibrations came from the commons area. It was from a voice. She didn't need an eidetic memory to be able to pick it out of any crowd anywhere. Duncan. She couldn't hear the words he spoke, but the sound alone made her blood pressure lower several points. Yes. This was going to work.

CHAPTER 17

Hurst walked into the station at the same time as Duncan. Shaking his hand, Duncan squeezed hard enough to make his point without overstating. "Good morning, Special Agent. I believe we are the last ones to arrive."

Lifting his wrist free of his navy blue suit jacket, Hurst checked the time on his watch. "Did I get the wrong time? Eight o'clock, right?"

Stage one, complete.

An explanation as to why everyone had assembled early was not earned or warranted. So, Duncan nodded and said, "Yes, eight o'clock. Shall we?" he said and held open the door for him. They strode through security and to the elevator without speaking.

"It will be warm today," Duncan said as they rode to the top floor.

Hurst didn't answer, not that he'd asked him any question. He tilted his head toward Duncan and squinted.

Stage two, complete.

The common area silenced when they stepped out of the elevators in their suits and ties. No talking, no typing, no rustling of papers. Each beat officer who finished reports from the graveyard shift, the desk clerks and interns ducked their heads into work that suddenly encompassed them.

Stage three.

As they neared Captain Nolan's office, Duncan gestured for Special Agent Hurst to enter first. Dave sat behind his desk in full uniform. His wife, Amanda, sat in the farthest chair, wearing the scrubs she preferred to use when working with the homeless. Jess Larsen in a pair of jeans and a polo and Nickie sat in the next two. She was amazing. Beautiful, collected and poised. The chairs faced the back wall.

Stage four.

The group stood when they entered like they were in a courtroom. "I have coffee along the wall," Dave said. "Let's get started."

No introductions. No small talk. This was good.

No one went to the coffeemaker or moved from their seats but, instead, sat down and placed their hands in their laps. Except Nickie. Standing, she made her way to the back wall with an unrefined aura of street intelligence and cunning only his Nickie could display. She knew how to dress the part. Dark gray slacks that hung straight, hugging her hips and waist. Black boots and deep blue button-down blouse. She'd chosen her shoulder holster. Her Smith and Wesson M & P .45 ACP rested near her badge. He loved this woman.

"I have in my possession the planned locations of seven trafficking operations coming up within the next two weeks." Her words were for Hurst, but she spoke as if to the group. He would recognize this. Also, good.

She picked up a marker and tugged off the cap, giving the impression she was about to list the seven locations. Duncan knew otherwise. "Three of the seven are out of the country."

The large honey wheat waves moved with her as she rotated to face the empty dry erase board behind her. With the blue marker, she drew the numbers one through five in a vertical line on the left of the board.

Without explanation, she wrote her conditions.

Number one: No rescued child placed in juvenile detention facility.

Hurst placed his hands on the armrests and straightened in his chair. He lifted a finger as if to protest. Nickie didn't turn but, like a schoolteacher, seemed to have eyes in the back of her head and said, "I'm not finished, Special Agent."

Number two: Each agent involved trained by JL's CR certified trainers regarding alternative methods to handle processing victims.

He lowered his hand back to its place on the arm of the chair.

Number three: Civilians allowed in all operations.

This time she turned and took a step toward him. "Don't tell me you can't do this, Hurst. You had Slippery Jimbo Spalding practically leading your last bust. Make it happen or I'm out."

The muscles in Hurst's jaws flexed and released.

Rotating on the balls of her feet, she stepped back to the board. Her actions weren't forceful or condescending; they were simply honest and strong. She lifted her writing arm.

Number four: JL and AN in charge of coordinating safe houses.

"Locations I will provide if and only if you agree to these conditions."

She capped the marker and placed it on the tray at the bottom of the dry erase board. Number five remained empty. She strolled to the coffeemaker as she said, "Amanda?"

Amanda stood and walked to the marker board. Her small size should not be mistaken for weakness. Nickie upturned a mug from the wall and poured a cup from the decaf pot.

"I am Amanda Nolan. I am not only the wife of our NPD captain, but I oversee the homeless shelters in the Northeast and have connections up and down the East Coast. I have available safe house locations for rescued children across the east side of the country."

"You've been given the locations?" Hurst asked.

Amanda darted her eyes to Nickie. Nickie looked to the floor but nodded. "I've been given potential areas but no specific locations."

"Over the years," Nickie said from the side of the room. "Amanda has become a large presence in the area of shelters for the homeless around the Northeast as well as up and down the East Coast." She strolled back to the board with the steaming mug in her hand. Duncan found it difficult to recognize his Nickie with a mug of coffee in her hand instead of a Diet Coke.

"Her connections are solid as are her decades of expertise with housing humans in need. Thank you, Amanda. You're amazing. Jess?" Nickie gestured to Jess Larsen, who took his turn in front of the list of conditions. "Hello, Special Agent. It's good to see you again. Some of the locations are in the west, friend. Yes, Nickie's given me the general areas, and, yes, I can find solid places for the rescued children. Listen to her. I think she's got some good ideas."

Nickie had given Hurst her demands, then solutions to some reservations that would be going through his head. Duncan was married to the smartest, most beautiful, selfless woman there was.

She took a deep breath. No one else in the room would understand why, but her last condition would be the most difficult for her to express.

"Along with the locations of these seven trafficking operation locales, I have obtained the coordinates of four likely mass grave sites." Her fingers flexed and released before she turned and wrote.

Number five: Before sting operation, four qualified teams search potential grave sites.

When she turned, the expression on her face was not to be toyed with. "No exceptions. No negotiations. These are my conditions. If you don't agree to my conditions, I give you back Dale Parker and wash my hands of it all."

The silence could have been cut with a knife. His Nickie stood tall, her hands straight at her sides. No pacing, no rocking back and forth or fidgeting with her fingers.

"My superior still thinks Dale Parker is in Maine."

"Less than two weeks, Hurst."

"Why the grave sites beforehand?"

An agreement was close. Duncan could feel it.

"While your question is understandable, I am not going to answer it. The men needed to search and potentially excavate the sites are not the same men you'll use for busting human trafficking rings. You have the manpower for both. I do, too."

This was not entirely true, but his Nickie was an expert at not entirely true.

"Yours is faster. That's all," she finished. "What's it gonna be, Hurst?"

"What are the dates?" Hurst asked. Nickie said he would ask this and planned to give it to him as a breadcrumb.

"Date," she corrected, inhaled deeply and said, "July 2nd."

He nodded and ran his fingers over his jaw. "If I agree, you'll hand over Parker?"

"After. I need him for collateral."

He pulled his cell from the inside pocket of his black suit jacket. "With the press of a button, I could have you arrested for obstruction of justice, kidnapping and disobeying a direct order."

"Except you are responsible for the incarceration of sixty-three abused and molested children. Your organization is responsible for the breach in the Maine witness protection location and for the escape of Jun Zheng."

Duncan winced at the low blows.

"And you're a good man. A good cop. You have the power. This is in your hands."

Hurst held out his hand. "Okay, Nick. You've got a deal."

The corners of her eyes loosened. Her blink was a longer than usual, and her shoulders dropped. No one else would see it, but Duncan did.

* * *

The muscles in Nickie's neck ached like she'd just swum three miles. Unfortunately, she hadn't. Her purpose for this planet rode on this operation. There was no time for stiff muscles.

Lunch was over, but her stomach still growled. It threatened to toss back anything that went in. Jess caught his flight, and Dave took Amanda back to work.

Hurst, Duncan and she were left to hash out details. For now, she sort of wanted it that way.

The dry erase board with the conditions she'd given Hurst remained. Instead of erasing it, she pulled a clean one over the top of it. Before she numbered this board, she glanced to Duncan. He believed in her and, for whatever reason, loved her.

If she could get through this…if she could take down the organization that stole eighteen months of her life and continued to decimate the lives of children everywhere, she could focus on that starting a family thing. A brief image crossed her mind. She and Duncan as they held an infant between them. They were in a home in the—

Duncan cleared his throat. Shaking her head clear, Nickie blinked and spun around as she lifted the marker in her hand.

Number one: Professional boxing—Manhattan, NY.

Number two: Horse race—Cleveland, OH.

Number three: Car race—Daytona, FL.

Number four: Horse race—Louisville, KY.

Number five: Poker Tournament—Baraboo, WI.

Number six: Horse race—Albuquerque, NM.

Number seven: Celebrity poker tournament—Las Vegas, NV.

Plus a poker tournament in Lima, Peru, and horse races in Vancouver, but these were out of his jurisdiction. As they were out of hers. She glanced to Duncan. His subdued expression read confidence and support.

She drew a horizontal line between Daytona and Albuquerque. "Amanda Nolan will handle the placing of rescued children for location numbers one through three, Jess Larsen four through seven."

"This," she said as she circled Vegas, "is the rescue I'm leading. I have connections—" Or Duncan had connections, "—with sources who can get Slippery Jimbo inside the tournament." She hoped.

"Where will Detective Lynx be in all of this?" Hurst asked.

He knew exactly where Eddy would be. Nice try. She shrugged.

He walked to her, then around her. Picking up a red marker, he pulled the cap off with his teeth.

Across the top in all caps, Hurst wrote the words OPERATION FU HAIZI, then underlined it in one quick swipe.

CHAPTER 18

The new brushes Duncan ordered from Canada had arrived. Windsor and Newton. The studio he created in Andy's guest room didn't have a suitable easel or seating, but it had been so long since Duncan had painted, he dove in like a child in a candy store. The outline of his Nickie formed on the free hand paper in front of him. It was as he remembered her that day, standing in front of the room full of people she respected, presenting the most perilous proposal of her life.

He needed proper lighting, a bigger canvas and more comfortable clothing. None of it mattered that evening. His Nickie, his partner, his wife. She was coming closer to grasping her purpose, her meaning. Not that precise moment, of course. Currently, she was thirty minutes into her standard forty-five minute shower. The true meaning that had become her life had become his as well. He assumed this happened to people who became as one.

A deep charcoal created the lines of her hips and thighs as they fit beneath the slacks she'd chosen that morning. The purest of blues created the curves that filled her blouse and her posture. Golden browns helped express the way she spoke with her hands.

Most of his life had been marred with his memory, his curse. He searched from location to location and occupation to occupation for his reason for being. He spent his childhood pretending it wasn't real, his high school and college years using it for selfish ambitions.

He'd searched for purpose in the armed forces and left with post traumatic stress disorder. Painting for the rich and famous? The time had been the pinnacle of his failed attempts, yet its essence was what brought him and his Nickie together.

The sound of her hair dryer ceased. In the few years spent with this woman, he'd been part of rescuing more abused children, finding more missing women and saving more captive persons than he could have dreamed of in his wildest imagination. And he had a vivid imagination.

Her boots deserved the deepest of his blacks. He chose the medium that would leave the best impression of the black patent leather ones she'd chosen for that day. The door to the bathroom cracked but didn't open. He assumed she released the moisture from the air inside.

They were going to succeed. Operation Fu Haizi. The words written in Special Agent Hurst's handwriting would be etched in Duncan's mind for the rest of his life. Red and in all capital letters. In less than two weeks, they were going to gather the rest of the damning data from the Peru headquarters database, rescue the children from the eight locations, arrest the pedophiles identified on the hacked databases and put Jun Zheng and Edward and Ivanna Monticello away for the rest of their lives.

He blinked at the movement from the corner of his eyes. His Nickie stood in her pajamas, a new pair of shorts she'd purchased since the fire. They had pink ruffles around the bottoms and matched the color of the lacy tank she'd put on. She wore pajamas, yet she styled her hair. Closer scrutiny revealed she wore makeup as well.

She tilted her head and walked around his makeshift art studio. The ruffles were a numbing distraction, as were the thighs beneath them.

"This is quite a set up you've made," she said and laid her lips on his cheek. She stepped away before his brain caught up to the other parts of his body and he had a chance to grab hold of her. Curiosity won over as his eyes followed her purposeful movements.

Placing his brush in the case next to him, he waited patiently. She took the chair from the desk and set it in the center of the room. Then, she strode to the side of the bed and picked up her cello stand. The physical reaction to this was more than acceptable. It was like Pavlov's dog. Did she realize how many hours he could paint when she played her cello? Yes. The muscles in his face relaxed. She was well aware of this.

She set the stand down, stepped away and judged the placement before readjusting the black metal piece of equipment he'd purchased for her. Twice. She could adjust it another dozen times if it meant he could watch. Her thighs and calves tightened, flexing with each shift in her body weight.

The cello was next. It took less adjusting. His eyes closed, and he contemplated starting a new painting. His wife in one of his most cherished spots, playing her cello as he painted.

Looking at the paper that rested in front of him, he noticed a spot on the forearm of his drawing that needed adjustment. So, he picked up the smaller brush.

Without pretense and just as if it were something as simple as showering or placing her instrument, she took hold of the lacy tank and pulled it over her head. Every corner of his lungs emptied. Beneath was nothing but the creamy skin of his wife. The paintbrush fell to the floor. Had he covered the bristles with paint? He had no idea and no plans to investigate.

With the most ordinary, methodical expression on her face, she stepped out of the ruffled pink shorts and underwear in one single swoop. Her bare toes were painted an aqua blue. Had he noticed this before? She smiled at him as she rosined her bow.

As his mouth was certainly shaped in a wide O, he imagined his chin hung close to the floor. As only his detective could do, she slung a bare leg over the top of the chair and sat. She adjusted the cello between her legs, tuned it for the longest few moments of his life, then pulled the bow across the strings.

The expression on her face was part peaceful bliss and part ornery blonde. He had no idea which he preferred, but found himself switching to a canvas and starting a new painting. His fingers couldn't move fast enough. The cello, the stand. His wife. The position on the chair caused her hip to protrude like an invitation.

She planned this. She styled her hair and put makeup on just before midnight in his brother's home. He was certainly the luckiest man alive.

The fingers on her left hand danced along the neck of the instrument like the legs of a spider as her head moved back and forth with the bow. Part peaceful bliss.

Never once did she give the impression she was naked. "I find it interesting that in the fleeting moments we've had to replenish material possessions, you've chosen clothing and makeup before home goods," he said to her. Part ornery.

A single eye opened to him. "Interesting or disturbing? Didn't know you're stuck with a material girl, did you?"

"Material as in one who needs next to nothing in the way of shelter, possessions, vacations or vehicles?"

"Oh no. My vehicle is huge. Size matters."

He nearly choked on his tongue, but kept his pretense and dipped his brush. "Agreed. However, when the price of said vehicle is ten percent of the cost of an average vehicle, I say nay to the materialism."

"What about you?" she asked.

"Hmm?" World War III took place within him.

"You're used to living in big houses, with the best furniture, indoor pools—wow, do I miss that by the way— ginormous vacations, and the best cars money can buy. Except, all you've bought so far is painting stuff."

"And a cello."

That made her smile. "A Stradivarius. Sometime we should probably think about a place to call home."

"This is ridiculous," he said and set his brush down. "What kind of restraint do you think I have?" He walked to her, took the bow and set it on the desk. She plucked the first several lines of the Jazzy Cello at Barbas. He remembered.

He held out his hand and, without disagreement, she accepted and stood. He placed his hands on the sides of her face, lacing his fingers into her hair. Looking into each of her eyes, he noted that the steel gray was both peaceful and ornery. It was a familiar yet sparse expression in the past few months, and he looked forward to helping her keep it there.

First things first. Slipping his hands behind her bare knees and naked back, he lifted her from the light oak floor and carried her to the bed.

Nickie offered to take a turn at riding the perimeter. The sun would go down soon. Without a cloud in the sky, the bright orange blinked in and out between branches as she rode in the trees.

Clean air blew through her hair and her mind. Abigail trotted her happy trot. Nickie missed their rides together. Xena's tail wagged like mad as she zigzagged and circled around her and Duncan. Yet, it did little to erase the wrong or unjust in her world.

As she came to the highest spot outside of Andy's property line, she slowed Abigail to a walk before stopping altogether. From this vantage point, the blackened spot that was once her home showed through the trees. The unjust.

Xena came and sat in front of her, then tilted her head the way dogs did. "I don't know what that means, girl." It made Nickie smile. She gave the command, "Free," and the pup took off. She sniffed and searched and romped, but kept within eyesight of Nickie and Duncan.

He led the horse he rode next to Abigail and stopped. Leaning over, he stroked the white spots that covered

Abigail's golden brown snout. Her long tail swished behind them as she snorted happily and stomped a foot.

"What are you thinking?" Duncan asked her.

The wrong. How the abuse she suffered both internally and externally likely left her unable to have a child. "I was thinking about how life is ten percent the shit that happens to us and ninety percent the way we react to said shit."

"Introspective and forward thinking, and spoken as only my Nickie could."

She smiled and dipped her chin. The setting sun warmed the side of her face and left the jacket she'd tied around her waist unnecessary. "What about you?" She turned to him. When was the last time they had a moment like this? His expression did not look like he considered anything wrong or unjust. The wind in his dark brown hair made him look sexy.

He reached out his arm and opened his hand. She placed hers in his. The ring that sat on her left finger rested on top like a flower on a wedding cake. He laced his fingers in hers as he turned his head from the left to the right.

She joined him as they scanned the area for signs of wildlife, a passerby or any Fu Haizi insurgents waiting to shoot them. The scene was like a picture. The lush green that came with late June was everywhere, but not only ninety percent everywhere. Ten percent of what she saw was the brown of the tree trunks and the occasional dead tree.

"I am thinking," he answered. "That we cannot make a fire until all of this is finished."

Reality, yes. The tracks in and around the vast area that surrounded Andy's home belonged to his horses and their Rottweiler with thin trails of deer hooves and thinner yet where rabbits ran. The location of Dale Parker at the Reed Ranch was safe. For now.

Their fire circle. It was hidden to the west between them and the black pile of rubble that once was their home. Smoke signals would not help their concealed state. The small circle of stones with fallen logs arranged as seats around it would have to wait for the end of Operation Fu Haizi.

"I am also thinking," he continued and squeezed her fingers, "that although we cannot make a fire, we can still take time to paint and play."

Paint as in finish the nude he started the night before, and play as in her new Stradivarius. She liked this idea.

"I believe you should be required to finish what you started," he said.

She had started last night, hadn't she? It made her blush and look around like someone might hear him out in the middle of nothing but trees. That was when she saw it. Movement to the north. A deer? Coyote? "Xena!" Nickie commanded. The pup raised her nose from deep in a pile of brush, then turned her head in the direction of Nickie's pointed finger.

Xena sprinted in a straight line, zigzagging only when she needed to avoid a tree or sapling. Duncan's heels flew out to the side, then nudged his horse. Abigail took off like a thoroughbred out of the gate.

Through the trunks, she spotted him as Abigail pushed the limits of her speed. Dressed in black, he mounted a motorcycle. Stray branches whipped Nickie's arms and legs as they left the beaten path. She searched for others as she and Duncan converged. The engine of his bike revved and his tires spun, but it was too late. A few yards to go, Xena leaped. She soared through the air with her four legs extended as the bike fishtailed and moved.

The girl landed on his back and sank her teeth into his shoulder. He wailed as his arm flew back and struck her. Xena went down. The man went down on top of Xena, the bike on top of both of them. The throttle was stuck as the back tire raced circles.

Nickie and Duncan hit the clearing just as the bike slid from the man's legs, cut out and died. Xena snarled and bit like a rabid animal. The man covered his head and ducked.

In a volume Nickie rarely heard from Duncan, he commanded, "Xena, heel."

Both Nickie and Xena jumped at the sound. Xena didn't heel, but she did let go of the man and sat. He thrashed and gripped his shoulder. Binoculars fell out of his pocket.

Duncan looked to her. "It's time to relocate," she said and dismounted, pulling her handcuffs from her belt.

CHAPTER 19

If anyone tried to tell Nickie she would be back at this place a second time, she would have doubted it. But a third? And to stay for who knew how long?

The moment she'd spotted the Fu Haizi scout near the Reed Ranch, she knew where to relocate. Maybe subconsciously even before then. It was the only location she could hide Parker that Fu Haizi would never check. A place Jun Zheng had abandoned himself.

"It's difficult for me to imagine this neighborhood ever recovering from the housing crash," Duncan said as he turned onto the drive in the blistering desert heat.

"Same tall weeds covering the driveway," Nickie said. They smacked the bumper as Duncan crawled along the gravel until he reached the single car, detached garage.

"Fuck," Parker said under his breath.

"Anytime you want us to send you to the wolves, Parker, just let us know."

She checked the surroundings. No tires had driven on the property in weeks, maybe months, but she did notice a narrow trail worn in the weeds that led from the alley behind the garage to the back door. It was thin, like the ones made by the deer in the woods behind Andy's place.

"We went from a mansion in Maine, to a ranch in Northridge, to this," Parker whined. "Just sayin'."

"Shut up, loser," Eddy barked, "Or we keep you in the basement."

He was justified. The bullet wound Parker put in Eddy's gut wasn't even healed yet. "There is a basement, right?" he asked Nickie.

She nodded as the car came to a complete stop. "It's part of the reason we're here." Opening her door, she climbed out and stood. It was her turn to mumble. "Dry heat, my ass." It was like standing next to the fire circle. The sweat was instant and useless in the zero wind.

Duncan and Eddy got out too.

A footpath led from behind the garage to the back door. Duncan stared at it, too, as he walked around the front of the car. "It could be squatters."

She hoped it was squatters. Movement from inside the window she remembered went to the kitchen made her elbow Duncan.

"I see it," he said.

Nickie cracked open the car door. "Stay in the car," she said to Parker, then shut it again.

"Hey, it's hot in here." His voice was muffled from inside the car.

She considered ignoring him altogether, but chose a shrug.

"You wouldn't keep a dog in here."

Duncan opened the door and tossed him the keys.

"Go ahead and escape," she said through the windows. "Jun Zheng would thank me."

"To serve and protect," he said as he crawled into the driver's seat and turned on the AC.

Duncan led the way.

"I'll keep an eye on the back," Eddy said as he crossed his arms and locked his knees. Nickie assumed he meant Parker. Good call, considering.

The back door wasn't latched. He eased it open and stuck his head inside. The hinges creaked and the sound was followed by the thumping of running feet. A door slammed open against a wall in front.

Duncan waved a hand to her, then pointed to his chest before turning it toward the front of the house. She loved it when he used military signals. She nodded and stepped toward the basement door. Not many homes had basements in this area. The temperature was cool in basements, although that was relatively speaking. It was why she assumed the homeless chose this empty house as a place to hang rather the other dozens of empty ones in the area.

An open palm pressed against the center of her chest and stopped her. She looked at Duncan's hand, then darted her gaze to his face. He shook his head. She did not love it when he did that. Pushing his hand away, she stepped toward the basement.

He followed. At least he didn't step in front of her this time. She knew this house. She wished she didn't know it as well as she did. The FBI had first requisitioned her personal knowledge of child trafficking systems in a case that involved this home.

The homeless weren't the only ones who chose it because of the basement.

Fu Haizi used it to house children. As she turned the corner, she noted that the locks on the jamb to the basement door hung covered in dust and cobwebs. This was a good sign.

She already knew what the basement would hold. Other than a potential scattering of homeless, mostly runaways, it would carry leftover evidence of trafficking specific to Fu Haizi.

Creeping down the stairs, she dodged a spider's web. The familiar sound of shuffling and grunting came from within. As she reached the bottom, she peered around the stairway wall. They didn't notice her. Statistics said they were likely to be under the influence of something cheap and easy to obtain.

Covered in grime, an old outlet strip hung from the wall. Scrapes and scratches next to it and on the concrete floors matched the sizes and shapes of the cages Fu Haizi used for children. Aged blood and human excrement stains colored the concrete where mattresses would have lined the floors.

"Police," she yelled.

Duncan pulled his brows together and turned to her.

She looked right back at him as she said in an equally loud voice, "We are here to relocate you to a safe place."

It worked. They scattered like flies, taking turns scrambling out the single accessible window that was barely large enough to fit a child.

Duncan placed his hand around her upper arm, and tilted his head at her.

"We don't have time. It was the easiest way to get rid of them."

"Why are we getting rid of them? We can find them homes. You did so for the boy we found the last time we were here."

"He wanted to be found. Not all do."

A single female stood in the center of the room. She was filthy. Eyes dilated, she swayed back and forth.

"You the guard, the decoy or the sacrifice?" Nickie asked.

She was ready to catch her if she fell, but instead she spoke. "Are you Detective Savage?"

It made Nickie blink several times. Had they been made? She double-checked around for perps, but all she saw was garbage, random clothing and strewn mattresses.

"Johnny said you found him a place to live. He trusts you." The clarity in her voice was a contrast to her appearance, but Nickie knew all about how appearances could be deceiving. She paused before stepping toward her.

Jonathon Cleary. He'd called himself Jane Doe. "Yes," she said. "I am Nickie Savage, and I can help you too."

"Duncan," she said over her shoulder. "Secure the rest of the place, please, and get Parker and our luggage from the car. I think I have something in my bag that will fit this young woman."

She turned to him. His expression was impressed, peaceful and proud. It seeped into her very soul.

The ringtone said it was Duncan's pilot calling. Parker didn't flinch his attention from his ereader, and the girl called Sylvia slept soundly on the dirty living room carpet. He extracted his phone from the front pocket of his pants. "This is Duncan."

"Good afternoon, sir. Do you have an estimated time for takeoff that you would care for me to arrange with the Henderson airport?"

"Hello, Andrew. Yes. It won't be until late, I'm afraid." He smiled before he said, "And call me Duncan." It was a dance of words he and his pilot continually bantered over the years they had worked together.

"A late night departure. That will work quite well, sir."

Smiling, Duncan disconnected and continued his search of the home. The living room, kitchen and guest bathroom areas were clean of any electrical surveillance or tracking devices. However, he was reluctant to think of the word in conjunction with anything in this home.

He still had the master bath and two bedrooms to search. It would be nice to finish before Nickie returned. She would undoubtedly torment him mercilessly at the prospect of working surveillance cameras in homes long deserted by the people they searched for.

The rooms were void of any furniture. Other than food, they truly didn't need anything in way of furnishings. They'd brought a folding table, chairs and air mattresses with them. The truck stop located at the end of highway 95 would suffice for bathroom breaks and showers. Duncan had survived with less and his Nickie on much less. The heat was an entirely different issue.

He ran his fingers along the inside of the master bedroom closet frame with one hand as he called a local hardware store with the other. A simple generator and a few window air conditioners should solve that problem.

Dale Parker stepped behind him, his ereader device in one hand and the earbuds for it in the other. "It stinks in here."

"Indeed," Duncan said and pulled down the useless smoke detector.

"I need to get to wifi."

He searched the smoke detector for bugs of the electrical kind but found only that of the live and kicking variety. And a few that were not alive or kicking. "And why would a prisoner in witness protection need wifi?" Duncan asked.

Dale held up his device as if Duncan were dense.

"You'll need to wait."

"I have to use the bathroom."

"There isn't one. You can use the backyard or it seems any corner of the basement. You wouldn't be the first."

"It's not the standup kind of bathrooming."

Dale opened his mouth, but Duncan didn't let him finish. "We're not leaving the child, and I'm not waking her," he said and replaced the smoke detector to its spot on the ceiling.

"The pound wouldn't allow a dog to be treated this way."

"Yes, you've said that before. The difference is that shelter facilities don't care for dogs who have served as police department moles for child traffickers or who have shot the volunteers and left them for dead." Duncan left for the kitchen area.

His cell rang again. This time it was Nickie's ringtone. "My wife," he said as he answered.

"Not quite, Pretty Boy." The voice of Eddy Lynx caused his teeth to grind.

A small battle of wits ensued as to who would speak first. Duncan had endless patience as well as complete faith in his wife. Eddy used her phone for a reason.

"Nick wants to know if you need anything. She's in the shower."

The truck stop shower, which was not what Eddy alluded to. She hadn't wanted to leave Eddy at the house. She and Duncan would be leaving for South America soon. This was Eddy's last moment away from the prisoner in weeks. Mostly, Nickie didn't want to leave Eddy and Duncan without her to mediate.

"Bug spray," Duncan said.

CHAPTER 20

The seat recliner didn't recline. One of the hinges on her tray table was stuck, and Nickie ended up in an aisle seat. Not that Duncan hadn't offered his, but it was in the middle between hers and Dr. Byrd's, who landed the window seat. She appreciated the bomb expert's willingness to tag along and everything, but he was close to getting airsick. How could someone who dealt with explosives—defusing bombs specifically—be airsick? The aisle seat turned out to be the lesser of two evils.

She'd used Duncan's plane for so long, she had become completely spoiled. The guys at the station never even gave her shit about using it anymore. When did she become a married cop who was trying to get pregnant and whined about riding coach?

Andy rode next to Gloria somewhere in the back. She would trade seats with him as soon as the seat belt sign went off. The plane jumped. Again. Who knew when that was going to be? She tugged on her blouse, fanning her chest.

"I have Dramamine," Duncan offered.

"The turbulence that's coming from the plane isn't the kind of turbulence that is the problem."

He placed his hand on hers and curled his fingers around it.

"I should be in Henderson with Eddy and Parker."

"I know."

"I should be in Vegas with the Lyonses."

"I know."

He knew? "I should be in Daytona with Hurst and Dave."

"I know."

Did not. "Gloria should be home making plans for Sunday dinner with her family."

He turned her hand over and traced the lines with his thumb. A melody of clarity washed from the side of his thumb, through her hand, her arm and over her shoulders. "Are you going to be okay with all this?" His thumb stopped. She referred to the flashback he'd had the last time he was in Peru. He would know this. And he wouldn't be able to answer her. It was a low blow. "I'm sorry."

He reached beneath his seat and took out his tablet. She wasn't forgiven. She didn't deserve to be. He didn't just have PTSD. He had an eidetic memory. It was much of what brought them together in the first place. She'd been suspicious of him. He recalled details like he was reading from a text book. She thought it was a memorized alibi. He had something to hide.

Then, his sight became invaluable. He was able to memorize scenes, remember details others had missed. No camera needed.

At first, she thought of it as a gift, but crystal clear memories of learning his parents died in a plane crash when he was four years old were not a gift. Neither was helplessly witnessing the beloved aunt who raised him like a son as she was blindsided with a baseball bat. The time he was a boy and used as bait in the attempted murder of Brie. Memories of his time in the Middle East. "I'm really, really sorry."

As he worked his tablet, he placed his free hand on her knee.

"One way or another," she said. "This will all be over soon."

Seat belt sign be damned. "Screw it," she said and released the buckle. She stepped into the aisle, tiptoeing in her boots. Two of the nearest stewardesses turned to her. "Bathroom," she mouthed and pointed to the back of the plane. Grabbing the tops of the seats as she staggered, she cursed the fact that she'd chosen her four-inch heeled boots instead of the two.

Andy's eyes met hers as she reached him. His expression matched the stewardesses'. She pointed a thumb over her shoulder. "Your brother wants you."

He unhooked his seat belt and pulled himself up using the top of the seat in front of him. "Liar," he said and smiled as he maneuvered around her.

She slid in and grinned at the stewardess police as she buckled her seat belt. "I thought we could sit girls and boys," she said to Gloria.

No response. Turning her head to the only true mother she ever knew, Nickie recognized the look. Distant, serious and sad. "What's the matter?"

"Why?" Gloria asked and shook her head slowly.

Why had Gloria bullied, insisted and barged her way into a life-threatening operation? Why had she gotten involved with a girl who attracted trouble like flies at a picnic?

"Why children?" Gloria asked. "Why not guns or drugs?"

Nickie sighed. The forever asked confusion. The question.

She wrapped her hand around Gloria's. The contrast in color meant nothing. Neither did the thin, crepe lines next to Nickie's taut skin. Together they were humans. "Guns and drugs are a onetime sale. Humans can be sold over and over again."

Gloria's nose dipped but not her gaze. She stared at the back of the seat in front of her. "We will take these men, yes? Tell me we will take them and save the children."

Nickie clasped her hands together. "Count on it."

* * *

As they exited customs, Duncan placed his hand on Nickie's back. Warm muscles flexed beneath the cotton. It wasn't just the stress, but also the humid climate that would immerse them for the next twenty-four hours.

His legs ached from the sedentary flight. The drastic changes his body had gone through in the past few weeks were catching up to him. He and Nickie didn't have a private pool in their basement with which to exercise their bodies and quiet their minds. No longer did they have a basement. Neither had they taken the time to swim in a public facility. Since these were all first world problems, he chose to both keep them to himself and shake them from his thoughts.

The Jorge Chavez International Airport was sparse this time of night. Or was 3 a.m. still considered nighttime? Jess Larsen waited on the other side of customs as did his driver Duncan remembered as Samuel.

"Nickie," Jess said and opened his arms.

Duncan knew this about Jess Larsen, yet it was unfortunate. He didn't interfere but watched for how Nickie responded.

She held her arms out longer than appropriate, then patted him on the back as he pulled her in close. "I hope the flight was smooth," he said as he pulled away.

Nickie's reluctance at physical warmth with others. The corner of Duncan's mouth lifted. It was the highlight of his day, and it had barely started.

"The flight was fine," she lied. "It's good to see you." She rotated her body and stepped away from him. "This is my—" She lowered her brows and looked at Gloria.

"Mother," Gloria finished and held out a hand to him. "I am the one who will pose as—"

"And this is Dr. Tyler Byrd." Nickie interrupted, saving Gloria from speaking publically of their operation. Dr. Byrd adjusted his Indiana Jones hat along with the collar of the suit jacket he wore over the open-necked button down shirt that would, even in the South American winter, smother him as soon as they stepped outside. "You know Duncan and his brother, Andy."

"Good to see you again. Thank you for your time and service." Jess smiled.

Said the man who dedicated his life to the rescue and rehabilitation of victims of trafficking.

"Shall we find more suitable accommodations for private conversation?" Duncan asked.

Jess nodded, turned and led them to the sidewalk outside the building. Duncan didn't recognize the car, but he was glad Jess had brought one that would fit the seven of them. It was a VW van, Duncan guessed around a 1962 model. The driver, Samuel, was a local. Although under the radar, Duncan considered him a key player. He knew the land, the people and was worthy of trust.

Duncan spoke to him as he rounded the end of the van. "Samuel. How have you been?"

Samuel nodded and held out a hand. "Good, my friend. Good. Welcome back."

Duncan and Andy assisted Samuel as they secured the luggage on the top of the van. The rest of the group took their seats, but not before Dr. Byrd removed the suit jacket and puffed out his chest. "It's good to be here, friends. Good to be here." A large oval sweat mark had formed in the center of his back. "I've always wanted to be part of a mission trip, and here I am."

Andy paused and glanced at Duncan.

The van had three rows of seats. A single spot was left at the edge of each. Jess took the front passenger seat, Duncan the middle next to Dr. Byrd and Andy in the back with Gloria and Nickie.

Looking down at the floor of the van, Duncan noted the carpet was missing, exposing the painted metal from end to end in the vehicle. The vinyl seats were cracked and padding escaped, but Samuel had covered them with bamboo beads. The windows were down and the ride was quite comfortable.

Dr. Byrd removed his hat and ran his hand over the top of his sweaty head. Samuel pulled away as Jess began. "Is anyone hungry?" he asked.

Dr. Byrd opened his mouth, but Nickie answered from the back. "Can you drop some of us off at the safe house and take the rest on a tour to get the lay of the land?"

The doctor inhaled then let out a visible sigh.

"Of course. Nighttime in Peru is a beautiful sight to remember," Jess said and turned around.

The drive to the safe house took them around a section of the slums of Lima. Rows of single-room homes made of shared corrugated metal walls and roofs stood butted up next to each other. Alleys, most not big enough to fit a vehicle, wound between a few of them and disappeared in the city of metal sheeting.

It was surprisingly dark and quiet for an area filled with so many people. Chickens squawked as they stirred from their sleep from the noise of the van. "Everyone except me will stay the duration between now and the day we infiltrate the compound. Two others come next week."

Jess kept an eye out the windshield but turned his head enough to allow a view of his profile. "I understand Miss Gloria will be creating her presence as a potential buyer during her stay."

"Buyer of what?" Byrd asked.

Duncan slowly turned his head to the seat behind him. "Of children."

"Oh yes, of course," Byrd sang.

A mother walked alone in flip-flops along the side of the road, cradling a crying infant.

"Which brings me to the question of what your needs will be, Dr. Byrd," Jess asked.

"I will be collecting materials for an EMP." He spoke of the highly illegal bomb as if he were discussing planting flowers on Mother's Day.

Andy choked on air. Duncan found himself checking around the van as if someone may have heard them as they passed.

The doctor was oblivious to the inappropriateness of his words.

"EMP?" Jess asked.

Byrd nearly bounced in his seat as they made the turn onto the street that led to the safe house.

"Doc," Nickie raised her voice and interrupted. "That is not something we are going to bother Jess with. I am sorry, Jess."

The safe house was easy to spot. It was the only two-story structure for a quarter mile in each direction as well as the only brick structure. With the uncomfortable silence that encompassed the inside of the van, the only sound was that of the tires as they pulled alongside the building.

Oblivious to the reaction around him, Byrd finished by saying, "It will take me some time to gather the materials and create the device. In between times, I want to help the peasants."

Duncan closed a single eyelid. His face physically winced.

"Lesson one," Jess said, smiling, as if Dr. Byrd hadn't just mentioned a highly illegal bomb.

Samuel opened his door and exited the vehicle, but Dr. Byrd's eyes and body remained cued to Jess's every word. "These people are not peasants. They are intelligent, motivated people, working to survive in less than ideal conditions. They have a fierce loyalty to their country and their people and, although they will accept handouts, they prefer to work for their money."

Dr. Byrd blinked several times. "Oh."

Duncan grinned. Jess carried exceptional character.

CHAPTER 21

It was Nickie's first time in a foreign country. She didn't count the short trips she and Duncan took to the Bahamas or Cancun. Those didn't take her to the heart of the people who lived there.

She carried her single carry-on piece of luggage. Unfortunately, she didn't need more for the short time she would be here.

Everything was foreign. The air, the smells. They were pleasant, albeit different. The safe house resembled more of a dorm. Packed dirt surrounded the perimeter. Other than a large greenhouse that stood to the side, the place had little yard space and a tall fence surrounding the entire area. She stood outside the entrance, taking it all in.

Jess stepped next to her. "It's not to keep people out, but to keep the ones inside safe."

She hadn't questioned the motive; it was interesting nonetheless. Duncan followed as she stepped inside. Three small children were awake and up. Jess spoke to them in a dialect that wasn't as familiar as the Spanish spoken by her foster family. All three of them were girls. They looked to be around seven years old. Two of them ran to Duncan. "Mister Duncan," they said in a thick, harmonic accent.

He hadn't shared this part of his trip here. She had no idea he'd spent time in the safe house with the children. A strange sensation of estrangement ran through her.

He squatted low on his heels and wrapped an arm around each of them. They lifted their wrists and showed him the bracelets they wore. If he didn't understand what they were saying, he faked it well.

The third child tugged on Nickie's shirt. Copying Duncan's movements, she squatted. The girl didn't hug her but said something in her special dialect, then looked at her like she waited for an answer. Nickie looked around for anyone who could help translate.

Gloria stood next to them, her eyes glossing over. "She asks if you are here to save more children."

Nickie looked to the child. She had the prettiest brown eyes. Brushing a strand of hair from her face, she tucked it behind her ear. Nodding, Nickie smiled and answered, "Soon."

"Shall I show you to your rooms?" Jess asked.

To the right was a large living room area. Block brick walls surrounded a concrete floor. In the middle was a large straw carpet with mismatched couches that circled it. Duncan set their luggage out of the way in the room and turned.

Nickie shook her head. "I'll wait here, Jess. Thank you." Duncan and Andy took a step closer to her, one on each side.

Dr. Byrd tossed his jacket over the arm of one of the couches. "I'm not missing a moment," he sang.

One at a time, Jess looked to each of them. "All of you?" He scratched his head.

Gloria lifted her nose. "I want to see this compound."

"Oh my gosh, there's a cockroach," Dr. Byrd squealed.

Andy whispered in her ear, "We could always tell him we saw cockroaches in the van."

"Maybe poisonous snakes," she said as they went out the door in a line.

They piled back in the vehicle, and Samuel craned his head around the driver's seat. "I am taking five gringos on a tour through The Hill in the middle of the night?" he asked.

"Only if you're willing," Jess answered.

"Only if they're willing," Samuel said and started the engine.

Duncan was a much better seat partner. She pressed her thigh against him. The small, platonic connection was just what she needed. "What is The Hill?" she asked as they pulled away from the compound.

"It is a local name for a mountain. Many people of Peru come from rural areas to Lima in search of work. They live on the mountains. There is no running water and the electricity is little. Some have learned to use old car batteries to charge cell phones and box fans. The place next to the compound you call Fu Haizi is The Hill."

The road became increasingly sparse of homes or signs of life. Dr. Byrd spoke a mile a minute, but by this time, no one was listening. The sights, sounds and feel of the country were too much to ignore. A single coyote ran in front of the headlights. With a backdrop of climbing mountains, millions of stars filled the sky. She fully expected to see this on a canvas in her living room someday.

The sound of the engine lowered as they climbed. Duncan leaned closer to her. "We did not raise elevation like this the last time I visited the area."

"Let's hope Samuel and Jess aren't using us as collateral, then," she whispered and smiled.

The road thinned. Samuel turned off his headlights, leaving only the parking lights to brighten the path. Duncan said, "I can't imagine a vehicle making it up here in the daytime hours when populated."

Samuel spoke up. "The best view you will have is near the top." Except, he let his foot off the gas.

The outline of four men in dirty white T-shirts stepped into the middle of the street. Large men. Muscular large. As soon as the van reached them, the two on the ends broke off and sauntered around to the sides of the van before stopping. Keeping guard.

Samuel glanced to Jess. They seemed to communicate without words. "Don't get out," Samuel said as he did exactly that.

Not that anyone was planning on it.

"Don't get out? What does that mean? Who are those men?" Dr. Byrd's voice cracked as he said the last word.

As Samuel approached to the men, she noted how each of them was a full head taller than he was. When Samuel stepped out of the beam of light, the men dropped their folded arms to their sides. One held up an arm.

Duncan placed his hand on the door handle. What was he going to do about it?

"Is this okay, Mr. Larsen?" the doc asked from the back. "What is going on? Is this going to be okay?"

Samuel smacked the extended arm, then executed a complicated handshake. Nickie sighed with relief. They gave one another a one-armed hug and patted each other on the back. This male greeting of testosterone must be international.

Using the crank, she rolled down the window and lifted a single hand in greeting to the one guarding her side. The look he gave Duncan confused her. It was a mixture of surprise and anger. She really just wanted to hear what was being said and leaned her head out into the nighttime air.

She didn't catch much other than the words school, church and donations. The one Samuel hugged handed him a folded piece of paper. Samuel opened it. He looked at it for a long time before nodding and sticking it in the back pocket of his jeans.

Jess explained, "Samuel is a central part of this community. He's building a two-story concrete brick school in the center of the slums. He's provided many of these people with jobs and rice for their families."

The guard from her side of the van walked away from his post as Samuel made his way back to the driver's side.

"The road ends here," Samuel said through the open window. "We park and walk now."

Dr. Byrd asked, "You want me…I mean us to get out?"

Everyone ignored him and followed Samuel's directions.

"Stay close to me," Samuel said and led the way.

She'd already had the urge to hold onto his belt loops before he said that. As the pathway became small enough to warrant a single file line, Duncan maneuvered her and Gloria into the middle of the group.

Not much was said as they walked and walked. Random clucks from chickens became more frequent with the rising of dawn. Nothing was in a straight line in this place. The group wound through the rusted metal. Women emerged and stared at the gringos. Getting their fill, they squatted near fire circles and placed whole fish set on stones to heat around the smoke. A break in the metal caused Nickie to pause. They'd come high on The Hill. So high that the homes ended.

"Look," Jess said.

She turned and there it was. The compound they came to infiltrate. To dismantle. To destroy. Her breathing quickened. This could be it. Her end. Her happily ever after.

The place seemed alive. People, cars. All moving amid bright lights. "Look there," Duncan said. He wasn't speaking to her, but to Andy.

"Yes," Andy agreed. "That's quite an increase in foot patrols and vehicles, and there wasn't this kind of activity in the morning hours when you were hanging by your wrists."

Wait. What? "Hanging by his what?" she asked too loudly and made a dozen chickens squawk and dogs bark.

Duncan removed the set of binoculars hanging from his belt. He scanned the area. She let him take all the time he needed since he was recording the entire compound in his memory. "I see the electrical box," he said.

Andy responded, "Nice!" at the same time the doc said, "Where?"

"In time," Duncan said. "All in due time."

* * *

Duncan yearned for some place quiet where he didn't have to unwillingly memorize everything he heard, smelled, tasted, felt and touched. A pool. "Do you think Peru has a YMCA?" he asked Nickie sarcastically as they rode to the safe house.

Her expression softened. "A pool would be good."

"If we have nothing else in our new home," he said. "We must have a pool."

"There," she said and joined hands with him. "You said something about a new house."

With his thumb, he rubbed the ring on her third finger in circles. "That I did." By this time, the sun had risen over the tops of the mountains. Gloria and Dr. Byrd were asleep in the backseat, Byrd with his head resting on Andy's shoulder. Andy ignored him, watching out the window.

Her head turned to him. This look was not soft but filled with lines that formed between her eyes. "You said pool." She would recognize his reason for speaking it. A place where he could muffle the intake around him. A place where he could work his muscles hard enough that it distracted the pace of his eidetic memory.

The safe house appeared quite different from when they'd left it a few short hours beforehand. Children of all ages ran in and out of the front door. They played as if nothing amiss had ever occurred in their lives.

A safe house. A place for orphans and runaways who had been abducted into human trafficking. Mostly girls, but some boys. A place where children traumatized from their experiences could heal before transitioning fully back into the places they called home.

His Nickie was never afforded such a luxury. She had become a risk the day she discovered her parents' holding room for trafficked children in the basement of their home.

"Duncan."

Ivanna Monticello allowed Jun Zheng to abduct her only child from her bedroom at gunpoint in order to silence her.

Why not make a dollar while ridding herself of potential scrutiny?

"Duncan."

Now, her organization reached as far as Canada and South America.

"Duncan. Open the door, man," his brother said from the backseat. Samuel and Jess were already out of the van. He looked to Nickie.

"They are inside," she said. "It's okay. You're tired. We all are. Just open the side door, and we'll go inside and eat breakfast."

He did so and stepped out. The sun warmed his face and arms. There was much to do in little time.

"Other than an orphanage for trafficking victims, the building serves as a daycare center for the children of victims as they get back on their feet," Jess said as he led the group inside. "We also carry a work study program. You might think of it as a junior college or a trade school. Everyone who comes here works here."

Children of all ages ran to Jess and hugged him. His legs, his arms, his waist. They all but ignored the group of gringos who stood in the foyer.

Samuel stepped to Jess and whispered in his ear. Jess listened, then pulled his ear away and looked to Samuel. He rubbed his hands across the back of his neck and nodded.

"Who is hungry?" he asked.

CHAPTER 22

E ggs and scallops. Nickie understood this was an ocean front city, but she would have never thought to put the two together. Since many in this country went without, she ate every bite and thanked the cook.

Most of the group was dead on their feet. Gloria had been able to sleep on the plane, but she and Dr. Byrd slept in separate back rooms anyway. Nickie needed some level of planning and communication before she could think about sleep.

In the living room area, she played backgammon with one of the girls. Everything smelled musty, but it was better than the scent of blood and urine she'd become accustomed to while in captivity. That was what the children in the Fu Haizi compound endured at this moment.

The straw carpet that covered most of the floor was really quite comfortable. Soft but durable and wouldn't attract mold in the humid temperatures. The couches were another story. They were fabric and smelled like they had been in a home in a warm, humid climate with no glass on the windows.

Not all communication was done through speech. It had been too long since she'd played backgammon. The kid was kicking her butt. Duncan and Andy spoke about hacking and explosives. They would have to give her the Cliff Notes version at the planning meeting. That is, whenever, the doc and Gloria woke up.

Nickie was somehow able to exchange names with the little girl. Ariel. She called herself Ariel. Or else, she really liked Disney. "Doubles again," Nickie said, hoping her expression trumped her lack of Spanish. "You're killing me."

Ariel giggled. She had a tiny laugh although she was probably high school aged. As Ariel reached to move her chips, Nickie spotted something at the top of her back. Two raised lines peeked from beneath the collar of her T-shirt.

The girl must have noticed that Nickie stared, because she sat back and fast. Her expression was like she'd done something wrong. Of course it was.

Nickie set her fingertips on the back of Ariel's hand. The child pulled it away but looked up at Nickie. That's all Nickie had wanted. She smiled warmly and turned her back to the girl. Sliding the bottom of her shirt up, she exposed her scars that matched the child's.

When she turned back to Ariel, the child's eyes were as round as saucers. They darted from one side of Nickie to the other, searching her mind for answers to her questions. Nickie recognized the moment that the child realized there was only one answer. She pushed the game to the side of the ottoman and curled up next to Nickie. It was that moment in time, the small event that would mean nothing to anyone else, that made Nickie hate Fu Haizi more than she ever had.

Nickie's aversion to touching anything that wasn't her husband washed away. Lifting an arm, Ariel snuggled in and sat in the arms of someone who knew, someone who had moved on with her life, coming out on the other end working as a cop, married even.

There would never be a got-over-it. That was something Duncan helped her understand. Never a got-over-it but a move-on. She and Ariel would move on with their lives as best as they could, batting away the self-doubt and crazy each and every day of their lives.

Jess stepped into the area. "We're ready," he said, then led the way.

The room looked like a classroom. Nickie supposed it was. A dozen chairs sat around two durable folding tables. She sat down in one of them. Andy and Duncan were there as well as the driver, Samuel. No sign of Gloria or Dr. Byrd.

Jess arranged some maps over the top of the tables as a young boy ran in. He ran around the table, grabbed a soccer ball from the corner of the room and ran out.

Gloria and the doc weren't far behind. They sat in their circle of seven. Nickie stood. This wasn't much more comfortable than leading the meetings for the FBI sting or the plans with Special Agent Hurst, but the end was in sight, so she stood tall.

"Gloria has one mission over the next several days," she said as she stood at the front of the room. "Duncan will assist her as she makes her presence known in the community as a Spanish American woman looking to purchase trafficked children." Bile gathered in Nickie's throat. Gloria didn't even flinch.

"Dr. Byrd first will spend time in purchasing materials for his part in this."

"Nickie," Jess interrupted.

Yes. Nickie understood. She'd been intentionally vague about the doc's role in all of this. Child Rescue was a respectable, safe organization. Nickie would not include him in anything that could hurt his mission or the relationships he had built here. "I'm gonna get to that in a minute," she explained. "The doc and Duncan will shop for the materials. In three days, I leave to finish arrangements for the U.S. portion of Operation Fu Haizi." She lifted her chin and stood tall. "They will be creating a device while I'm gone. Andy's going to be staking out the compound to find the best time and location for infiltration."

Samuel leaned in toward Jess and started whispering again. They'd been doing a lot of that. Jess cleared his throat. "Excuse me, Nickie, Duncan. You might want to rethink some of this."

Duncan nodded and kept his eyes on Jess. Samuel pulled a folded paper from his pocket. Nickie recognized that paper. It was the one the big dudes handed him last night on the mountain. He held it out for Duncan.

He took it and opened it slowly. It was bad. She could tell by the look on his face. Really bad. Nickie did everything she could not to rip it from his hands. This patience thing was for the birds. After the longest damned time, he turned it for the group to see. Some words were at the top. She didn't need to be able to read what they said. It was a frigging wanted poster, and Duncan's picture was in the center.

"How much is 750,000 pesos?" she asked.

"About forty grand American," Samuel answered.

"So, you can't be seen," Nickie snapped. "No shopping with the doc. You have to stay hidden." Why didn't the men on the mountain take Duncan then and there last night? Forty grand. That must be three lifetimes worth of money for them. Duncan was right. Samuel was a key player in all of this.

"Or maybe come back with me to the States. It's saf— smarter," she said.

"Thank you, Samuel," Jess said. "This is very helpful."

"You're a good man." Duncan understood the magnitude of what Samuel had done too.

"I leave tonight to work the operation stateside. Gloria's son and Duncan's uncle arrive in six days to help with manpower." More like because they had browbeat, threatened and insisted their way into all of it. "There are three phases to this plan. Phase one, Gloria gets into Fu Haizi as a buyer and keeps the attention of key Fu Haizi players as—" She held up her thumb. "Duncan plants...distractions and—" Keeping her thumb up, she added her pointing finger. "Andy hacks the database—"

She added a third finger. "And the doc prepares his piece in this. Phase two, the distractions are ignited. Andy gathers the rest of the records as Byrd finishes his prep work. Final phase, the doc dismantles the compound and Duncan, Nathan and Gil save all the children." She took a look around and realized she was the only one who carried doubts. These people believed in her, even though she would be in Vegas when all of this happened.

She turned to face Jess. "Which brings me to your question. Obviously, much of this is covert. Although we will gratefully accept and appreciate your hospitality, we are going to also find a remote location to complete some parts of the operation I…we refuse to involve you with."

"I agree, but you need a better code word for explosives than distraction."

She grinned. "Understood."

"Have you slept since yesterday, son?" Dr. Byrd asked Duncan.

"No, and calling me son will not help with an amicable partnership." Duncan stood next to the doctor at the end of the drive that led to and from the safe house. It was where Duncan requested pickup from the cab company Jess had recommended to him. Jess also gave him the address of a motel he knew was safe and in a tourist area of the city.

"Right-o," Byrd said.

Children who should be in school ran between the corrugated metal rooms that doubled as entire homes for their families. They wore sweatshirts and sweatpants, but their feet were bare. One stopped to stare at the two white men who stood at the edge of the road as if they were lost. He was a boy about eleven years old. His shirt read, Kiss Me. I'm Greek. Duncan winked, and the boy smiled and ran away.

"So, you keep a low profile, Duncan." The doctor enunciated Duncan's name, then laughed as if that was funny. "That's quite a ransom you have on your head. Here is my list."

He handed over a handwritten, laminated index card. Duncan took the time to memorize it before handing it back to him.

"Oh no, no, no," Byrd said and held up a hand without taking the card. He stuck his hand in his pocket, then pulled out another laminated list. "I have my own."

Duncan's nostrils flared. "If one of those were to become misplaced, it could cause a national emergency."

"Oh." The smile faded from Byrd's face. "I can see what you mean."

Had he truly not thought of this before? The doctor stuck his hand back in his pocket just as the cab arrived. He pulled out a pile of matching, laminated index cards. Duncan rubbed his hand over his face, and then opened the door to the back of the cab.

"Hola," Duncan said to the driver. There was no barrier between the front and back bucket seats, so he held a hand over the seat. The driver took it and began the same complicated shake Duncan had witnessed between the men on the mountain and Samuel. He remembered it, of course, and returned the gesture.

Duncan handed the man a paper with their first location written on it. Lines formed on the driver's forehead, but he nodded and took the paper.

The car reminded Duncan of Samuel's VW van. Old and worn, yet tidy. It was cleaner than any New York City or L.A. cab he had been in. "Gracias, amigo," Duncan said to the man.

As they pulled away, Duncan held out his hand with his palm up and said to the doctor, "It would be best if you handed each of the cards to me. I will store them in my money belt. It is quite secure." Or he would throw them away in the first garbage can he found.

"I am thinking a few pieces at each store." Byrd winked at Duncan as if the driver couldn't see them in his rearview mirror. This was going to be a long day.

The landscape changed as they drove. Downtown Lima was waterfront to the Pacific Ocean. Tall buildings, restaurants with valet parking and people who filled every corner. This was definitely not the casino strip Gloria would need to infiltrate.

The first place they came to was a common drugstore. On a side road, it nestled between a hairstyling business and a coffee shop.

"Ah, yes, the basics. This is good." Byrd bounced.

Duncan needed a few personal items as well as the ones for Byrd's device. He considered dying his hair, since he was a wanted man.

"Stay close," Duncan said to him. The prospect of losing the man was better than if he'd brought the child with the Kiss Me sweatshirt.

CHAPTER 23

Nickie stood in the center of the motel room. It was accessible from the ground floor. The car could back right up to the door. Jess had given her the names and addresses of three motels that he considered safe. She chose the one that seemed the most under the radar. The desk clerk spoke decent English. Nickie booked it for ten days, no housekeeping needed.

For the next several days, this would be home for Duncan, Andy and Dr. Byrd. They had work to do here, things to build.

She hadn't slept in going on forty-eight hours. When Fu Haizi was finally dismantled and her parents and Jun Zheng in prison, she was never going to miss a night of sleep again as long as she lived. If everything went to hell and she ended up six feet under, her sleeping problems would be solved regardless. Six more hours before her flight back to the States.

She eyed the beds. The room had two along with a pullout sofa. Very American. There were several nice hotels in this city. This was not one of them. It was clean but worn. It reminded her of Samuel's van.

She would just pull back the comforter and rest her eyes for one short minute. Reaching for the one on the bed closest to the door, she heard his voice. She would be able to pick it out in any crowd. Instead of pulling back the comforter, she turned and pulled back the blinds. He carried a small box in one arm and two bags in the other. The doc dragged his feet and reached for the door with his free hand.

She opened the door wide and used the chair as a doorstop. The doc wasn't nearly as spunky as usual, and although that was probably a bad thing, she looked on the bright side. Silence.

"There you are," Duncan said to her after he paid and thanked the driver.

He passed through the door, blowing the scent of his barely there cologne and male shampoo over her. It was a much-needed reminder of home amid the uncertainty.

"Is this it?" she asked. "I expected more bags."

"This was trip number one. Purchasing all of the materials at once for an EMP would bring unwanted attention." He wrapped his arms around her waist and pulled her into him. PDA was not generally her thing, but she was leaving in a few hours and appreciated that he could read her need. "I stayed in the cab. I am a wanted man, you know."

She pushed him away. "That's not funny. What about the cab driver? Cabbies would be the first to know about wanted men."

He pulled her back and clamped his arms around her. "The driver was a friend of Samuel's."

"He seems to have a lot of connections."

"Indeed."

"What does EMP mean anyway? I get the zing and the woosh and then the nothing, but not how that works without killing everyone in radius."

"Electromagnetic pulse," the doc said from the doorstop/chair. He didn't seem to be sleepy now that the bags were all in. "Is a transient electromagnetic disturbance. A short burst of electromagnetic energy."

Duncan let go of her to drag the doc's seat away from the door, letting it shut.

Doc didn't seem to notice the hostility, scooted his butt to the front of the seat and kept right on talking. "Although it may be a natural occurrence, in this case, the origination of the pulse will be a man-made, radiated electric current." Oh yeah, he was awake now and talking with his hands.

"If large enough, the electromagnetic pulse interference, or EMP, will not only damage any and all electronic equipment in the radius of the pulse, but can damage buildings and aircraft structures." Byrd rubbed his hands together and spoke faster and faster. "The type of energy along with the range and spectrum of frequencies present can be manipulated regarding the materials and creation of the device. Shape, duration and amplitude, each is a product of development and interrelated depending on the Fourier transform." He shook his head. "It's basically two different ways of describing the same pulse." He snorted. The doc snorted. "These devices can be nuclear or non-nuclear." He held up his hands, palms out as if he were offering a compromise. "Ours will be non-nuclear, of course. Non-nuclear."

She looked at the pitiful box and bags and said, "So, you have a lot of shopping trips left."

Duncan grinned. "My wife is succinct."

"Indeed we do, Detective. Duncan here thinks we need to shop at a minimum of six separate stores using six separate cabs."

"Okay." She faced her fate and turned to Duncan. "This is goodbye for now."

He looked at her and lifted a brow. "Absolutely not. I will be taking you to the airport. I will pick you up at ten. That should leave us plenty of time for your twelve thirty flight."

Why did this bring her such joy?

It was after ten. Duncan had the cabbie pull all the way up to the safe house this time. "We'll be right out," he said.

The driver must have understood his meaning. He nodded and shifted the car into park.

The house was quiet. His Nickie waited just inside the door. Her hair and makeup were done, but it could not hide the loss of color in her face or the dark rings beneath her eyes. She was the most magnificent, beautiful woman he'd ever laid eyes on.

Her bottom lip. There was a time he considered it too large for the upper. His mind was shallow then, his interests more into L.A. and painting for politicians or Oscar Award winners than it was in helping others.

Her perfect lips opened as if she was going to speak, then she simply stepped to him and reached an arm toward his ear. She took hold of a lock of his hair and twirled it in her fingers. "This is interesting. You look older."

"Gray does that," he said and kissed her on the forehead. "I dyed it between trips to tradesman stores. I think the doctor fell asleep before his head hit the pillow. I don't want you to be late. Do you need to say your goodbyes?"

She shook her head. "Already done. Everyone is sleeping. It's been a big day."

Peru was only an hour behind Northridge, yet between the plane ride, adrenaline and mission, people could only take so much. "For you as well."

"I'll sleep on the plane."

"No, you won't." Not unless it was on the sofa affixed to the center of his private plane.

She took his hands and laced their fingers together. "There will be time for sleep later." She smiled as if she thought of a joke, but then decided against sharing it.

Turning to her luggage, he said, "Shall we?"

She nodded. They may have ridden in silence, and she may have looked out the window as they drove in the dark, but her grasp on his hand was tight. It was much the same for him. "This is the right thing to do," he said as they approached the exit to the airport. He wasn't sure if he tried to convince her or himself.

"I know." Her voice was without inflection.

"And we are sure this is right?"

Her chin still faced the window, but he could see as her lids closed before she answered. "Yes."

She would go to the States and coordinate with Special Agent Hurst. Duncan suspected he was already angry with Nickie that she had been inaccessible for the past forty-eight hours. It wasn't as if she was going to tell him where she was headed or what she was doing in the midst of the national operation she requisitioned.

"I won't let you down," he said. This caused her to turn to him and squint.

She glanced toward the cab driver. "Pull over here, please," she said.

He did. Duncan tried to come around and open her door, but by the time he motioned for the driver to wait once again, she'd already gotten out and had her luggage in her hand.

"You never let me down," she said. Her chin stood tall, her shoulders back. Her eyelids closed halfway as they did when she closed off her feelings and relied upon her autopilot. "I love you, and for whatever reason, you love me back. I want to get this over with. I'm tired, Duncan. I want to be normal. A wife. A mother. I want our own little Ariel someday."

"About tha—"

She put her fingers on his lips. "I can't. Please. Let me walk away now while I can still make my legs leave you."

She squeezed the tips of his fingers, and his Nickie walked into the sliding airport door.

Even though Hurst yelled on the other end of the phone, Nickie had a hard time hearing him. Someday rental cars would come with built-in hands-free devices. Until then, her phone sat on the dash with the speaker on. "Hold on, I can't hear you."

Pressing the mute button, she turned to Slippery Jimbo. "And you can't hear a thing. Got that?"

He drew a pretend line across his mouth. "My lips are taped, man."

"Ears, Jimbo. You don't listen with your lips, and it's sealed, not taped." She couldn't believe she let herself get caught up in this conversation with him.

She turned off the air conditioner and the fan. There. No background noise. "Okay, go ahead." Go ahead and yell as she sweated in a hot car in Nevada with the windows up.

"Are you in or not? You make demands, then disappear. I'm starting to get questions about the prisoner." Hurst turned out to be a loud yeller.

"I'm on my way to him right now. I'll meet you at the Lyonses' home in Vegas tomorrow noon. Slippery Jimbo is with me."

"I want an update on Parker's condition. I want you at the Vegas location by twelve o'clock and the Daytona location the day after tomorrow."

Now might not be a good time to mention the grave sites, but Nickie didn't do wait-for-a-good-time well. "Will do, boss. And the Upstate New York grave site search is scheduled for tomorrow?"

Silence. That was okay. She was patient. Sometimes.

"If." He emphasized the word. It was ridiculous. "You show up in Vegas with an update on the prisoner. And a picture. I want a picture of him safe and sound."

"Oh, good grief."

"Sah-weet," Jimbo said from the passenger seat. She punched him in the shoulder with a single knuckle.

"Ow," Jimbo said.

The second Hurst disconnected, Nickie rolled down the windows and turned the air on full blast. She turned onto the driveway on the side of the Henderson location.

Nickie heard voices. "Shh," she said to Jimbo, and stopped the car. Shit. She'd just told Hurst she had everything under control. Tire tracks had matted down the weeds in the drive. She didn't like that. It looked inhabited. And there were voices. "Shh," she said again as she listened.

Shifting into park, she cut the engine. Here would have to do. Holding up a finger, she said, "Wait here," and opened the door. She got out and pressed it closed again.

Two males. The voices came from the back. Setting one foot in the gravel, then the other, she placed her hand on the butt of her gun. As she reached the corner to the back of the house, she peered around enough for a single eye to see what the freaking hell was going on.

Eddy sat in shorts on a vinyl reclining lawn chair with his feet up. A boy stood next to him, shooting the shit like they were friends. "Where the hell is Park—" she started as she rounded the corner. "Our friend? Where the hell is our friend, and who the hell is this?"

"That would be her," Eddy said to the boy as she marched toward the two of them.

CHAPTER 24

Was Eddy giving away the location to everyone now? "This would be who?" Nickie asked.

"Detective Nickie Savage, this is…" Eddy gestured to the boy to answer in a way that said he had no idea who the boy was.

The kid said, "Blake." Dirty jeans hung from his bony hips. His shirt had a ring of sweat around the neck and under the pits.

She took a cleansing breath.

"They keep coming, Nick." Eddy crossed one foot over the other. "Say they want to talk to the cop who can hook them up in a safe place."

"Your name is Blake." She didn't know what else to say. This wasn't her jurisdiction. She had a hard enough time finding a place for Jonathan Cleary. Harder yet for the Sylvia girl.

Eddy folded his hands behind his head. "Give him food and a dozen more show up."

She couldn't believe he said that and kicked the crossed leg to the ground.

"Just sayin'. I tried it. That's what happens. And our friend is inside."

He had been feeding the homeless?

Parker. She turned and looked through the window in the back door that led to the kitchen.

He sat on a matching lawn chair. She could see him through the window. The earbuds were becoming a permanent fixture. His hands were folded on his lap and his legs crossed at the ankles.

Turning back to Eddy, she said, "The generator is working. There is air conditioning. Why are you out here in the heat?"

"Because he's in there."

"Blake," she said and dipped her chin. She needed a moment to grind her teeth in peace. "I need to speak with my friend here." She dipped a hand in her pocket and pulled out a business card. "This is my card. I want you to call me at this time tomorrow. Can you do that?"

He nodded and took it.

"Thank you." She pulled out her cell. "And say, cheese." She took his picture and saved it in her photos.

He slunk away in the heat to the alley behind the garage.

Eddy said, "I talked to the captain."

The captain. She closed her eyes. How long had Eddy been helping her out?

"He said, and I quote, 'This shit happened in my house.'" His imitation of Dave was spot on. How could he make her smile at a time like this? "You are officially," said the fake Captain Nolan, "unofficially staying with the witness until this is over with. Feds be damned. If you ask me," Eddy added in his Eddy voice, "the captain likes defying them, even if Hurst is on board with this crazy train."

He leaned to the side and looked around her. "I thought you said you had Slippery Slimeball Jimbo with you."

"I told him to wait in the car."

Swinging his legs around, Eddy popped to his feet. "Get him out. You're on babysitting duty. I'm going to town."

Her shoulders fell forward. "I sort of need to go. There's a place I have to visit."

"Oh hell." He sat back down, crossed his legs again and swiped open his phone.

"And I sort of need to go alone."

His chin turned slowly to face her as he realized she was leaving Jimbo with him.

"You can go all night when I get back," she said. "I swear. I'll take watch and keep the slimeball. The store closes in an hour, and I need to talk to this someone I know."

"You mean that cranky woman at the convenience store?" He rolled his eyes.

"You have no idea," she mumbled as she made her way to get said slimeball out of the car. He was watching for her. She motioned for him to get out.

"Detective Lynx, dude," he said as he walked to the back of the house. "What's new, man?"

"New? I got a new checking account," Eddy said without taking his nose from whatever he was doing on his phone. "That's what's new."

"Sah-wheet, dude."

Nickie saw it coming. Jimbo had no idea.

"I got a free toaster made for the bathtub," Eddy said. "It's all for you, man."

She drove down the only strip of road that had any kind of goods or services. The trip wasn't just to talk to the woman Nickie remembered as Janet. She needed grub for dinner and breakfast, and she kinda had to pee. It wasn't like she could go in a bush like the guys.

She sent the pic to her captain. He would check up on the young runaway who claimed to be Blake. A run through CODIS and NCIC would help with identifying him. It reminded her to send a pic of Parker to Hurst. It was an old one. That was cheating, but it wasn't like Parker was dead and she was lying.

Henderson was a bigger city, but this was an outskirt of the outskirts. Sidewalks crumbled. Paint eroded from the lampposts and few people were out in the midday heat.

As the tires of the rental rolled over tiny pieces of concrete, she looked through the open garage door of the only auto shop. A man leaned under a hood as another lay on his back beneath one of the dozen cars in the place. On the other side of the road, she spotted two men through the dirty windows of the barbershop. One sat in the chair and the other worked buzzers over his head.

Pulling up to her destination, she noted the closed sign. The overhead lights were on as well as the ones in the coolers along the side. She shifted the rental into park and turned off the engine. As she craned her head, she noticed the woman she was here to see. Young and plump with long, dark hair. It was Janet. Nickie couldn't recall her last name or if Janet had ever offered it.

They'd made a connection the two times Nickie had been here before. Janet held Nickie on a pedestal she didn't feel she earned, but a pedestal nonetheless. "My child plays in the streets because of you," she'd said. Her child was a pre-adolescent girl who had been hidden for the months Fu Haizi had embedded itself in this town.

Nickie got out of the car, left it unlocked and wandered in. The lines on the woman's face had deepened, if that was possible. For having a pre-adolescent daughter, she looked more like she was in her sixties.

Is that what having children did to a person? Of course not. Nickie knew plenty of moms who looked much younger than their age.

The bell that hung over the door jingled as Nickie walked in. Janet didn't turn to investigate or greet her customer but turned her back to Nickie and her attention to the counter behind her.

She began doubting her vision. The woman might not be who she thought, so she picked up a worn plastic basket and loaded it with bread and peanut butter and gallon jug of water.

Since they were the only two in the place and they weren't in Manhattan, Nickie said, "Hello," as she dropped some instant coffee in the basket.

The woman glanced over her shoulder. If it wasn't Janet, it was an older sister or relative. She paused before shuffling to the back.

"Come," the woman said and disappeared to the right where Nickie remembered the break room was located.

She found herself in this kind of predicament often lately. Deserted shop. Closed sign on the door. No backup. Should she just go on back and have a sit down with a woman she wasn't sure she knew?

She set the basket on the counter near the cash register. Resting her hand over her Smith and Wesson, she walked around it and through the back door.

The woman sat at a round table to the side of the back room. It was her. Nickie was sure of it. What had happened to her? "Would you like to talk about it?" she asked as she took a cautious step toward her.

In contrast to her shaking head, Janet answered, "She's gone."

Her daughter. The feisty young girl with ideas and confidence. Nickie had to grip the edge of the counter that dug into her side. Her head spun with possibilities. Fu Haizi wouldn't dare come back here. They'd been made in Henderson. There were plenty of other places to abduct and keep children.

Her mind pieced together possibilities. The Belmont Stakes. Their numbers had been depleted. They had a huge gig in less than two weeks and their numbers had been depleted.

"Janet."

"Do not say my name. She is gone. Do you understand?"

Nickie put her hand on her shoulder. The woman jerked it away. Regardless, Nickie said quietly, "I am so very sorry. I am going to do everything—"

"Do not," Janet repeated. "I do not want to hear these things."

"I need to know," Nickie said apologetically. "When did this happen?"

"Last week," Janet mumbled.

And for the question she really didn't want to ask, "Are there others?"

The woman nodded, her face empty of light. "Many." She placed her face in her hands and cried until her shoulders shook.

Nickie sat in her rental in front of the closed convenience store and dialed her partner's number.

"You get my soda?" he asked as he answered.

"Not yet, no. Is everything okay there? Parker is good?" You weren't ambushed by a team of Fu Haizi?

"Since fifteen minutes ago when you left? I killed Slippery Jimbo. I hope that's okay."

"And Parker? Can you still see him?"

The phone rustled, then Eddy said, "Still listening to his stupid…wait. Shit."

"Eddy? Eddy!" She cranked the ignition, shoved it into drive and sped down the road, oblivious to the shouting she earned from the residents. She redialed Eddy's number three times, then broke down and called Jimbo.

"Detective," he said as he answered.

No Detective Dude. That was bad. "What's going on? I'm almost there."

"I do not know. Eddy made me wait by the garage. It's okay. I pulled his chair back here."

"What. Is. Happening, Jimbo?" she yelled as she fishtailed around the corner to the neighborhood.

"I can't see from here. Eddy ran into the house. The back door is open. I don't know, man. It's quiet."

"Go to the door."

"What!"

"You don't have to get close. Just go to the door and tell me what's going on in the kitchen. Hurry up."

"Okay, okay," he said like a junior high boy.

She could hear the crunching of the gravel beneath his feet. He wasn't walking fast enough.

"So, okay. Yeah. I see Eddy. He's standing in front of the prisoner."

She slowed down for some teenagers on bikes. "Is there anyone else there?"

"No, not that I can see. Oh, fuck me."

She heard the distinct sound of the phone dropping to the ground, so she gunned the engine after the bikers passed. She was dialing him again when her phone rang. Caller ID said it was Jimbo.

"Jimbo. Are you hurt?"

"I'm a dead man," Jimbo said as he answered.

"I'm almost there. Are you hurt?" she repeated.

"I'm gonna be. He spotted me."

"Who spotted you?"

"Who do you think, Detective Dude? Eddy. Eddy spotted me."

Her left eyelid twitched.

"He told me to wait by the garage, and he spotted me. He's going to kill me with his toaster. I'm never taking a bath again."

She slowed a block before the witness protection site. "What is Eddy doing? What is the prisoner doing?"

"No way. I am sitting my butt next to the garage. Did you get some grub? I'm starving. Is there any liquor in that there house?"

She clicked off and tossed the phone in the passenger seat. She had her door open before she shifted into park. Jimbo waved from his spot on the lawn chair in back. She ignored him.

Something made her pause at the back door before she went in. Eddy was on his knees next to him. Parker's feet were no longer crossed and the arm closest to the back door hung on the floor next to the lawn chair.

She gave herself a short moment, only long enough to exhale. She rested her forehead on the back door and closed her eyes. Inhaling, she turned the knob and walked in.

CHAPTER 25

"He was fine a few hours ago," Eddy said without turning to look at her. "Fuck, fuck, fuck."

Nickie stepped over the body and checked for a bullet, foaming at the mouth or bruises around his neck. Anything. Something wasn't right, but hell if she could tell. His skin was cherry red.

Folding both hands on the top of his head, Eddy paced and said, "I'm sorry, Nick. I'm really sorry."

He'd been working 24/7. The captain would say for the department, but it was really for her. And after she'd fallen for the scheme that pointed to him as a department mole. "You're a good cop, Lynx. We'll figure something out."

"Like what? He was the only witness. He was key."

"And they knew that. It's not safe here."

Jimbo. She ran out the back. He still sat on the lawn chair playing with his phone. Upright. Not with earbuds in his ears. "Get your ass in here, Jimbo."

Without taking his eyes from her, he slowly turned his chin away.

"Now!"

He jumped to his feet and scurried to the house.

She took out her phone and swiped it open.

Eddy put a hand on the screen.

"What?" she asked.

"Let's talk about this before you call Hurst."

"Oh hell. I'm not calling Hurst. I'm calling Duncan's pilot to see how fast he can get here so we can get the body back to NPD."

Nickie sat at the edge of the loveseat on Duncan's plane. Eddy was next to her, scooted to the front edge of the recliner. Since everything was screwed to the floor, they couldn't get close enough for a private discussion.

"What the crazy shit is this?" Jimbo squealed like a happy girl from the back. He'd already sifted through most of the plane.

They were flying with a dead body on ice in the luggage compartment. She was going to jail, to detective jail and possibly divorce court over this.

"I have no freaking idea how to break this to Hurst."

"Yeah," Eddy said.

"He's gonna renege on his offer to search the grave site."

"Yeah."

"He's got the deets on the July 2nd locations. He might just take me out of the equation. He could do that."

"Yeah."

She frowned at him. "How is that helping?"

He shrugged.

"We both might be put away for abducting Parker and killing him."

"You might want to keep an eye on your informant over there."

She turned and found Slippery Jimbo living up to his name. He slipped two whiskey glasses into the pockets of his trench coat.

"Put those back or I break your arms."

He pulled the glasses out and set them gently back on the bar. "Heh," he laughed. "I thought those were complimentary."

"When we land," Eddy said as he scrolled through his phone, "we can have security go through his luggage, pat him down and do a cavity search." It was the first time she'd seen a smile on Eddy's face since...since she didn't know when.

Jimbo stuck a finger in his mouth and pulled his cheek out. "I ain't got no cavities."

Eddy lowered his voice. "You gonna call Hurst?"

She shook her head.

"Chicken."

She had called the captain and messaged Duncan. That was good enough for now.

Parker is dead. Using your pilot and your plane to transport body to Northridge.

It was as good as any love note.

"I want to see what the ME says first," she said to Eddy.

He tipped his phone away and looked at her. "What are you going to say to Rickard when you drop a former NPD officer onto his table in the lab?"

"Captain says Rickard owes me. He's on board." She hoped.

Her captain waited on the gravel in the dark staff parking lot. He held up a hand as they entered. Nickie pulled up next to him in her ancient Cadillac Eldorado and rolled down the window.

Jimbo spoke to him from the backseat. "Just for the record, I'm in the back because there was no room in the front seat. I repeat. I am not in trouble."

Dave spoke like he hadn't heard him. "In the garage. Back up the car to the staff basement entrance."

They were all going to cop Hell because of her.

She did as he said, then got out and walked around to the trunk. Dave and Eddy stared at Jimbo. Awkward silence. More awkward silence.

He threw up his arms. "Wait in the break room. I get it. I get it." As he walked away, he mumbled, "They promised me I'd be in Vegas right now pulling slots."

Nickie popped the trunk. The larger-than-life package was tucked inside.

"At least he doesn't smell, yet," Eddy offered.

She tilted her head and said, "We double bagged him."

"And stuffed icy coolers around him."

Dave rubbed both hands over his face. "I've got a stretcher." Using his key card, he swiped open the lock to the staff basement door. Eddy held it open as Dave and Nickie hauled Parker onto the stretcher. He'd stiffened since they left the small Henderson airport.

Once in, she turned to Eddy. "Will you park my car?"

"Yep. I'm adding it to your growing list of you-owe-me's."

She got that.

She and Dave rolled the body to the service elevator. "It's going to be okay, you know." Of all the things for him to say. He'd always been more of a father to her than a boss.

"How? How is this going to be okay?"

"All for the greater good."

Her brain hurt.

The elevator opened and Nickie jumped. Medical Examiner, Benjamin Rickard, waited inches from the metal doors. He adjusted the collar of his short-sleeved plaid shirt that was buttoned to the top. "Hello, Detective." He rubbed his hands together like he was waiting to dive into a steak dinner. It was damned creepy.

Regardless, she was grateful. "Hello, Rickard. Thank you for coming in at this hour."

He maneuvered to the back of the stretcher and pushed it himself. He practically pranced on the way to his lab. "This is *the* Dale Parker," he said like he was a news anchor. "The infamous department mole, killed while waiting to testify."

It was all true, but neither Dave nor she acknowledged him.

Sliding the stretcher between two metal tables, he adjusted it, and then readjusted it until it was perfectly centered. Nickie clasped her fingers together. Never shake a baby.

He put on his lab jacket and a pair of latex gloves, then rubbed the palms of his hands together once more before using a surgical pair of scissors to cut through the black garbage bags.

The expression on his face fell. "Oh," is all he said. What the hell did that mean?

"What a disappointment. The autopsy will be a formality. The cherry color of his skin shows carbon monoxide poisoning."

"Holy what the hell?" Nickie yelled. "Was this an accident? Did Parker die from the generator? From faulty window air conditioners?"

"On the contrary, Detective. The amount of carbon monoxide needed to create this color could have only been purposeful."

Eddy walked in at that moment. He didn't speak but moved his eyes to each person in the room, dead included.

"Does a generator running window air conditioners count as a new heating system?"

"Ah. Indeed, Detective. Indeed it does. Find the seller of the equipment and find your killer."

Byrd snored as Duncan took one of the blankets from the empty double bed and spread it out on the floor in the corner. He dumped the contents of each bag onto the blanket. Before he organized the materials, a knock came at the door. He was expecting his brother, but he had a large underground ransom on his head. He stepped lightly to the door.

Glancing at Byrd, he checked the peephole. He yanked open the door and pulled his brother inside, then locked and bolted the door. Blinds secure. Door secure.

"Toys!" Andy said and walked to the pile of materials on the floor.

Bombs were not Andy's expertise. Dr. Byrd was the professional, but Duncan carried the knowledge he gained from his time with explosives in the armed forces and Andy brought his natural talents as a builder. Andy's gift for placing inanimate objects together was one he held since he was a child.

Duncan logged on to his local cell phone to check for messages.

Another from his office manager. She wasn't doing so well without him. And another from his aunt and his pilot. He chose his Nickie's message to open first.

Parker is dead. Using your pilot and your plane to transport body to Northridge.

He checked the time. Nine p.m. That was hours ago.

"What happened?" Andy stood next to him.

Duncan turned his head to his brother. "They got to Parker."

"You mean the murdered kind of got to?"

He nodded. "I need to get back to her." Picking up his jacket, he patted the pockets to make sure he had his wallet.

"Whoa," Andy said and sat on the floor next to the blanket. He looked over the piles of supplies as he said, "What would Nick want you to do?"

"Don't."

Andy shrugged. "You know you can't. Beat yourself up if you need to, but it's annoying."

"As are little brothers who are annoyingly forthright."

"Job description." He lifted from his butt and organized the materials.

While Andy worked, Duncan responded to Nickie.

I'm sorry. Are you okay? Do you want me to come home?

To his surprise, she messaged back.

Rickard said homicide.

He had more questions than messaging allowed.

What is next?

Vegas planning meeting today.

Still? He didn't have a chance to respond when his phone vibrated again.

Potential mass grave site excavation tomorrow.

It was one of the most helpless moments of his life.

Say the word and I can be with you in less than twenty-four hours.

I've been through worse.

That she had.

Nickie considered herself well rounded. Raised as a Maryland Monticello snob, she scratched her way through college after floating from foster home to foster home.

Nothing could have prepared her for Johnny and Bebe Lyons' Vegas house. She expected big from an Emmy Award winner, but this was nuts. Stopping at the entrance, she squinted up the winding drive. The house was up there. She could see it, but it looked like a postage stamp at the corner of an envelope.

"Now, this is what I'm talkin' 'bout," Eddy said from the backseat.

"You're not staying here, Jimbo," she said as she shifted the rental economy car into drive. Even at double the price per day, she second-guessed her decision to turn down the convertible.

Eddy sneered from the passenger seat. "That's right, Slimeball. I saw a nice place for $29.99 a night near the interstate on the way in. Free cable."

She spotted the main entrance as she drove. The ginormous set of glass front doors stood framed by brick. White stucco covered the outside walls. Duncan had been here. Why were there no paintings of this place in his collection? Or in the ashes that used to be his collection?

Mrs. Lyons came from around the back before Nickie reached the house. Bebe stood in spiky heels and a sunbathing robe, waving her hand in what Nickie liked to think of as a parade wave. Nickie lifted a hand in return.

Bebe's smile was sincere. "Just make sure to stay in the car, Jimbo," Nickie said to him.

"At least the break room at the station had donuts."

Nickie and Eddy got out of the front seat but left the car running for Jimbo.

"Hello, Nickie. It's so good to see you again."

"Thank you, Bebe," Nickie said. She could smell Bebe's floral perfume from where she stood. "This is Detective Eddy Lynx. Due to recent events, he has become available to oversee this part of Operation Fu Haizi. He's an excellent detective with extensive expertise with trafficking."

Crooked at the wrist, Bebe held out a hand like she might have expected Eddy to kiss it.

"Um, yes," he said and shook using the tips of his fingers.

Bebe leaned around him as she smiled and peered in the car. "Um, Nickie dear. Your car is running." She dipped her head a few inches. "And you have a man in your backseat."

Nickie waved a hand like she was shooing a fly. "That's Jimbo. James. Jim. He's going to stand in as an undercover pedophile."

Eddy added, "He has extensive expertise in being a scumbag."

"Any friend of the Reeds is a friend of mine." Bebe stepped to the car and waved for Jimbo to come out.

An image flashed in Nickie's mind. It was of her waving her arms in big circles as she yelled, "No!" as if Bebe was about to unleash The Cracken.

From the backseat, Jimbo looked around the car like she must have been gesturing to someone else. He pointed to his chest, then smiled from ear to ear. He reached over the seat and turned off the car. Spilling out of the car, he smoothed his greasy hair over his ears and then held out an open hand.

Bebe stared at Jimbo's outstretched hand as she said, "Welcome, Mr. Jimbo, James, Jim." She patted him on the shoulder instead of shaking. "Shall we?" She gestured to the trail of stepping stones that led to the back of the place.

Flagstone stepping-stones. As the group followed her, Nickie leaned close to Jimbo. "If you touch one single thing, I will personally push your eyeballs through your sockets and blind you for life."

"Why you gotta be like that, Detective Dude?"

"Because of the other set of whiskey glasses from Duncan's plane that were found in your carry-on. And no talking, either." In case he didn't hear that part, she zipped her lip.

Ducking under the low-hanging vines that covered an arbor leading to a fenced-in pool, Nickie stood for a moment in awe. An hourglass-shaped pool stood in the center of a ton of plants. They weren't even fake plants like the ones in their Maine vacation home. It must have taken an entire crew to keep it all watered. She was going to try hard not to leave this house filled with bullet holes.

Johnny Lyons sat at a glass table. He stood as they entered, taking off the reading glasses that sat on the end of his nose. "Nickie! It's good to see you. Welcome. Please," he said and gestured an arm around the table. "Sit."

"This is Detective Lynx and Jimbo, James, Jim," Bebe said as she sat next to her husband.

"Just James," Nickie corrected. Turning to Jimbo, she explained so all could hear. "Special Agent Hurst is due at any moment. This is his operation. The Lyonses will get you a ticket into the Celebrity Poker Tournament. That is all. They have agreed to keep their eyes open, but they will not be involved beyond that."

Eddy pulled out a tourist map from his back pocket. He'd circled the meeting spots in red. He laid it on the table and said, "This is where we meet the night of the 2nd. Fu Haizi generally uses rooms inside casinos, so look for a long hall with lots of doors. It will be disguised as business meeting rooms and might be labeled as a conference area."

"I just can't believe anyone could do this," Bebe said and put her hand over her mouth.

Me neither, Nickie thought.

CHAPTER 26

━━━◆━━━

Duncan woke fully clothed to the sound of snapping wires and clinking metal. Hints of the rising sun peeked through the window screen in his peripheral vision. As he blinked awake, his focus rested on the ceiling. It was plaster and cracked in several places. Water stains gathered in spots, mostly at the outside wall corner.

As he turned his gaze to the rest of the room, he first spotted his brother. His mouth hung open on his razor-thin pillow. He'd at least had enough sense to change into more comfortable clothing before sleep.

The clinking came from the blanket Duncan had spread out the night before. An ironing table had been set up next to it since he had fallen asleep in the late hours the night before.

The doctor faced the wall and worked furiously. The weight of his backside lifted from the chair as his elbow raised and lowered. Then, he craned his head to one side and lifted his chin as if he was looking through trifocals.

Watching him work reminded Duncan of himself as he painted. Hair disheveled. Wrinkled clothing. His face shined as if he hadn't showered in days. Understandable. It occurred to him that Byrd was in the same spot when Duncan fell to the bed with his clothes on the evening before.

"Good morning, Doctor," Duncan said and set his feet on the floor next to his bed.

He felt a short wave of guilt from the fact that he had arranged Dr. Byrd's materials. He would not at all be pleased if someone had rearranged his paints, brushes, canvases, or studio.

He stood and walked around to investigate what had gained the doctor's undivided attention. On the ironing board sat a contraption that resembled the engine of a car. Spools of wire attached to the outside like a bad hairstyle.

He hadn't gotten a response from the doctor. Duncan recognized he hadn't actually asked a question and tried again. "Have you been up all night?"

The doctor grunted and continued his work. The haze was one that Duncan recognized. This was Dr. Byrd's painting. His instrument. His passion. Like any artist, he was in his element, not to be reckoned with.

Instead, Duncan studied his creation. His piece of art. His bomb. His electromagnetic pulse device. Any attempts to earn a response from the doctor were fruitless. Duncan understood and appreciated this. He tiptoed toward the bathroom door with a newfound respect for this man.

Nickie sat with her phone in her hand. She waited in her car outside one of the possible grave site locations Dale Parker had given her. It was a dirty trick. Levels of dirty, really. Dirty because she'd failed Parker, the one who gave her the tip. Dirty because it was Special Agent Hurst who provided the manpower for the search, and she hadn't told him his only witness in the case against her mother and Jun Zheng was dead. Dirty because the sole reason she hadn't told him was because she didn't want him to pull this dig from her. That and the fact that she truly was chicken.

A small army of vehicles, supplies and earth-moving equipment arrived and gathered around the perimeter. She pressed the send button on her phone and closed her eyes.

"Nick, what's up?" Hurst asked. "Things are coming together."

"That's good but—"

"Captain Dave's wife and contacts from Jess Larsen's Child Rescue have locations set up and ready to accept children."

"I have something I need to te—"

"Are you at the grave site? Has the team arrived yet?"

He was psyched. She got that. Every good cop she knew got that way ahead of a bust of any size, let alone one of this magnitude.

"Stop," she said as loud as she could without yelling at him.

Silence.

"What's the matter?"

"It's Parker."

"Oh fuck. They got him."

She could have been calling to say she'd got him to talk. Or that Parker had had an epiphany about his time inside Fu Haizi, but Hurst must have recognized the tone in her voice. It's not like she tried to hide it. "Carbon monoxide poison in the air conditioning set up."

"Fuck," he said again. She got that, too. "Where's the body?"

"NPD."

"Did anyone else get hurt?"

No inquiry. No accusations or threats. "No. Our ME did the autopsy. Said it was cut and dry, but I'm sure you'll want to do one on your own."

"You've had time to do an autopsy?"

Oops.

"I didn't want to tell you until I knew the cause of death." It was partially true, but she didn't kid herself. She had to have this site searched. Needed it. There were likely the bodies of missing girls in the field in front of her.

People she didn't recognize moved around like a well-oiled machine. One of the cars had wire crisscrossing all the windows in the back. Search and rescue dog.

"This is screwed up, Nick. I need to think about how to deal with it."

"What can I do?" she asked.

"Promise me your tip is good, and Fu Haizi will show up at the five locales."

"I promise." She had nothing left to lose.

"The Belmont Stakes wasn't a complete fail," Hurst added. "I've got the MO of this organization now and have been able to brief the team leaders at each location."

"Stop being positive."

"What?"

A woman got out of the K-9 car. She wore a black shirt with a patch on the chest and pants tucked into tall brown boots with flat heels.

Search and rescue dogs, plural, Nickie corrected herself as the woman opened the back. Two German shepherds bounded out, then sat in front of her.

"I gotta go, Hurst. I'll let you know how today goes."

He clicked off, and she got out of her car.

Shaking her mind clear, she adjusted her attitude and walked to the woman with a smile. "Hello, I'm Detective Nickie Savage." She held out a hand.

The woman nodded and took Nickie's hand. The dogs didn't get up to greet Nickie. How did the woman get them to do that? They stared at their owner like they were ready to ask how high at her command to jump.

"I'm Special Agent Johnson. I am the human remains detection expert."

Nickie's confusion must have been evident on her face because the agent clarified. "Human remains detection. Cadaver dogs." She turned and looked over the area. "Search and rescue dogs are trained to find live humans. Cadaver dogs are trained to locate body parts, tissue, blood and bone. They can find dead people fifteen feet under."

She would be lying if she said she wasn't impressed. "How old?" she asked.

"I'm assuming you're not asking about the age of the dogs but about how long the remains can be underground and still be detected."

Nickie nodded.

"Hundreds of years," Johnson said and pursed her lips. "This is going to take a while. If you'd like to leave, I can call you if we find anything."

Shaking her head, Nickie said, "Not on your life."

Gloria sat on one of the couches in the safe house with a book in her hand. Like a teacher in front of her classroom, she read book after book written in the language of children who only begged for more. It was easy for Duncan to see why Nickie loved her.

It was too early for Gloria to go to work. She did this in the evenings. Entertainer of children by day, undercover pusher of trafficked children by night.

Duncan suffered a similar daytime fate as he'd somehow found himself on the other side of the room with a small sketchpad on his lap, drawing pictures of individual children.

They were accustomed to missionaries coming and taking their pictures but only saw the photos on the screen of a phone soon to be deleted.

This one was of a boy. His name was Rico. He spelled it for Duncan and told him he was six.

Six years old.

Six years old and had been through more in his short lifetime than Duncan had in his thirty-three years. Jess explained he had been mute for the first two years here. Now, he had found his voice and learned to read and write and trust again. To save a child, even one single child, was more than anyone could ask of their lifetime.

His eyes were a dark brown, almost black, and his chocolate-colored hair long enough to wave over his ears. Duncan couldn't get him to smile but drew the corners of his mouth turned up in a grin regardless. No need to etch his sadness permanently on paper.

Rico pulled on his pant leg and said something Duncan didn't understand.

"He wants to know if you will give the paper to him when you are done," Gloria said between pages. Women were such good multitaskers. "Si," Duncan said to the boy, ripped the paper from the pad and handed it to him. A small smile formed around the corners of Rico's lips. Yes. It was how Duncan had imagined it.

Before his next customer arrived, Duncan messaged his multitasker.

Sitting in her Eldorado, Nickie watched out her windshield with her boots propped on the dash. The dogs had done their lay thing the trainer, Special Agent Johnson, had taught them, giving the signal that they'd found a bone. Or body parts, or tissue, or blood. Johnson had given them a rope to play with as their reward. They had a measly ten minutes to play, then the whole thing repeated. About a dozen times.

For days, Nickie had carefully stuffed the possibilities of this day in a safe spot. Deep in her subconscious, under the rug or wherever else people shoved this kind of stuff. Potential grave site. Maybe even plural. Potential Fu Haizi grave sites of a decades-old, now international human trafficking organization. The grave possibilities were endless.

So far, excavation equipment dug in five of the twelve locations. Like most police work, it was excruciatingly slow. White plastic markers stuck in the grass, labeling the spots that equipment hadn't gotten to yet.

Her phone vibrated in the seat next to her. Glancing over, she saw it was Duncan. She sighed a small breath of warmth.

Thinking of you. How is the dig?

Her shoulders relaxed.

Amazing. Unsettling. Still digging around. You?

I'm drawing sketches of children. Gloria is reading. There is a boy. I want to come back here when all is said and done.

Okay.

There were still seven remaining spots marked with white plastic markers. This was going to be a long day.

This is but a season in time. In eight short days, we will be together.

Special Agent Johnson headed her way.

Gotta go. I love you.

Pulling her feet from the dash, she opened her car door.

"Detective Savage," Johnson called.

Nickie walked toward her. The dogs heeled one on each side of her.

"We have unearthed the remains."

It had been a few hours but all things considered, that was fast. "Can you tell me what that means? Do we know if it is human remains?" Nickie walked in a quick clip toward the deepest hole. She wanted to know. She didn't want to know. Story of her life.

The agent's face tightened like she'd just taken a bite of a bad apple. Nickie stopped and lifted her brows. "What did I do?"

"Cadaver dogs have a ninety percent success rate."

Whoa. Nickie had definitely hit a wrong button.

Ninety percent was impressive that meant…her eyes grew big as she looked around the field. Five mounds of dirt were piled in separate locations. Seven more white plastic markers. "Okay," Nickie said and walked faster to the initial site.

Peering into the hole, she didn't need to be a crime scene tech to know what she saw. The skeleton of a small-framed body lay on its side. Nickie assumed female. She was curled in a ball with an arm cocked unnaturally behind her.

Pulling out her cell, she said to Johnson, "I'll call for a crime scene tech."

"Detective, there's no need. I've already alerted FBI, CSU and the pathologist. They're flying out via helicopter as we speak."

Oh, right. Bureaucracy. Red tape. Hands tied. She didn't even care anymore. Placing her cell back in her pocket, she stood over the hole. Who was this child? Was she missed? How did she die? How long was she captive? How old was she when she was murdered?

"Detective?"

Nickie nodded. "Okay, okay. We'll wait for your CSU."

"They've found something in hole number three."

Which one was hole number three? She followed Johnson to a grave that was much shallower. Sweat instantly covered her scalp and her upper lip. Grasping her hands in tight fists, she knew she should say something but words wouldn't come out. She had a powerful need to run. To hide.

This body was not a little girl. It was large. Larger than female. The only thing left were the bones. The bones and fragments of a leather belt. The silver belt buckle was not fragmented. She knew that buckle. She knew this man. This was George Kruger. She had strangled him with his tie when she was fifteen years old.

CHAPTER 27

H e was coming. He was coming and she was ready.

They'd put her in the red room. They named each room for its color like it was the real White House. The white house. They made her wear the yellow, lacy bra with matching panties. That was what they liked to call them. They never put makeup on her. They wanted her to look like she was a virgin. They'd taken that from her a long time ago.

This one liked her. They'd brought him to her before. He called her Savage like the rest of them. She'd show them a savage.

"That's a good one, Mr. Kruger." The man named George Kruger came in with his deep voice laughing about something she didn't know. Lifting his arm once to the guard, he shut the door and turned his eyes to her. She scrambled to the edge of the bed and curled her legs tightly into her. It was only partly an act.

He huffed a half-laugh and emptied his pockets like her father did when he came home for the day.

"I'd hoped you'd be that way, honey," he said like she was some sort of little girl.

She shook with fear, more from her plan than of him.

He tossed his jacket over a chair and pulled at his tie.

"They…" Nickie could hardly find her voice. "They record us, you know."

His hands stopped. He didn't turn his head, but moved his eyes from one side of the room to the other.

"There," she said, pointing to the lion's head on the wall.

He continued with his tie, tossed it on a chair, then untucked his shirt, exposing a brown leather belt with a silver belt buckle. She needed that belt.

He didn't believe her. He had to believe her. Please believe her. He was going to ruin everything.

He took his shirt off. His blubber hung over his pants so far it covered the belt buckle. Taking his jacket from the chair, he walked with it to the far wall.

She took her chance and reached for the tie.

He tossed his jacket over the lion's head before he came to her. "There we go, honey. Just you and me."

She put her mind somewhere else. Somewhere safe. Her lip trembled as the weight of him sank the bed and tilted her toward him.

"Now, where did we leave off last time?"

Bracing, she let him pull her legs until she was horizontal. His clammy body pressed against her. The stench of cigars and alcohol filled her nose as his hands searched and squeezed.

She found it. She found it and she was going to do it. She grasped his tie and started thrashing like a fish. He'd expected it. That was why he chose her. Always be the smartest person in the room, she told herself, as she wrapped the tie around his neck.

Startled, he stopped. It gave her enough time to scramble around to the back of him, twist the tie around his neck and pull until her arms shook. Lifting, he turned from side to side, reaching for her. But he was too fat, and she was too strong. Like a savage, she held on. Even when the muscles in her arms ached, she hung on. Even when he quit moving and fell forward, facedown.

Her arms kept shaking, part from the ache of what she'd just done and part because she really did it. Her eyes jerked from his lifeless body to the door, to the covered lion head, to the window. As she'd planned in her head a hundred times, she ran to the lacy robe they made her wear. In the pocket, there were old slices of bread and some Cheetos.

She didn't even think to put on the robe; she just ran. Ran to the window, opened it and jumped to the ground, dropping the food. She picked up as much as she could before she sprinted to the trees, to anywhere away from the white house. The dogs were coming. It was okay, she reminded herself. She knew what to do.

She stopped, stuck one knee to the ground and held out the food. The dogs wagged their tails when they spotted her. She'd worked for months gaining their trust. One of them whined at the side of her bed. Opening her eyes, she adjusted her focus to the snout of Xena, who sat inches from her face.

Blinking, she turned on her back and looked up. Her hair was wet with sweat, and her chest sucked air like she'd had the wind knocked out of her. Oak wood crown molding crisscrossed the painted ceiling. Rolling over the side of the bed, Xena scurried back as Nickie emptied her stomach on the floor.

Breaking her own rules, she let herself cry. Cry until her stomach ached with cramps. It was him. The man named George Kruger, whose name she discovered only weeks before. The things he'd done to her. She was just a child. Her arms trembled with fatigue just as if she'd killed him at that moment, not seventeen years ago. The adult cop in her knew she would never go to jail for what she'd done but also that murder held no statute of limitation and that she could face a lengthy and brutal trial.

She curled into a fetal position and stuck her arms between her knees. Her arms were as wet with sweat as her hair. Wiping them on the sheets, she noticed it wasn't sweat on her arms but blood.

She sat up, patting her body, for what, she didn't know. A bullet? A knife wound? She wasn't completely awake and still halfway into her dream when she realized where it came from.

A loud knock on the ER patient room door was followed by a call from the hallway, "Miss Savage, are you dressed yet?"

Nickie buttoned her pants. "Yep," she called.

The nurse walked in holding a clipboard with a pile of papers attached. Concern radiated from her every move. She probably had a body that worked just fine. None of this was the nurse's fault. Nickie pulled on a boot.

The nurse turned the clipboard around. "Are you sure about this, miss?"

"Yep," Nickie repeated. She couldn't get out of there fast enough.

"This paper says you're checking yourself out against doctor's orders."

Nickie refused to blink. She ground her teeth together and took the pen, scribbled her name and stood.

The next visitor wasn't gentle or proceeded by a polite knock. Rose barged in, gasping for air. "I'm back. My mom's got A.J. How are you doing? What happened?"

"My sister-in-law," Nickie explained to the nurse.

Rose stared as Nickie pulled on her other boot. Holding her arms out, she barked, "Why are you getting dressed?" Rose turned to the nurse. "Did she tell you there is blood on her bed?"

The nurse looked to Nickie. "It's okay. She's my ride," Nickie said.

"The papers say you should stay in bed and drink plenty of fluids. If the spotting continues or gets worse, call your doctor." The nurse placed the papers in a plastic bag, then held it out. "The doctor should be back any minute. Are you sure I can't convince you to stay? You might pass the—"

"Stop," Nickie said. She didn't need to see the doctor again. She knew what her body did and what to do about it.

Tears filled Rose's eyes. Her hand lifted to cover her mouth. She stepped to the nurse and said between her teeth, "She had a miscarriage, and you're letting her leave?"

The nurse opened her mouth, then closed it.

"She can't stop me," Nickie said and tossed her jacket over her arm.

"I repeat," Rose yelled at the top of her lungs, "this woman had a miscarriage and you're just—"

"Rose, don't." Nickie put a hand on her forearm. "Please. This is my doing." She would not recover if a single tear fell down her face.

"Nickie."

She knew what Rose was thinking. "I'm leaving, Rose. I'll call a cab if I need to."

Rose nodded and placed a hand under her arm.

Nickie waited until they neared the exit. Her heart started to race, her breathing in short bursts. "Rose, let go. I have to pee."

Rose stopped and looked at the bathroom door next to them like she considered coming in with her.

"Single room. Sorry. I really just have to pee." Nickie stepped in and leaned her back against the door. She grabbed hold of the sides of her head, clasping hunks of hair on each side. Her chest heaved and sweat dripped down her temple. She ran to the toilet and dry heaved as quietly as she could. The tears won.

"It's me," she heard Rose say through the door. "It's bad. I can't tell you. I don't know if she wants anyone to know. She's going to be okay, but it's bad."

Nickie squeezed her eyes shut and placed her head against the sidewall.

"No," Rose continued. "No, no. He died. Yes. The key witness. The only witness. Who cares about that? What?" She wasn't whispering anymore. "I don't care if this happens to people all the time. Who cares about infertility stats? You don't get it." Silence.

Nickie sank to the floor at the side of the bathroom. She clamped her eyes shut as her lungs heaved. Dale Parker's lifeless, cherry red face. The silver belt buckle. The scars on little Ariel's back as she curled under Nickie's arm.

The van could be traced, so Duncan had his office manager wire cash to buy a used conversion van. After working solely with Andy and Samuel, Gloria had asked Duncan to join them that night.

She sat silently in the passenger seat. Her expression was much the same as it had been for most of the trip. Determination. No wonder Nickie found solace with this woman.

A brown patterned wrap covered her legs. Her flat sandals could almost be considered house slippers and her hair was tall and covered in material that matched the skirt.

If she were a stranger, he would most certainly be reluctant to cross her.

Her nightly excursions had narrowed her search to two separate trafficking organizations. Others were offers to hire adults. The two involved child trafficking specifically.

Duncan spoke up. "Two separate groups cause a potential issue regarding which one is Fu Haizi and which is not."

"Yes," she said. "Turn right at the next block. I have considered this. It is why I ask you to drive."

"The two groups are likely rivals," he said.

She inhaled slowly, then released the air in one quick breath.

Right at the next block took them through a warehouse district. Duncan added, "I am more comfortable when Samuel serves as your driver."

Gloria shook her head. "This is beyond acceptable to ask of this Samuel. No one will recognize you sitting in the driver seat."

He adjusted the rearview mirror and judged his appearance.

"Your hair is gray and you have beard. Size is same. Nothing else."

Had her English gotten worse since they'd arrived? He supposed his disguise worked well. The backward ball cap and jean jacket finished the look.

"You to tell me if these men are this Fu Haizi. You will know. I don't. We are here."

"Here?" Duncan looked around. Nothing was here. No stores, homes or people.

"The green one," she said and pointed to a large, green warehouse with no windows, two closed garage doors and a single entrance door visible from this side. He had little desire to check for an alley entrance in the back.

"I wait on bench."

He craned his head around her. There most certainly was a rusty park bench between the green building and the white brick building next to it. For fear of someone watching, he refrained from rubbing his hands over his face and chose instead to grip the steering wheel.

He was a foreigner in a third world country driving an unregistered vehicle in an unpopulated area. With. His. Mother-in-law.

Checking beneath the seat, he felt for the only firepower he carried. The small explosives he'd been building for Operation Fu Haizi. If the situation became dangerous, his only recourse was to blow up the front of the building. Nickie would kill him if she knew he allowed all of this to happen.

This may have been routine for Andy and Gloria, but Duncan was sick to his stomach. This should not be routine. He checked windows and mirrors, then Andy stepped out of the back and opened Gloria's door. Andy left his door ajar. She sat on the bench, adjusted her skirt and placed her bag on her lap. Andy stepped away and stood with his knees locked.

They waited for ten minutes. Gloria stood and turned to face the green building. She spoke a tirade of Spanish to the wall as if someone stood there. Some of the words he recognized. He was without his Beretta once again.

The door opened, and a man came out. He wore black pants and a matching mock turtleneck. Identification complete. Duncan's purpose fulfilled. "Let's go," he said loud enough for only Andy and Gloria to hear.

They ignored him.

The man spoke quickly, and then disappeared into the building. Gloria sat back down. When the door opened again, Duncan's shoulders reflexively fell forward. He turned his ball cap around and dipped his chin. Ivanna Monticello. She marched out with purpose as if she was on a schedule. She wore a three-piece tan suit and matching thick pumps.

Brushing pieces of his dyed hair over his ears with one hand, his other moved to his thigh, closer to the ammo. It wasn't enough.

CHAPTER 28

Gloria stood and lifted her chin as Ivanna spoke what Duncan considered perfect Spanish. His jaw flexed and released as he silently willed Gloria to accept whatever Ivanna offered and to get in the damned van.

"No," Gloria barked.

Duncan winced.

She waved her arms like a madwoman and released a slew of rhetoric. Duncan was able to pick out the word for tomorrow, but he was more worried about Ivanna recognizing him. Gloria pointed toward Ivanna's chest before nodding once and crossing her arms.

Ivanna stuck out her hand to shake. Gloria shook, then walked toward the open back door of the van and came to a stop. This confused Duncan, but he dared not ask or turn his head. The door adjacent to the single back door opened, shining in light from the streetlight into the van. With his chin low, Duncan looked out the driver's side window.

Ivanna sounded like she was inches from him. The voice of Nickie's mother. It reverberated through the backseat as she investigated the van.

A few more words were spoken, and Andy and Gloria slipped into their seats, Ivanna and her bodyguard returning to the green warehouse.

"She has nine girls she will sell," Gloria said as Duncan's hand trembled on the steering wheel. His shaking hand pulled the gearshift into drive, and he pulled away. He did a U-turn, and headed back the way they came.

He found it difficult to coax the words from his lips. "That was Nickie's mother."

Gloria's mouth opened in a small O. She looked around the van as if she was looking for something she lost. "I am Nickie's mother. That woman is spawn of the devil." She pretended to spit on the floor of the van. "She wanted to sell the girls July three."

He turned the corner, checked and rechecked his rearview mirror while trying not to lose his dinner from listening to Gloria speak of purchasing children like she was at a farmer's market.

"I say, 'No!'"

Yes, Duncan had heard.

"July one, I say to her or no. I gave her 5,000 pesos."

She did? Duncan had not seen that.

She waved her hand in front of her face in circles. "It was…how do you say?"

"An advanced payment," Andy finished for her from the backseat. "We meet at noon."

"Tomorrow, then. During the day. That will be trickier. Let's hope for wind."

"Wind?" Gloria asked.

"Yes. The wind creates a dust storm and, therefore, cover. There is little cover in the dark, let alone the daytime hours."

Much to Duncan's relief and disbelief, they made it to a public area safely. "Noon. That is earlier in the day than we had expected, and a day early," he said.

Silence followed and consumed the van. They'd purchased a getaway van, built black market explosives and were making an EMP bomb. There was no turning back now.

It was a risk to many. Each knew this. They remained not just because of Nickie, although anyone in the group would have stayed the course if for her only. They were here for the children. Tomorrow they would rescue not only the children Gloria feigned purchase of, but also the rest of the ones held captive in the compound.

The following day, a rescue of countless others in the United States. Followed by a complete dismantling of Fu Haizi through Andy's data drop. Anticipation bubbled in the silence. It was like a tunnel vision of focus. One that took his mind from his destination.

Autopilot drove him back to the safe house. Shifting the van into park, he craned his head toward the entrance and leaned over the steering wheel. Something wasn't right. Not the children. They ran in their usual circles. He checked his watch. They'd missed dinner again. It would soon be dark in this South American winter, and dark meant stay inside.

Voices carried through the van door as Gloria opened it. Gloria's son and Duncan's uncle were due in that evening, but neither were the voice he heard. Checking his local cell phone, there were no new messages. For the first time in his eidetic life, his memory played tricks on him.

He turned off the engine and locked up the van as Gloria and Andy made their way inside. Leftovers would be plenty. The boy named Rico sat on the front step. Duncan squatted in front of him and reached to tap his nose with the end of his finger, but the boy reached out and wrapped his arms around Duncan's neck. He wriggled his legs around Duncan's waist and linked his fingers near his shoulder.

The boy's legs clung so tightly to him, he may have been able to release him without the boy falling. With one arm, he hung on to the child and stood. As he stepped inside, he heard it again. The voice. A distinct mixture of euphoria, confusion and frustration painted over him. Sliding Rico from his hip, he shooed him along.

Andy's voice came from the classroom in the back of the house that Duncan considered their meeting room. "Child Rescue has a needed presence here. And by here, I mean this country."

"Yes," Jess said. "We've earned the trust of many."

"And deservedly so. Forgive us if we, therefore, talk in a code of sorts."

Neither Jess nor Andy was who he came to see. Duncan didn't understand exactly why his feet were reluctant to step into the room, but he made them do so regardless.

It was just as Duncan's eidetic memory had told him. She sat with her back to the door. Her hair up in a rare ponytail, she nodded as Andy finished.

Andy took a breath and sat back, then caught Duncan's glance. His brother's eyes darted from Duncan to her, then to the table at his folded hands.

Her shoulders stiffened. It was slight enough that no one else would notice, but no one else was her husband. Yet, he seemed to be the only one unaware of which continent she occupied.

Jess took a breath. "Our rehabilitation, orphanage and work study facilities will be here for you when you return."

"If we return," Nickie said.

Two sets of walking feet came from behind him. He recognized both and should have been overjoyed with at least one of them. "Duncan," his uncle said and embraced him with a bear hug. Pulling back, Nathan set an outstretched hand on Duncan's shoulder. "Look at you. A beard. The gray works."

Gil stepped around him, smacking him on the back of the shoulder as he did. "Good to see you, man."

Greetings to Nathan and Gil went around the table.

He was at a loss. Should he walk away? Step in and add his opinions? Take her by the shoulders and make her look at him?

He chose the second option, or possibly his feet chose for him. He passed her. She didn't waver. He passed Gloria. He passed Andy. He passed Jess, then he sat. Gil, Nathan and Dr. Byrd sat on the other side of her.

She didn't make contact with him. "Explain to me the plan, please," she said.

Dr. Byrd cleared his throat. "May I?" he said but didn't wait for an answer and, instead, scraped his chair on the concrete flooring as he scooted out. He bounced to the maps and charts that hung from the wall.

Nickie's gaze followed him. As her face turned in the light, he saw the color of her skin. Gray. Not the brilliant steel gray color of her eyes, but the kind that went with the dark rings that hung beneath her eyes. He hadn't seen her in several days, but swore she looked like she'd lost fifteen pounds.

No longer did he care about her motives. A tsunami of worry blew through his very fiber. Dr. Byrd spoke in excruciating detail. Duncan didn't want to listen, but his eidetic memory never allowed that.

"Thanks to our nationally renowned artist—"

Fuck you, Byrd. Hurry up.

"—we have this beautiful sketch of the compound. You'll see here," he said and pointed to the largest building near the north side, "is the largest structure."

"Yes," Duncan snapped. "Everyone can see that the building is the largest. Can you hurry along?"

His words only caused Byrd to stutter and stammer through the next few sentences. "We've been by a dozen times and have only seen a few children. We began, you see, to wonder if possibly the children were kept in a different location altogether. That was, of course, until our amazing Gloria arranged for the fake purchase of nine children from the site. So, we think they are kept in the largest building and simply not let out unless by truck."

He tapped a finger to the sketch of the white box truck.

Should Duncan stand and stop the meeting? He and Nickie were becoming the elephant in the room. The only one who didn't sense it was the doctor.

"Andy and I come in from the south. He cuts east toward the cable box. I cut west to start running wire." He drew a pencil line over their map as if it was a kindergarten dot-to-dot ditto. "Gloria and Gil come right through the front door, so to speak, here from the far west. We think they are going to meet about…here," he said, tapping a point midway to the compound. "Duncan and Nathan come from the north and set their…" Pausing, he moved his glance to Jess, then corrected. "Dis-trac-tion," he said as if Jess might not hear. Then, he spoke quickly. "I must say I am mighty impressed with the boy's abilities."

Duncan stared at him with a death glare. Byrd winked in return.

"Gloria gets the girls. Duncan takes care of the distractions. Andy downloads the rest of the data from the compound drop box." Words bounced off his tongue as if it was a full proof plan. "I ignite my creation. We get the rest of the children, bring them here to the safe house and provide an anonymous phone call to the local authorities."

Nickie said, "I'm going in with Gloria."

That was it. Nickie had lost her mind. "I believe your own mother might recognize you," he said as the first words they'd exchanged.

"No, she won't. I'll make sure of it. I didn't come down here for nothing."

"And why exactly did you come down here?" he asked.

"I'm tired. I'm going to bed." Nickie rose from the table. Duncan followed her into the hall and circled her arm with his fingers. Cold and tight, the connection was still tangible.

For the first time in their relationship, she physically pulled away from him. "Girls room is that way," she said.

"Nickie," he said, desperation in his voice.

"I'm really tired. Jet lag and all that." She didn't hurry. Didn't storm down the hall. She simply turned and left him standing alone.

She'd used Broadway cover-up to make her skin several shades darker. The black hair dye didn't take over her blonde hair. It was a dark rusty brown. Good enough. After several attempts, she maneuvered a dark brown contact in one eye. Blinking, she judged her hair.

Duncan was right. She looked too much like her.

Duncan. She squeezed her eyes hard enough that she popped out the contact.

After punching the concrete wall three times, she ignored the blood that came across her knuckles and took out a pair of scissors from the top shelf behind the mirror over the sink.

Taking a clump of hair, she cut it just below her ear. She kept going until she'd cut it all the way around into a short, dark brown bob. Placing the contact in the palm of her hand, she forced it back in, stepped back and threw her chin up.

One more to go and she would be someone else.

She checked the dressings the ER nurse had given her. The bleeding was almost done. Over. Finished. She zipped her pair of black jeans. Staring in the mirror, she disappeared altogether.

One of the toddlers cried and ran away as Nickie stepped into the hallway. She found the group in front of the building, emptying boxes from the conversion van to the rental sedan. No one noticed her at first.

Not even him.

He rubbed the top of a small boy's head before he loaded one of several spools of wire.

"Test your audios," she announced to the team as she approached. Gloria and Gil were exempt since Nickie's mother would, without a doubt, search them for wires.

Everyone stopped and stared. Her foster mother wore a floral wraparound skirt and scarf over her head. She put a hand over her mouth. Andy's eyes grew large and he rubbed the back of his neck. Nathan took hold of Duncan's forearm and grasped.

The little boy Duncan had touched walked slowly to her. He wrapped his thin arms around her thigh and squeezed. She looked down at him and felt something stir in her heart, so she stepped away and repeated, "Test your audios. We leave in thirty."

"The one underside the dash of the van is working, little sister. I checked," Gil said.

Byrd lifted a finger. "May I? This is so very important. I cannot emphasize this enough. You must remove the batteries of anything you don't want annihilated. That includes cell phones, watches all the way to car batteries." He rubbed his hands together. "And wrap the device in cardboard. I know," he said, turned his chin away and held up a hand. "It's strange. But if you ever want to use your equipment again, you'll follow these rules."

No one considered not following them.

"Sync your watches with the times on your phones," Nickie interrupted. "You'll want a backup in case one or the other fries. We keep on schedule."

Byrd inhaled and opened his mouth.

"Almost time," she said. "Finish loading up."

CHAPTER 29

The conversion van pulled away. It was like watching a firstborn son leave for active duty. Nickie drove. She was nearly unrecognizable. Her hair. Duncan couldn't care less about the color or the length, but nearly unrecognizable left a hole in his heart.

He leaned toward his uncle. "Is this what you and Brie felt when I left for the Middle East?"

"Some, yes, only you were buzzed rather than dyed."

"I don't know, man," Andy added. "I got no words for that."

Duncan turned to his brother. "You talked to Rose."

Andy nodded. "Yeah. A lot of cryptic girl shit. Something happened. Has Nick done this before?"

Duncan didn't know if his question was in reference to the hair and makeup or the portcullis she'd dropped between them. Nonetheless, he said, "Not like this."

"We've got ten," Andy said. "Let's lament about women in the air conditioning."

Their heads turned to the rental sedan. The trunk was loaded with the dozen small explosive devices Duncan had created and the EMP bomb. Dr. Byrd waited in the passenger seat.

Duncan paused and took this in. Three Reed men, standing in a line. "Come on." Duncan shoulder-checked Andy as he passed. "It's time."

Duncan drove. The clouds were thick enough to cause mid-day seem like dusk. It was unseasonably warm. Fortunately, the wind he'd hoped for blew in angry wisps of warning. It whipped small bits of trash around in small tunnels as he drove.

His mind fought with his heart, and he ground his teeth together and held tight as he took the corner with exaggerated control. Would they succeed today? What happened to drive his Nickie into such an abyss? So many people he loved would put their lives in danger this day. He turned onto the gravel road Samuel had advised. Regardless of the unanswered questions or risks involved, one fact remained a constant. Today had to work. Failure was not an option.

Small groups of children who should be in school laughed as they ran through the wind tunnels. Stray dogs seemed to sense the coming storm, ducking their tails between their legs as they ran with bits of food down the alleys.

"Thank you," Duncan said, breaking the thick silence that filled the inside of the vehicle.

"To who, brother?"

"The three of you."

"It's been the highlight of my life," Byrd said. "My eyes have been opened and my heart filled. Whatever happens today, this has been the best week of my life."

The terrain changed as brush hit the bumper of the rental, reminding Duncan of the driveway next to the home in Henderson. A thick forest of oncoming saplings forced him to stop altogether. He shifted into park. "This is it, men."

"I live for this shit," Andy said.

"I hate it when you say that," Duncan answered. He exited the vehicle and walked around to the trunk. Nathan popped it, and the four of them stared at the contents. The EMP was in a box with two protruding handles. As Duncan stood guard, Andy wrapped his fingers around one side, the doctor the other. "You have your laptop?" Duncan asked Andy as he judged the size of the backpack he wore.

"And a tablet as backup. I have flash drives and the camera in my phone in case all of it goes to hell. I'll get the names and dates, brother. Count on me."

And he did. Reaching out, Nathan grabbed Andy around the shoulders. Not a one-armed hug as they were accustomed to but a full three-second hug that meant something.

"It's so beautiful," Byrd said and grabbed Duncan in for a hug, then Nathan.

"Remember to remove the battery and put it in this box," Byrd said, wiping tears from his face. He handed him a cardboard box with a lid. "Then, cover the vehicle with this." He pointed to a complicated array of cardboard that was folded like a box. "You can replace the battery thirty seconds after I ignite the pulse."

"At 12:45 p.m.? How will I know if you're running late?"

Byrd's smile was one to cause a healthy concern. "You'll know," he said.

Duncan watched the only brother he had walk away, carrying one side of a disabling device. Checking his watch, he swore under his breath and got back in the car. He needed to back out at least hundred yards before he could turn around and make his way with Nathan to the other side of the compound.

Although several more in number, his materials were much smaller. "We may be without guns, but we have plenty of firepower," he said to Nathan.

"Let's just not get caught. I have a feeling what we're packing might be worse than guns in the eyes of the authorities."

Duncan thought of the children in the safe house. The twelve-year-old child who carried a child in her womb. He thought of Rico. Of his Nickie. "Dad, I worry for her."

"I know. Give her some room. She has a lot riding on this day."

That was true. Somehow, that gave him a possible needed reason for her distance and change in appearance.

"She tends to close off in a crunch," Nathan continued. "She always turns around in the end."

Duncan's lungs filled. "I was quite angry at your insistence to join in this."

"I know that too," Nathan said and smiled.

"I, now, find myself overwhelmingly relieved."

"Me, too. You are a son to me and Nickie my daughter. Reeds stick together."

The spot Samuel told him to park in was far enough away from the compound, it was likely out of range of the electromagnetic pulse, but Duncan pulled the lever to pop the hood anyway. In the humid air, he put on the hip-length trench coat with the many pockets full of the explosives he needed.

The Hill towered over him like a watchful mother. Or possibly a mob ready to pounce. He removed the car battery and put it in the empty cardboard box in the trunk. Then, he covered it with the blanket of cardboard the doctor had given him. He didn't bother to lock up. If the car was found, it would be stripped regardless.

He shut the door and placed the keys in the inside chest pocket of the coat and walked around to stand in front of the car. He checked the surroundings. The country was truly beautiful.

Today, he would do his part to make this country safer for children and families. Buttoning the three buttons on the jacket, he and Nathan took off in a jog to set his small explosives, ready to ignite at precisely 12:30 p.m. Fifteen minutes prior to Byrd's EMP. Too much rode on timing.

Nickie's wrist hung over the steering wheel. "It's not too late to back out," she said to her foster mother. "This is crazy shit, you know. It's not safe."

"Language," Gloria scolded and gestured two fingers forward, urging Nickie on.

"Come on, Ma. Nickie's right. You don't have to do this."

Rotating in her seat, she let out a tirade in Spanish to Gil, then turned forward again. Nickie guessed she wasn't changing her mind.

A mile or so from town, cars became fewer. The roads became thinner with more potholes and divots. The mountain stood next to them like a prison wall void of windows. Single-room homes with the rusted metal roofs that were common in the city slum areas butted up to each other, reaching high into the clouds.

The compound came into view. Few lights were on and little movement came from between buildings. The road was nothing more than a worn line of soil that led from the highway, over the plain to the tiny village of buildings that sat in the center of barren area.

"Entering the compound grounds," she said into the audio bug under the dash.

The heart she had so carefully turned off sank. Places to keep cover were few and far between. Men with rifles hanging from their shoulders, however, were plenty.

Duncan, Nathan, Andy and Dr. Byrd. How could they do this?

Nickie didn't veer from the road and considered how she would turn around since each side of the road was dotted with rocks and holes.

A guard stood in the middle of the path. It seemed like he didn't see the van, but she knew this wasn't the case. This was business as usual. Another day in abusing and selling children. Her fingers wrapped around the steering wheel and squeezed.

There were almost a dozen vehicles parked randomly throughout the compound. Most wouldn't be drivable, but some would. More may be stored in the larger structures.

She looked up at the dark clouds that threatened to open, and she imagined the storms could be fierce enough in this expansive area to warrant shelter for the more important vehicles. Her mother's Mercedes.

Large warehouse structure to the north. Smaller sheds to the south. She stopped twenty feet from the man. He turned and looked at her, then pulled out a radio from around his neck and spoke into it.

"Don't get out," Nickie said to Gloria and Gil.

Gripping his rifle in both hands, the man leaned his head from one side of the van to the other as he walked around it. He would think the driver was of little consequence and stopped only when he got to the passenger door.

Nickie paused before rolling down Gloria's window.

"Ivanna Monticello," Gloria said in English. "She knows I am here."

He stepped away and used his trigger hand to pick up the walkie again. He spoke in Spanish. Nickie didn't make out any of the words, but Gloria dipped her head a single time in a nod.

It took only a few minutes before a shiny, black BMW rolled from one of the smaller shelters. It crawled down the road toward them. The guard stepped from the path but continued to point his rifle at the van.

Nickie couldn't see through the tinted glass, but she knew what was in the car. Who was in the car. Her mother. And two to three men with heavy artillery. Nickie turned her chin down and away.

This was a business. Ivanna needed customers, but she didn't need cops and would check every move from the people in the van.

The passenger door opened and a dark-haired man in black pants and a mock turtleneck stepped out. He stood tall and opened the back door. Ivanna Monticello stepped out and stood. She brushed off the pants of her linen aqua pantsuit. Lifting her chin, she walked toward the van.

"Now," Nickie said under her breath.

Gil got out of the back and opened the door for his mother.

"You brought a different man," Ivanna said in English as she looked Gil over like she considered buying him. Even over the residual odor of the fresh hair dye and the dust that swirled around them, Nickie smelled the perfume she remembered from her childhood.

Her vision blurred. Sweat dripped from her temple down her cheek. Images of her mother forbidding her from the horse stables and pleading with her to ride English-style and not bareback brushed Nickie's mind.

"This one is your son," her mother said to Gloria.

"That's right," Gil said and stepped to her.

No, Gil. Not so much.

"Where are the children?" Gloria asked. Her demeanor was unsettlingly collected.

"Where is the money?" Ivanna said.

"I stand in your territory. I have money. First, I see what I buy."

"Bring the children," Ivanna called to the single guard behind her.

He hesitated, but then spoke into his walkie.

Nickie's eyes burned holes in the sides of her mother. Flashes of her childhood threatened to take from her needed focus. Flashes of Gloria as Jun Zheng held her captive, taunting her for Nickie's namesake.

She closed her eyes. Only for a few short seconds. When she opened them, the white box truck crawled down the dirt path, rocking as it hit uneven roads. She imagined the inside of it. It would smell of dirty bodies. Handcuffs would clink as they hung from the sides. They were there as a reminder. They would not be needed. The children would've given up hopes of running away.

"I am a business woman," Ivanna said. "You understand." She smiled. It was sarcastic and evil and all wrong. "Where did she get you?" Ivanna squinted her eyes as she asked.

Where did Gloria get who? Oh no. A breach. It was a breach. Nickie considered calling for help into the audio bug affixed to the underside of the dash. Instead, she pulled it off and smashed it with her foot. She opened the driver's side door, then slipped out and under the van.

Police emergency autopilot took over. Down the man with the gun first. She rolled all the way under the van and kicked the gunman's legs out from under him. "Take cover!" she ordered as she wrestled his gun from him. Not before it shot off three rounds in the air. A swift elbow to the side of his face and he was down.

She grabbed a spare magazine from his belt as she rolled back beneath the cover of the van. It rocked above her and the doors slammed shut.

"Get down," she yelled as she pulled the trigger again and again. Man down. Shoot downed man's gun away from reach. Repeat. Two down. Three down.

A single empty click and she released the magazine. In the split second it took to replace it, a hand gripped her ankle and yanked her along the hard ground. Simultaneously, she kicked her feet as she secured the clip in the stolen gun and shot the arm that pulled her.

Except it was followed by another arm and another until there were four of them, one on each of her limbs.

Gloria. No, no, no. Please, not Gloria. She thrashed like a fish out of water. Freeing an arm, she grabbed the one on her leg by his hair and head butted him. The stars she saw from the blow didn't slow her down, but made her aim off. She found herself hauled to her feet with her arms craned behind her back and legs secured. "One move and I break your neck," a familiar voice said into her ear. She didn't need to see him. She could smell him.

Jun Zheng.

CHAPTER 30

Nickie's lungs beat like mad. Her toes brushed the dirt as the men dragged her around to where Ivanna stood in her business heels. Gloria and Gil stood next to her, angry tears running down her foster mother's caramel cheeks. Neither had any men grappling their limbs, but each had a pistol pressed against their temple. Nickie could hardly move, but she thrashed anyway. The backs of her eyes burned as panic set in. This couldn't be happening.

Jun Zheng held Nickie's neck like a vice. "Do you think I would not recognize my own daughter?" Ivanna barked, lifting a piece of Nickie's dark brown hair and flicking it against her face. "You have crossed the line this time."

"Murderer," Nickie spat. "This isn't over."

"This time, my dear Nicole, it most definitely is. You see, I did not keep you alive because I feared public attention from your murder. I own public attention. And the police? They are mine. I kept you alive in hopes that you would come to me. Your mother. The one who gave birth to you, raised you from a baby."

Gloria yelled, "You are not her mother!"

No, Gloria. No, no, no. Stop talking. Traitorous tears poured down Nickie's cheeks. She blinked them away, so she could watch what she didn't want to see.

Ivanna cocked her head to Nickie, then moved her attention to Gloria. Stepping nose to nose with Gloria, Ivanna smiled and asked, "And who are you? Really."

"I am her mother. The one who raised her. The one she comes to."

Ivanna looked down her nose from Gloria's headdress to her sandals. "Mr. Zheng," Ivanna said. "You may take Nicole to do with as you please. The woman and boy? Put them in the cellar with the others."

It was too late. The timers would be set by then. They were all going to die.

The crunch of a foot cracking brittle sticks caused Duncan to freeze where he squatted in the brush. Fifty yards of barren plain separated him and Nathan from the largest building at the northernmost end of the compound. Fifty yards and three guards, if Duncan counted correctly. One toward the east, one toward the west and the third who was apparently a few feet behind him, crunching sticks as he stalked the area.

He turned his head ever so slightly and caught the glance of his uncle. Nathan nodded. Wrapping his hand into a tight fist, Duncan used his legs to propel him, his fist sinking into the man's temple. An expression of confusion ran over the man's face before he fell toward the ground like a fallen tower. Duncan caught him and lowered him gently as he checked any movement from the other two. Taking the man's gun, he shoved it in the back of his belt.

Adjusting his backpack of explosives, he ran east on the balls of his feet. This guard stopped to light a cigarette. Duncan slipped the backpack on the ground, threw an arm around the man's neck and spun. This one seemed equally surprised but didn't go down with just the single punch to the cheek. Duncan was happy to accommodate with another and another until the man staggered.

As Duncan pulled his fist back for the final blow, the barrel of a rifle prodded his back. The guard in front of him fell unconscious while Duncan held his arms out in surrender.

The barrel of the weapon disappeared and the guard grunted. Duncan spun in time to see Nathan shoving the butt of the weapon into the man's diaphragm. As the guard gasped for air, Duncan used the gun he'd confiscated to hit a blow to the side of his head.

Lifting his brows, he smiled at his uncle, put a finger to his mouth and pulled him low. He and Nathan squatted on the backs of their feet and checked for movement. It was then that he spotted the van. Nickie had already announced through the audio bug that she'd arrived on the grounds. He could barely make it out in the dark clouds and whipping dust. It sat parked in the center of the drive.

Pressing his watch near his mouth, he whispered, "Brother, do you copy? Out."

"Busy workin', dude. Out."

"How close are you? Out."

"Not very. Out."

"Aren't you going to ask me, son?"

Duncan waited for Byrd to signal he was done talking, but realized it wasn't going to happen. "How close are you, Doctor? Out." He enunciated the last word.

"Done. Pack up your goodies, ladies and gentlemen. Oh. What?" he said far from the bug. "Ah, yes. Out, then."

Duncan needed to hurry. Checking his watch, he saw he had less than fifteen minutes, smacked Nathan's shoulder with the back of his hand and ran for it. The fifty-yard dash to the nearest shed left him breathless. He was trained for this and controlled his breathing.

Simultaneously, he checked for patrols as he unzipped the bag. The dark clouds and wind reduced visibility, but Duncan didn't need a map. He'd studied and memorized the grounds from afar. Seven buildings. Discarded vehicles that served as useful occasional cover.

Nathan appeared then disappeared around the east side of a central building. Foot patrol. The man in black passed. It took Duncan seconds to secure adhesive putty to the back of the first explosive and affix it to the side of the shed against his back. Nathan was quick for his age and landed next to him.

Duncan's heart yearned to check on the progress his wife made. He couldn't see the van from this vantage point. The core of her being rode on the success of this operation. He dipped his head around the side of the structure.

Two of them. Pressing his back to the sheet metal wall, he lifted two fingers toward Nathan. He counted to ten in his head, and peered around again. The backs of the second guard's shoes disappeared behind the largest shed. Duncan ran around a rusty truck and placed an explosive beneath the front bumper. He considered, then placed another at the back.

Nathan did the same to a smaller shed south of the large one before ducking behind the rusty truck with Duncan. Together, they waited for a third guard to walk by with his rifle resting on his shoulder, far too ready to shoot. They continued until the backpack was empty. The entire east side of the compound was going to light up and, as far as he could tell, the incapacitated north guards had not yet been missed. Nathan stopped and crouched under the single back window of the shed where Duncan hung from the ceiling joist a few weeks before.

Pressing his fingers against his rib, Duncan dug in. The tenderness was gone. A raindrop hit the back of his hand. He looked up. The dark gray spoke to him, mocked him. Water made little difference; he wanted to tell the sky.

Inches from his gray head, the window beckoned. It was nearly time. Nathan elbowed him in a rib and reached in the backpack. He removed the four small boxes big enough to fit two cell phones and two watches.

Swiping his phone, Duncan checked his social media messages once more before disabling it.

One from his office manager, another from Johnny and Bebe Lyons. How did life carry on as usual around all of this?

He and Nathan took the batteries from their cell phones and placed both in separate boxes. They repeated the same with the watches.

Left, right. No one was around. He shoved the phones and watches back in the backpack and stood. Raising his head to the side of window, he peered a single eye inside. Both the bag and the gun in his hand dropped to the ground.

CHAPTER 31

A topless woman with short, dark hair hung from the spot Duncan had weeks prior. Her head dipped low, her chin resting on her neck. She had six lines of scars on her back and three circular ones that were old cigarette burns. He knew these scars as if they were his own.

His Nickie. His wife.

Was she alive? Darting so that both eyes could see, he squinted through the dusty window. Stepping into view was a face he would know forever with or without his eidetic memory. Jun Zheng. Nickie adjusted her toes along the concrete. He knew what she was doing. She used her toes to try and stop herself from swinging in circles as well as lifting a portion of her weight from her shoulders and wrists. She was alive.

"Duncan. Son. Where are the others?" Nathan whispered as he looked through the window and saw what Duncan saw.

"Find them," Duncan said to him. He knew there was no entrance on this side of the building, but he checked the walls anyway. Nathan took off on the balls of his feet as Zheng strolled along side her, one foot and then the other. Running his fingers around the outside of the window frame, Duncan shook the metal every few inches.

He lifted the audio bug to his mouth and announced, "Breach, breach, breach. They've got her. He's got her. I repeat Nickie has been taken."

With little warning, Zheng pulled his arm back and swiped. The end of a bull rope struck her perfect back, leaving a raw trail of pink that turned into a thin line of bright red before his eyes. Her body didn't react to the pain.

Tucking his fist inside the arm of his jacket, he reared back and shoved it through the glass. He had the shards cleared and was up and through the window in seconds. The bull rope still dangled from Zheng's hands, but he'd had time during the breaking of the glass to pick up a long knife and hold it to her throat.

"Good day, Mr. Reed. I do not care for interruptions with my savage."

Nickie's head bobbed.

"The place is surrounded, Zheng," Duncan said as he tiptoed closer.

Zheng tossed his hair back and laughed. "It was hard enough to hear these threats on U.S. soil, but here? Do you see who I have with me?" He tightened his grip around her. "Your attempts have been futile all along. We regroup. There are always more children." His laughter was short-lived.

The explosion shook the ground. Duncan had affixed two explosive devices to this building alone and the others reverberated throughout the compound. Zheng swayed and darted his gaze from one side of the building to the other. Duncan lunged and jumped into a kick to the side of Zheng's face. He flew backward to the ground, his head hitting the hard dirt with a thud. The knife fell beside him.

Duncan's upper lip curled as he stomped to him and picked up the blade. He spun and used it to cut her free. Her limp body against him, her arms dangling over his shoulders. Gripping her waist, he was careful not to touch her fresh wound. Her right arm slid and bobbed next to her limp body. "I am here," he whispered in her ear.

Silence ensued between occasional remnants of pops. The rain had started. It drizzled over the small village now encompassed with fires.

Chaos erupted outside. Deep voices. Some yelled orders. Some just yelled.

"There is little time," he said and guided her arms into the sleeves of his jacket. "The EMP ignites in less than fifteen."

It was like she woke from a dream. Her arms snaked around his neck. She shook like she was cold, clinging to his head and neck. Tears drenched the shoulder where she dug her face.

Her head shook back and forth, and she mumbled into his shoulder. "George Kruger. Dale Parker. The blood."

Had Zheng drugged her?

"The belt. The carbon monoxide. My body."

Her arms squeezed him like he wore the only parachute as they jumped from a burning plane.

"They all kill."

There was no time. The bomb. They had to get the children out. "I am here for you. Do you know where Gloria and Gil are?" he crooned.

She dug her forehead into his shoulder, slowly moving her head back and forth. He took her by the shoulders. "My love is without condition. You are my detective. My Nickie. My wife."

The chaos continued around them. Zheng stirred.

"Where is your mother?" Duncan realized too late the double meaning behind this question. He didn't have a chance to explain. Nickie placed her hands on his cheeks.

Her wince changed to clarity, and her eyes grew large. "Duncan. I know where they are. All of them."

Zheng bolted upright. Crouched like an animal ready to spring, he blinked as he looked at Duncan and then to Nickie. "Ahh!" he yelled and sprang. Duncan stepped in front of Nickie, taking the full force of the blow. He and Zheng tumbled to the floor. "We have but moments before the entire compound is down. Go!" Duncan yelled to her as he wrapped his legs around Zheng's torso and squeezed.

Zheng lifted his clasped hands above his head and thrust them into Duncan's ribs. The air left his lungs. He coughed but staggered to his feet as Zheng kicked the side of his head. His vision went dark long enough for a fist to come up beneath his chin, knocking his teeth together.

Shaking his head clear, he spotted Zheng marching to the exit. Duncan scooped up the blade and roared, "No!" as he ran. He tackled him and straddled his back. Pulling him by his neck, he shoved the blade beneath Zheng's chin. "One move and you're gone. How does it feel?"

Zheng jerked and garbled something incoherent, but Duncan's arm wrapped tighter around his neck. If he just held on a little tighter. Jun Zheng. "You touched her. Hurt her." A little longer. "Left scars on my wife."

Standing, he let him drop facedown and stood over him. Zheng lay limp with nothing moving except his lungs. With fires and turmoil ensuing outside of the building, Duncan strolled to the table with the weapons, set down the knife and considered. Bloody blades, knives, a mallet, a handful of zip ties and a machete.

He walked back to Zheng, who coughed in the dirt. "Be glad I didn't choose the machete, you worthless scum," he said and tied his hands behind his back.

As drizzle sprayed her face, Nickie stood with her knees locked, feet spread. Chaos buzzed around her. She was the queen in the center of the beehive. Only these bees worked for another queen.

A Mercedes stood running idle at the edge of the compound. From inside, Ivanna barked orders through the open window. Nickie did not search for that mother. Duncan had known this. Unconditional love. No matter what she did or who she was. He was her everything.

She scanned through the small fires that seemed to be everywhere. There. In the dark, in the rain. A rusted metal door that led underground. Take them to the cellar with the others, the pit boss had said. Fear in the eyes of men who didn't understand made Nickie invisible. She walked tall through the mud. Through hell.

A chain and padlock covered the door over the ground that held crying children captive. She heard her mother's voice. Her true mother. Nickie closed her eyes. Gloria lived. Her familiar soothing voice crooned to the children who were with her. She had used the voice with teenage Nickie during spells of flashbacks and panic attacks. Her mother who loved her. Unconditionally.

She found tools. They were crude and filthy, but they weren't electric and didn't contain any wiring. Digging the crowbar into the pin at the hinge of the door, she pounded. The rust was too much. Below turned into silence. At least they were safe. The EMP would explode and they would live.

A hand rested on her shoulder. She reached to take it and flip the body attached, but the man was quick. He pulled his arm away. Ice blue eyes smiled beneath a head of salt and pepper hair. "Nathan," she said and smiled back at him.

He took the tools from her and released the hinge, then another and another until the door was free.

Covering her fingers with the ends of Duncan's coat, she and Nathan inched it from the cover of the cellar. Fingers appeared from beneath. They wrapped around the side of the metal and heaved. Heaved until she saw the face belonging to the fingers.

"Brother," she said.

"Sister," Gil answered and nodded behind the tears on his cheeks. "You came."

"Always."

"There are children down here. Help us."

"Not yet." She hesitated, convincing herself to have faith that Duncan knew exactly when and where to be when the bomb went off. She held out a hand to Nathan. "Come," she said. "This is his expertise. The war. He knows how to be safe."

Nathan shook his head as the tips of their fingers parted. "He is my son. I cannot leave him. Stay with the children." He smiled, spun on his feet and ran.

"Nickie," Gil said as children started crying again. She crawled in with them and looked around at the underground village. Gloria sat on the ground with children circling her. Her smile was warm. Nickie closed her eyes and inhaled. The area extended all around her like a dark city of mud.

"Bomb shelter," Gil said.

"Irony. Get away from the door."

His chin jerked toward her, then to the children. "Get away from the door," he yelled.

Leaving Zheng half-conscious on the ground, Duncan stepped out into the drizzle. It whipped around his face and hair, but did little to put out the fires. A trio of men, soaked with the rain and soot, walked around the burning rusted truck. Two explosives had been affixed to that vehicle. Vengeance was sweet.

He stepped backward into the shed and almost stepped where Zheng's body lay. Glancing down, he considered giving him a sound kick. He was gone. Zheng. He checked the area and spotted Zheng's backside where his hands remained tied, ducking into the shed that held the better vehicles. Duncan lifted a corner of his mouth. "Good luck with a working vehicle, Zheng," he said and eyed the window in the back.

Crawling through the way he came wasn't necessary. He waited for the trio to pass, then dipped his head out the opening once again. With the fires to the east, he marched around the west side of the building. The backpack with the cell phones and watches still lay, untouched, in the spot he'd dropped it.

A loud crack sounded behind him. It was followed by a heavy thump. He rotated on his feet and found Nathan straddling a man in black, placing a hard right hook to the side of his head. Blinking several times, he looked to his uncle, his father. "That's the second time you've done that for me today."

Nathan lifted from the perp, then huddled close to the building with Duncan. They had but a few moments before the electromagnetic pulse. "I took care of Jun Zheng," he said to Nathan. "Nickie is free and went to find Gloria and Gil. She thought she knew where they're located. All of them, she said, although I have no idea what that means."

"I do. Let's go to her."

"We are out of time," Duncan said.

CHAPTER 32

Nathan faced him. "What do we do? Where do we go?"

He looked around. "We stay right here," Duncan said.

"Here?" Nathan turned his head toward one side of the back of the shed to the other.

They were at the southernmost edge of the compound. In front of them lay over a hundred yards of barren brown plains.

"Are you suicidal?" Nathan asked.

"Possibly," he said, realizing he'd placed the lives of everyone in the hands of Dr. Byrd. "We're away from anything electrical or that contains or uses a fuel source."

Nathan didn't seem completely convinced. "You're smiling. That's it. You dyed your hair grayer than mine, and you're smiling. You are suicidal."

"I'm remembering."

"Tell me. And hurry. I want to know about this memory before we die."

"It is small. We sat like this fishing for palm-sized blue gills in the Black Creek behind your home."

"Our home, and we caught more crawfish and turtles than fish."

"You saved my life."

"I don't think the crawfish were that big."

What would Duncan and Andy have become if Nathan hadn't raised them as his own?

From his peripheral vision, Duncan noticed movement. A Mercedes SUV with tinted windows came into view. Mud kicked up behind the tires as it drove straight toward a plane at the end of the crude Fu Haizi airstrip. Duncan's autopilot checked his wrist for the time. "That's not a good idea," he said.

The propeller kicked on before the Mercedes came to a complete stop. "That is a really, really bad idea." He stood. It was minutes at best before the EMP exploded.

The driver stepped out. Zheng. A small battle ignited in Duncan's head. Part of him wanted to take off running and snap his neck once and for all. Part of him wanted to sit back down next his uncle and let the bastard die in the air.

Arms free, Zheng opened the back door of the Mercedes, and Duncan dropped his chin to his neck. Ivanna Monticello. Duncan started toward the plane. "There's going to be a lot of panic," he said as he walked backward. "This won't be like the power went out. This will be cell phones, watches, radios, cars." He pointed at the aircraft. "And planes." He spun around and took off running as he yelled over his shoulder, "I'll find you."

Zheng turned his head and looked at Duncan. He smiled.

Duncan waved both arms over his head as he ran. "No! It's not safe."

With one arm, Zheng guided Ivanna onto the step of the plane; with the other, he saluted Duncan.

Duncan's feet beat against the wet soil as he ran. The door of the aircraft had barely shut when it started to move. Skidding to a stop, Duncan could see Zheng leaning toward the pilot and talking into his ear.

It was like the end of days. The plane tipped into the air and started to circle back when a series of clicks sang between the sounds of burning vehicles and buildings. Then, everything went dark.

Zheng waved through the window. A flyover. The engine cut and the plane took a nosedive. It was a distinct sound and one Duncan remembered well. The crash pierced the air with a loud crunch. A mushroom cloud of smoke and fire encompassed the compound like a useless umbrella.

Nickie.

The rain stopped, and the screams started. He ran through the panic. A handful of men carried obsolete electrical equipment to useless vehicles. Others bent over raised hoods in attempts to repair what the electromagnetic pulse had destroyed. Most simply bolted to The Hill where dots of electricity said civilization remained.

He spotted her. Short, dark hair didn't keep him from knowing his wife. His feet slowed as the backs of his eyes burned. She stood with one foot in a cellar, helping one child after another emerge from the depths.

The children gathered around Gloria like a tour group. Nathan. Gil. They'd formed an assembly line. Lifting his chin, he turned in a complete circle, checking for the two who remained missing. Andy and the doctor. He saw nothing but confused men who walked like zombies and others who looted their own place of business.

The last child emerged as Duncan reached Nickie. She turned, blinked and smiled. Her face glowed, full of life and color. "There you are," he said and kissed her forehead.

She slipped an arm in his and used the other to guide the children down the single dirt road. There were dozens of them. A quick count said thirty-five. He had no idea how they would transport them all to the safe house. The conversion van hadn't been protected and the rental sedan would hold a dozen at most. No idea if Andy had gotten the data and secured it in cardboard before the EMP, but he had his wife and his wife had the children.

They'd walked the children nearly to the end of the compound when a familiar VW van turned the corner and headed toward them, toward the fire and the panic that was behind them. It was followed by two other vehicles Duncan hadn't seen before. Samuel.

It was the best-looking vehicle Duncan ever laid his eyes on. He would get one himself as soon as they returned to the states. Samuel slowed to a stop and rolled down his window. "I saw the explosion." He glanced behind him at the other vehicles in the line. "We all did."

Leaning out, Duncan saw that the drivers were the same men who wore the dirty white T-shirts from The Hill.

Samuel announced, "We need to hurry."

"We have to call the local authorities," Nickie said.

Samuel stepped out and craned his head around her and the children at the flames and smoke. "I think they will know," he said and opened his back door.

"It was awesome!" Jimbo paced as he spoke. "We, like, saved people."

Eddy stood from his seat in the break room and stretched. "They're called children, Slimeball."

Nickie sat with her boots propped on the table in front of her. Headlines scrolled along the bottom of the small television monitor in the corner. As Slippery Jimbo and Eddy bickered like a married couple, she read.

OPERATION FU HAIZI...FBI RESCUES 158 CHILDREN FROM HUMAN TRAFFICKING...

This time, Nickie knew they'd been truly saved. Each was either placed or on his or her way to a safe house. The parents of nearly each child on the Missing Persons list had been notified.

Slippery Jimbo ignored Eddy as he lifted to the balls of his feet. "We were like the good guys. I might even give up stealing shit."

"Aww," Nickie said and eyeballed the donuts. There was a Bavarian cream with her name on it. "It makes my heart melt."

Eddy rolled his eyes like a junior high girl and stood. "Can't take the drama. I'm gonna go work on the mountain of good guy paperwork." He stopped when he reached the doorway. "Never thought I'd see the day when I had to write up shit for the feds."

She smiled. "You're just nice that way, Eddy."

Jimbo grabbed the Bavarian cream and popped it in his mouth. She could have scratched his eyes out, but it made him stop talking, so it might have been worth it. "Official police informant exiting the prem-ee-sees," he said and walked out the door toward the elevator.

She blinked when the news frame changed to a picture of Hurst carrying a girl on his hip. Scrambling, she found the remote and turned up the volume.

"Each of the 158 have a place in rehabilitation facilities," he said to the set of microphones shoved in his face. He turned his gaze directly to the camera. "Nonprofit rescue organizations across the country have opened their doors to provide safe homes for the victims to heal. Y'all should consider giving your time and donations to help the little ones like this here Joy." The little girl clung to him with big, dark eyes.

"Special Agent, we understand that a few members of the FBI have been arrested as long as a well-hidden list of politicians."

"I am afraid I cannot comment on an ongoing investigation at this time. It's been less than twenty-four hours, gentlemen. A press release will be scheduled. Give us some time."

The video footage and spreadsheets Andy had been able to retrieve would take more than some time to go through. Years of footage. Crooked cops were few, politicians…not so much. It was an amazing feeling to know there was evidence to bring them to justice.

She turned to Duncan. He was staring at her. "What?" she said.

"Your face. It glows."

"It's the weirdest sensation," she said and shook her head. Commercial. She pressed the television back to mute.

"It is closure."

"What is what?"

"The sensation. It is closure."

Huh. She guessed that made sense. "What are you doing over there?" she asked. He wasn't like Eddy, who could sit and play on his phone for hours. Yet, he'd been doing just that for the past several minutes. "Why not your tablet?"

"This is not my phone," he said and kept scrolling.

It was hers. "Hey!"

"Infertility is not uncommon," he said.

"Not helping," she said, then regretted it. It had been his kid too.

"There are options. Many of them."

"I don't want to talk about this." The past few days had turned out so good. She was ready to go back to Lima and forget everything that was Upstate New York.

"Did you know that you have two messages from Special Agent Johnson and one from the hospital?"

"Special Agent Johnson? I'll get to it."

He held it out to her. "Either you do it, or I will."

"You," she said.

He sneered. "I already tried. Neither will speak to me."

She sighed and took her phone from him. She chose Special Agent Johnson first. She would leave a message. "Johnson," the agent answered.

"This is Detective Savage. I have a message to call you."

"Yes, thank you. The identity of one of the deceased has been acknowledged. I wanted to tell you myself."

George Kruger. She knew it. How did the special agent connect him to her?

"Nickie, I'm afraid it was your father."

What? "Who?"

There was a long pause before she repeated, "Your father. Edward Monticello. The autopsy is pending, but estimates say he had only been dead a few days. Do you know where we can find your mother? She has not been notified."

Yes. "No." That would have to come out in due time. "Wow." She knew that wasn't the appropriate reaction, but she was speechless. "Okay. Thank you. I'll make arrangements."

Duncan's expression was a mixture of concern and curiosity.

"They found my father's body. His own wife must have offed him. He truly didn't know about Fu Haizi."

"Nothing is black and white," Duncan said. "Life is a color palate of different hues of gray."

She nodded and sat back in her chair.

He shook his head. "Now, the hospital."

She held out her hand, but didn't give him the satisfaction of eye contact. The phone was placed in her palm. Lifting her nose, she raised a finger to swipe open the call. She recognized the number. She'd called it on several previous missions. It rang five times before she answered.

"This is Detective Savage," she said.

"Miss Savage. Hello. This is the nurse from the ER. I wanted to make sure you got my message."

"Right. Actually, no. I've been without my phone and—"

"Your discharge papers didn't say I could leave test results via voice mail."

"Well, here I am."

"The doctor says you're five weeks along now and that things look normal. The bleeding isn't uncommon, but it's not good. You need to get rest and…" Her voice trailed away.

The phone slipped from her hand onto the table.

CHAPTER 33

Nickie couldn't park in the drive. It was already filled with cars. Pulling to the curb, she chose a spot behind a familiar gray minivan. It belonged to Duncan's Aunt Liz. Nickie recognized it just as she could identify the owners to each of the vehicles parked in the drive and along the street.

This was her family now.

Her eyes burned from the long day at work debriefing Operation Fu Haizi. At least, that was what she told herself the burning was from. The paperwork from said operation may take another few weeks, but today was the Fourth of July, and everyone agreed they needed the night off.

As she walked up the drive, a breath of guilt blew over her. Not because she felt she should be at work, but because her hands were empty. Then there was the secret. She passed Duncan's Barracuda and shook her head. He allowed Xena in his Barracuda? What a good dad. Her feet stopped.

Dad. When had her life become normal? She closed her eyes, smiled and took a deep breath. The sound of children's laughter came from all sides of the Reed home. Deep bellows of male bantering provided the bass. Leaves from mature oaks and maples blew in the wind, cooling her face and creating a harmony to the melody.

She opened her eyes and continued her path. Few in this group were a traditional nuclear family. Aunts and uncles who raised their nephews. Stepparents, half-siblings and as Gloria's vehicle came into view…she added foster families to her silent declaration.

Since she had nothing to add to the spread that would be in the kitchen, she veered toward the side of the home. Her foster nephew and niece, Lela and Neva, danced around the pillars that stood guard near the front door on the wraparound porch. Evergreens towered at the corners of the home with a myriad of different plant things of colors that filled every space in between. The twins were so enthralled with their game that they didn't notice Nickie. Her eyes squinted as she smiled at them. They were at peace. They carried the childlike trust and safety every child should carry.

As she stepped off the drive, she glanced down at the grass that brushed the sides of her sandaled feet. The guys at the station had given her all kinds of grief over them. And the shorts? She would never live it down. If they only knew.

Before making the turn to the back, she stopped and watched. Duncan's uncle stood in the ankle-deep water of Black Creek that ran behind his home. It was the creek tattooed on Duncan's chest. She knew it so well, she could draw it herself, if she knew how to draw. The dark color of the water was an illusion created from the nearly black soil that lined the creek bed. Large stones scattered throughout. The arched bridge that crossed to the other side was weathered with age, making it all seem comfortable and right.

Andy Jr. may have been toddling fast these days but needed help navigating the stones at the bottom. She drew her brows together as Nathan hovered his free hand over the water. Craning her head, she noticed as his open palm and fingers inched toward the water. He thrust in his hand. A.J. squealed as Nathan pulled out a squirming, kicking thing about the size of his hand. Pinchers. The thing had pinchers. Oh, hell no.

She marched on around the corner and ran head-on into two of Liz's grandsons. Each carried an armful of water balloons, but Nickie was on the top of her game and dodged out of the way. One slid out of a frantic hand and smashed at her feet.

"We're sorry, Nickie. Um. Hello. Good to see you." Their faces turned red as they juggled the rest of the slippery weapons.

"It's just water. My legs will dry," she said.

"You won't…ya know…tell anyone about the balloons?"

She pretended to zip her lip. "Your secret's safe with me."

The trees in the back of Nathan and Brie's home were younger, replaced from a fire of their own. Life was full of crazy good and crazy hard. When the hard hit, people had a choice. Bitter or better. She nodded and stepped into the better that was this day.

Duncan wasn't sure if it was the hint of lavender that brushed his senses or the heartbeat of his wife that entered his proximity, but he lifted his head from the grill in front of him and spotted her.

She stood like a Greek goddess. The short waves of her dyed hair blew in the wind and exposed her bare shoulders. The lacy tank and khaki shorts were something he'd only seen her wear a handful of times. His chin nearly dropped to the charcoals at the sight of her thighs, her painted toes and the way the tank hugged her stomach. Her stomach.

She found him, smiled and dipped her chin as she made her way to him. "Nickie!" Duncan's cousin squealed and ran to her. Only because Hannah was raised as Duncan's baby sister did he allow her to interrupt the greeting between him and his Nickie.

He turned his attention to the grates full of burgers, brats and hot dogs as he overheard bits of their conversation over the noise. College water polo. Nickie's sandals. Graduation plans.

The two of them reminisced as Nickie's foster brother and his wife organized a pickup game of softball in the field behind Duncan's childhood home. Eidetic memory or not, he remembered each room and corner of this home and beyond every remodel and organization thereof. It was home.

Home.

He and his Nickie had much to decide. Where to live, to grow, to be. Could they ever create a fraction of what Nathan and Brie had created? A place. A home for their children and grandchildren. Their neighbors, colleagues.

No. They were not his aunt and uncle. They were Duncan Reed and Nickie Savage. The canvas that was their future was blissfully clean, their paint tray full of colors and brushes eagerly waiting to create and design.

His aunt came down the short deck stairs, carrying two platters of food, each with a mini tent of netting covering it from mid-summer insects. The three women laughed and reminisced until Nickie took one of the trays and followed Brie to the two eight-foot folding tables filled with food.

Nickie set down the plate and nodded her head as she listened to something Hannah explained. Nickie's sincerity would be without question if not for the way her feet backed up toward him as she did so. Brie placed a hand on Hannah's elbow, distracting her long enough for Nickie to get away.

"There you are," he said and took her by the shoulders. Friends and family be damned, he pulled her in and set his mouth on hers as he kissed her more than was appropriate for a family gathering. Catcalls erupted from spectators of all ages.

"Great. Now, the food is ruined," Eddy said from his lounge chair.

Duncan craned his head around Nickie's to see him clearly. "Please feel free to get your sorry ass up and man the grill, friend."

"Pretty boy burgers. Can't wait," he said and threw back the last swig of his can of beer. "Look at that. I'd better refill."

He walked toward the back door, passing Andy and Rose as they napped in the shade of the deck in the hammock that hung below. Andy slept behind her with his hand resting on his child that grew inside of her. Eddy took the stairs two at a time as Duncan's Aunt Liz passed him with two arms full of buns for the grilled meat.

Duncan set his chin on top of Nickie's head, inhaling her scent. Taking his wrists, she wrapped his arms around her waist. "I haven't seen you naked in ten hours," he whispered as they swayed.

"Mmm," she hummed. "We'll have plenty of time for that. Look." She lifted a hand and pointed to Jess Larsen. He and Nickie's foster mother sat in adjacent Adirondack chairs, leaning over the side table that separated them. "They're up to something."

"Making plans to save each and every trafficked child in central and South America, no doubt." His words were meant to be facetious, and yet.

She rotated in his arms, making the state of his pants inappropriate in mixed company. "Don't you and Andy have fireworks to prepare?"

"Ah," he said and tilted his head, memorizing every detail of the hair that lay around her face. "Our reputation of pyrotechnics withstands time."

The sound of a throat clearing from a familiar voice caused him to reflexively jump back. He turned his head and, indeed, Aunt Liz stood with her hands on her hips. Her gaze went from his face to Nickie's waist.

His body stiffened as Liz pointed to the hand Nickie rested on her stomach. "You're pregnant," she said loud enough for far too many to hear.

Nickie's gaze darted to his. Their eyes met. The steel gray that was his Nickie lit with light and peace. Together, they smiled from ear to ear.

EPILOGUE

S weat dripped down Nickie's back in the old school bus. She crouched behind the last seat, watching through the peephole drilled in the metal. Three others waited with her. Two were veteran Green Beret. The other was retired FBI. Former Special Agent Hurst had somehow squeezed himself into the floor space in the seat next to her. He was in charge of the recording equipment.

Picturesque mountains loomed all around. Distant patches of crops Nickie didn't recognize were dotted with Cambodian workers wearing large hats.

As beautiful as the scenery was, her attention zeroed in on the three who stood along a rotted wooden fence speaking with human traffickers. Gloria served as the undercover boss. Jess Larsen and Duncan were her underlings.

They were amazing. Gloria was amazing. She wore a floral dress with her hair tied on the top of her head inside a headdress that matched the dress. Her M.O.

Small children with no shoes fed the few chickens and hogs that wandered in front of a stone building. Large holes in the walls served as the windows and doors.

Gloria negotiated the agreement as Nickie and Hurst recorded the transaction for the local authorities. Nickie waited for any sign that said she needed to intervene.

One of the toddlers stopped his work and faced Duncan. A T-shirt several sizes too large that once was white hung on the child's shoulders. His curly hair was buzzed short and his dark skin shimmered with the sweat of the day. Bright, curious eyes stared at Duncan's face.

The child drew unnatural attention to a would-be customer. The boy should be scared of him. Was it a breach? Wait on it. Wait on it. Nickie wasn't in charge. She wasn't even second in command. Patience would never be her virtue.

The boy stepped closer to him, too close. His little head craned upward to see the face of the white man who lounged at the entrance to the camp. The traffickers glanced down at the child, but then returned their attention to Gloria and their negotiations. Gloria peered down her nose at the men and pulled her purse around, opening it confidently.

Tilting his head, the boy wrapped an arm around one of Duncan's thighs. Duncan stiffened and ignoring the child, lifted his chin.

There it was. Money was exchanged. Eleven children were summoned, carried and dragged to the bus. Eleven. This was good. Nickie kept repeating this in her mind. This was good. This was good.

But so many were left behind. The boy in the large T-shirt. He cried as well but for a completely different reason. The boy sensed it, the light that surrounded Duncan everywhere he went. Duncan put up an act, but he couldn't fool everyone. The boy knew. Duncan walked away as the boy reached out an arm only to be shoved back to the home.

It was all she could do not to rush the place and rescue each and every one of them. Patience. The recording would be given to the Cambodian authorities. They would come back if Child Rescue provided evidence. Today. They promised.

Duncan nudged Gloria and everyone stopped. With her chin lifted high, she rotated on the balls of her feet, pointed to the boy and barked out an order. Nickie didn't hear just what she said, but the man at the gate shrugged and shoved the boy in her direction. Duncan picked him up with a single arm before continuing his slow meander to the bus.

The hidden four watched through peepholes even as they loaded. They didn't dare show themselves for miles. As Duncan stepped in, his glance searched the back until his eyes met hers. He blinked a long blink then slid into a seat as if he hadn't noticed her.

The boy clung to him, his little arms and legs wrapping completely around him as his head dug into Duncan's neck. He, too, showed no surprise or interest in the men that waited in the back. She guessed the boy was used to that as well.

Twelve children saved. Safe. Free. Free to heal, to grow. They huddled in hot vinyl seats waiting for the abuse that would never happen again.

Their future would be hard, but they had a chance. Many had donated the funds for the mission. People waited at the safe house to care for the children.

Good people lived everywhere.

Jess Larsen and Gloria bumped along in the front seat. Her façade as a heartless purchaser of children was flawless.

"Clear," Jess said, then turned to Gloria as the strange mix of former Green Beret, FBI and detective crawled from their hiding places to care for the children. "You're a natural," Jess said to Gloria as she released her hair from the fabric.

It was true. And so true that the children were cautious when she came back to care for them. That was, until she brought out the crackers and chocolate. It worked every time.

"This," Gloria said to her as she passed out food and bottles of water. "Is my calling."

Nickie got that. Duncan's eyes closed, and he let his head fall back against the top of the seat. The boy squirmed until he was wrapped in a tight ball, curled in Duncan's arms. She wondered if this boy would end up like Rico. Did

Nickie trust herself to serve as mother to another adopted child along with Rico? Their Joseph was almost a year old now. Oh, how she missed him. He'd learned to walk just before they left on this mission. She rested her head against the back of the bus seat as it swayed along the rocky ground. Her life was already filled with boys. Why not?

An older child grabbed the food from Gloria and scurried to the space between Nickie and the window as if she could hide there with the food. She had smooth dark hair and the same filthy clothing as the others. The child may be older than the others, but she was also much younger than Nickie was accustomed to saving.

It seemed like short minutes before the food was gone and the girl let her head fall on Nickie, using her leg as a pillow. Turning her head to Duncan, Nickie found him staring at her. He mouthed the words, "I love you," the deep chocolate of his eyes penetrating her soul.

She did not mouth her response, but said, "Is it too late for me to become Mrs. Reed?"

*Turn the page for an
excerpt from*

ISLAND
SECRETS

The Island Escape Series
Book One

R.T. Wolfe

Zoe's mother turned to him now, shoulders, face, and eyes. "Find her, Dane."

"I don't know where she is." What would he say if he did find her? Where would he look?

"She's a woman, Dane. She loves you. Go find her."

And then, he knew. Butterflies burst in his gut. He knew where she would be. But what if he was wrong? What if the timing was off? He kissed her mother on the forehead, then ran out the door waving backward before jumping into his Jeep.

Zoe sat with her eyes closed and her legs crossed. She heard the quick rush of water between hundreds of fins as a school of fish darted in circles behind her. It mixed like a melody with the steady bubbles that released from her facemask serving as the harmony. It was almost July and the water was warmer, so she'd chosen her diving skins over her wet suit. A boat sped by somewhere above. She tried not to focus on anything up there.

She wouldn't put herself at risk as she had done with her brother. Carefully, she had used the charts and guidelines of underwater diving to ensure she wasn't coming down too often or too long. The last thing she wanted was to give herself decompression sickness or be the cause of her parents losing another child.

He was with her here, Seth was. She could feel him. The memories were crisp. Ones of him carrying her on his shoulders when she was a little girl, all the way to the last dive they did together. This was the location of that last dive, not fifty yards away from where she found his skull. They'd spotted a grouper and took a zillion shots of it.

Sensing something was watching her, she opened her eyes but didn't move. Slowly, she glanced to the left, then right, keeping her breathing in controlled rhythm. It could be anything. Hiding in the seaweed. In a cavern. Behind a rock.

Of course something was watching her, she grinned. She was in the Gulf of Mexico.

Rotating, she started kicking lazily the fifty yards to the spot she found his skull. The water was choppy. Choppy was normal. The day she found him it had been unusually calm. Staring at the spot, she realized she would have never noticed the cavern under normal conditions. It was a mirage. No dark blue tint giving hint to the protruding opening.

She came to within five feet of it and waited. They had an agreement, her and the moray eel that made this its home. It poked its head out and tried to scare the hell out of her. Then, it bolted out of its hole, darting quickly in an effort to, once more, scare her before escaping the cavern and into the crevasse below.

Here, she'd found the skull with a knife through the eye. Her brother. Not much had been disturbed by the police. No yellow crime scene tape, she thought, sarcastically. Each of the last few days she'd come down here, she expected to find some sort of disturbance. Maybe rocks that had been chipped to release her brother from the wall. Or samples taken from around. Other than a small, jagged hole about the size of…of a knife, there was nothing.

She placed her hands on either side of the small opening, letting her legs dangle to the open water below. She felt something brush across her calf and assumed it was her friend the moray eel. She would buy a new camera. A good one. Her brother would want that. She would take out a loan and buy a Seth-approved camera and come down here to take pictures of her friend. He brushed her leg again. It made her smile, and she slowly inched herself from the crevasse. Friend or no friend, it was probably not a good idea to piss off a moray eel.

She came face-to-face with him. He wasn't the eel, and fear was nowhere to be found. Her body reacted regardless. Not with fear but an overwhelming warmth.

He came for her. The words repeated in her mind. He came for her. His beautiful, amazing blue eyes, although blood shot, searched her face. She saw tenderness there and hoped she returned the same. If there was one thing she could have asked for at that moment, it would be to gaze into the eyes of Dane Corbin. He looked sad. She reached out and put her hand on his cheek. It was warmer than the warm water.

ISLAND SECRETS

available in print and ebook

THE
NICKIE SAVAGE
SERIES

SAVAGE DECEPTION
SAVAGE RENDEZVOUS
SAVAGE DISCLOSURE
SAVAGE BETRAYAL
SAVAGE ALLIANCE

R.T. Wolfe enjoys creating diverse characters, twining them together in the midst of an intelligent mystery and a heart encompassing romance. It's not uncommon to find dark chocolate squares in R.T.'s candy dish, her rescued Saint Bernard at her feet and a few caterpillars spinning their cocoons in their terrariums on her counters. R.T. loves her family, gardening, eagle-watching and can occasionally be found in a third world country helping others help themselves.

R.T. enjoys hearing from readers. You can contact R.T. through her website: www.rtwolfe.com